graphic
the valley

peter brown hoffmeister

TYRUS
BOOKS

F+W Media, Inc.

Published by
TYRUS BOOKS
an imprint of F+W Media, Inc.
10151 Carver Road, Suite 200
Blue Ash, OH 45242. U.S.A.
www.tyrusbooks.com

Hardcover ISBN 10: 1-4405-6203-2
Hardcover ISBN 13: 978-1-4405-6203-7
Trade Paperback ISBN 10: 1-4405-6893-6
Trade Paperback ISBN 13: 978-1-4405-6893-0
eISBN 10: 1-4405-6204-0
eISBN 13: 978-1-4405-6204-4

Printed in the United States of America.

10   9   8   7   6   5   4   3   2   1

This book is available at quantity discounts for bulk purchases.
For information, please call 1-800-289-0963.

Printed on materials certified by the Forest
Stewardship Council™ to be from responsible
sources to benefit communities, wildlife, and the
environment.

To J
Who is my

And to Kenny
As a memorial

PART I
Samson

CHAPTER 1

The Yosemite Valley tells the extinction of the wolf: broken sideways, .30-caliber bullet in his hip, licking the wet fur of a stillborn. The Merced turns a corner toward Bridalveil, poisoned meat at the cutbank.

You have to listen to me.

Tenaya rides a paint to the lip where striations took the granite. Not glacial sheer. He opens his eyes to the no longer. He was born a Mono to the north, and all of what you see became his, before the war. But this Valley is yours by birthright.

Tenaya scrambles along the ridge until he sees the half-circle and the meadow, the old growths swaying in the breath like a fire's gasping. We put our ears to the river boulders to hear the first story. The last. But do not wait for the smell. The smell of the water belongs to the liars, and they are all.

I'd slept against the bear box, the iron food cache cold through my sleeping bag, and woke when it was dark. I couldn't sleep a night without picturing her, eight years after, the way she lay against the river boulder, her right hand turned away, fisted, like it held a valuable.

I choked on nothing and sat up.

I leaned back against the box and looked out at the sleeping camp, the orange, blue, and red tents pieced together like cars in the Curry lot. I stood. Pulled on my wool hat and slid into my shoes. Started to walk.

Low clouds hung in the Valley, the ends torn as wet paper. I crossed at the T near the Lower Falls, toward the meadow, moving

7

south, spooking mule deer on the road, their hooves skittering against the asphalt like young horses'. Then they were gone. I had no headlamp to follow.

I stepped through the bracken fern and followed the dirt road up to the boardwalk, left across the meadow. Halfway into the open, I lay down, back flat on the fiberglass replacement boards that the Park Service bolted down the year before. Looking up at the sky, I couldn't see anything but gray, the mist backed with massing low clouds.

I lay shivering. Thinking of her at the river. Her body, and my mother. The stories I'd heard my whole life. I was fourteen years old, and I would not make it back to camp.

I braided my hair, three feet. Pulled my braids tight. A long-haired boy, never a hair cut, I'd been confused for a girl when I was younger.

I rolled over and did push-ups to stay warm, a trick my father had taught me. He'd say, *Lie back and wait for the blood to move.* I pictured him pointing with that missing index finger. People who didn't know him would just see a fist, no pointing at all.

I got up and walked the boardwalk, back and forth, waiting for the smell of wet granite and ponderosa, bark like puzzle pieces chipped into moving water. I slept away from camp now sometimes, but still I couldn't sleep. My mind pounded the Upper Falls in spring. I would add to that now. This morning.

He came alone, in the haze, and I didn't know who he was. I was pacing the boardwalk in the early light, near the Merced, no sleep, tired like two stones grating behind my eyes.

He walked up in a full suit, expensive clothes, rare in the Valley. There were all-night gatherings at the Ahwahnee, and I guessed at that. But his suit had no wrinkles, the suit pressed, a white shirt starched clean, and the pants creased to the outside. He had his right hand in his pocket as he stared off, standing on the edge of the boardwalk while the sun struggled to rise south of Half Dome.

That was how it looked. The sun there as a slit. My mind the big falls, 2,000 feet above the meadow, pumping into the daylight elevation. Me walking toward him.

I stopped.

The man said, "It's a beautiful morning, huh?"

I looked around. The mist was in and I couldn't see the details of the south side: the Shield, the Sentinel, the triple pillars of the Cathedrals. I'd seen more beautiful mornings in the Valley, but I said, "Yes."

He didn't say anything else for a minute.

I didn't know about his programs. I didn't know about his new park plan. How he'd moved from the private sector to the National Park Service three years earlier. I would read all of that later in the newspaper accounts of what was about to happen.

A few feet from me, he was a man in a suit, nobody I knew, a man with a belly like something hidden underneath his shirt. He was tall above his paunch, as if three people were put together: A thin man, the heavier middle man, then a third person's legs.

I smelled cologne and smoke. He brought the cigar up to his lips and puffed, the smell like two fingers snapping in front of my eyes.

The Valley was in me. The Valley yellow turning to brown, a thousand bears in late fall. I looked down at my hands, the dirty black fingernail ends, and I bit one off. Spit that into the blooming milkweed.

The man leaned down to mash out his cigar, marking a stain on the low rail. He flicked the butt on the same trajectory as my fingernail, following it into the green. Dark mud crawling up the reed stalks, black bottomed, waiting for the next rain.

He said, "Do you spend a lot of time in the park?"

"No," I said, the lie that my father had asked me to tell when I was eight years old, when I first found out that it was illegal to live where we did. That no one else camped their whole lives off of the Northside Loop Road near the 120.

The man stood in front of me. The Valley rolling its shoulders, ten thousand years, after the final ice receded, boulders sitting as terminal moraines, the chambers of the ancient volcano exposed in white-and-gray plugs, flakes weakened by freeze water and the sloughed granite crashing, the Domes shrugging awake.

"Not camping, huh?" The man smiled like a forest fire. "It's a beautiful place to camp."

"No," I said. I didn't walk away. Didn't explain. I was never good at saying what I was thinking.

He stepped toward me. That smile. I was fourteen that day, but not small, never small, and my hands were like the rocks that they climbed.

The man was going to hit me or reach out to shake my hand. I didn't know which one. His shoulder came up, twitched, and he started to move his right arm toward me.

But I pushed him before that happened. With two hands and hard. I didn't know what I was hoping for. There was the Valley, and the Valley was in me, and the Valley was with me.

It was only a few feet down off the boardwalk there, only four or five feet down to the ground, to the milkweed and the reeds, not far, but his shoe caught on the low rail near the cigar stain, and the rail flipped him. He went over, upside down, a scrub jay caught by a gust. I smiled as I watched him fall into the wet reeds and the mud, smiled as I imagined him scrambling back up, muddy and angry in his soiled clothes, yelling at me, chasing me.

But his left hand stayed down in his pocket, where it had been before he went over the rail. His right hand reached out in front of him, waving once, touching nothing. He hit a rock, a foot wide, with his head, and his face twisted around beneath him, under the weight of his body. His head turned six inches too far, and I heard something pop as his body rolled over the top.

I bit a hole though the front left corner of my tongue. Bit down, and the blood filled my mouth. A tongue can bleed, and fast. I coughed blood there on the boardwalk, spit and drooled it into my hand, my palm filling with blood before I dumped it at my feet.

But the man did not bleed. Not at all. His legs flattened and his arms twisted, limbs in the reeds like the loose limbs of an old doll.

Her doll. The way she dragged it, wet, that hand-sewn cloth doll, as it went through the pool above the rocks my father stacked to make a swimming hole at Ribbon Creek's narrows. I found her doll months later, under a blanket in the tent, blackening with mold.

The man's face was looking over his shoulder, his eyes open, and I stared down into those eyes. The mist came, new smoke above me, and soon there was nothing I could see farther away than ten feet. The man's body and the boardwalk. The flash of green leading to the river, the dark-bottomed reeds, the tongue blood in my hands.

The man never blinked or twitched. His eyes open, and I didn't mean that. Not at all. Like suffocating doves.

CHAPTER 2

Storm coming. Early 1850. This is true Yosemite history.
The start: a Glacier Point rockslide buries a boy, and his
friend cannot find him. He calls his name and walks the talus
field. Unsettled flakes creak under his feet, the cloud of granite
dust drying the membranes of his nose and eyes, coating his
throat in white.

Miners are in the Sierra Nevadas, looking for that other
dust. People hear the stories from the Paiutes in the mountains.
Miners are panning the creeks and rivers, building settlements
and taking wives. California new from Mexico one year.

Some of the miners still speak in Spanish. Others English.
Miwoks are there as well, living to the south at Mariposa, by
the big grove of trees. The Diggers.

James Savage is with them, the miner and trader who owns
two stores and five wives. Gaining wealth and purchasing
respect, his Indian brides are twelve years old and walk like
green-broke horses.

But your people wait to the north, here in this Valley. Some
call them The Grizzlies. Others The Killers.

The Miwoks tell Savage that the Yosemiti will never allow
people to enter this Valley. They will die for this place. Like you.

I slept in the backcountry, running past Illilouette, Vernal, and
Nevada Falls on the first day, past the asphalt and stone-cut steps
of the tourist trail built for pilgrimages to the near high country.
The first night in a meadow, loam thicker than the backseat of my

father's Plymouth. Snow plants bright red in the patches between moss strings. And the cold.

The drifts harbored the mosquito hatch, so I used bank mud as a face coat. But the granules dried by midnight and the mosquitoes came up my nose before that.

I kept my thatch tight. Wound reeds until I was worried about oxygen.

I read the news report at the Tuolumne store on the morning of July 4th. The story read, "Although evidence at the scene suggests a scuffle, no suspects have been arrested. The superintendent's concessions plan for the park was hotly debated, but e-mail and phone records uncovered zero threats to his life."

I was sure that the evidence they were writing about was my blood, the blood from my tongue. The hole in my tongue had swollen and become a canker sore, and I had to chew food now without closing my mouth.

I had no bear canister and a bear came after my food bundle the third night, peanut butter and syrup wrapped in half of a tarp, pulled up with cord. The bear shuffled around my hang-tree, then he came to my debris shelter, his enormous footfalls like logs dragged and set down. But I couldn't see him in the dark.

It was the night of Independence Day. July 4th. I heard someone light off an illegal firework in the Tuolumne campground over the next ridge. I'd seen arrests for that in Camp 4 when I was younger, the rangers zip-tying middle-aged men, lecturing as they hauled them up the trail.

The bear continued to smell me in my shelter. I wondered about the grizzlies in the old days. When my grandfather lived here before the Depression. Grizzlies with hook-claws four inches long. Standing nine feet against a tree, smart enough to pull on a rope.

I lay in the dark of my debris shelter and pulled the needles closer, slid piles over me, insulating inside the stick frame, the bear walking around outside, and the black above me staying black, but my eyes open.

Two faces came to me then. His eyes, the superintendent's, blank eyes over his shoulder at the turn of his neck. That expression like new burn. Then her eyes like waking up. Not dead at all.

During the day in Tuolumne, I worried about food. What my father said: "There is always water here in the Yosemite. So eat. Always think about what you will eat next." He patted my head. "You're stronger than you know," he said. "So think about the next meal, and you'll be fine."

And I was fine. Never too hungry. I found half of a bag of Krusteaz just-add-water pancake batter in a campsite box, mixed a cup each morning, and drank the batter. Then I found jam and a few slices of bread. Some crackers.

I spent a week checking campsites after people left, running food over the ridge to my tarp bundle, and my bundle grew. When it was full, I stopped foraging for food and began to hike during the daytime.

I found a group of climbers in the woods near Fairview Dome. They'd circled twelve camp chairs, five tents. Standard-issue backcountry bear canisters in the middle like an iron campfire for a story circle.

One of them said, "We have enough cheese and peanut butter for the apocalypse. Have at it, man. Stay as long as you like."

So I joined them in their camp. I hiked my food over to their location and added it to their group stash.

One of them said, "Whoa, that's a random assortment."

"Yeah," I said, "I found all of it."

They were on a climbing road trip, all of them in their early twenties, and they liked that I was fourteen. They called me "Young Jedi," and took me climbing with them each day.

I built a new debris shelter next to one of their North Face tents, and they asked me all about its construction, the low entrance, the woven door, insulation, and outer debris. Two of them abandoned their tents by the third night, and we all slept in our new shelters in the clearing, improving them each evening until they were sleeping warm enough.

One of them said, "Jedi, how long have you been living like this?"

I didn't know how to answer that because I wasn't sure of what he was asking. In a shelter? In Tuolumne? In the Valley? So I said, "A while?"

He laughed and handed me my first beer. "Good enough, son. Good enough."

After a week, the mosquitoes were less active and I could leave the shelter thatch open at night. The days were long and hot, and we swam in the creek after climbing.

The guys taught me how to lead climb with trad gear, how to build anchors, how to avoid losing gear in retreat when afternoon lightning storms came in, the air turning first like wet wool, then static iron, a taste on the tongue.

My tongue healed with one little knotted scar where I'd bitten through, and when I gritted my teeth there, it felt like a piece of bone lodged on top of the muscle.

The climbers were impressed with my climbing barefoot, so I taught them how to jam cracks without shoes. I said, "Keep the toes together and slot straight in. Then drop your heel." One of them climbed barefoot with me after that.

At night, I listened to them tell stories about high school and college, parties and girls, failed sex attempts, and I laughed frantically, wondering about that other world beyond camping and fishing and climbing in this park. I wondered about a world full of girls.

One of them said, "Jedi, where'd you go to middle school?"

"Middle school?" I said.

"Yeah, you know, sixth to eighth grade."

I said, "I guess I didn't do that." I'd had two beers. I wasn't hiding anything.

They all looked at me. The first climber said, "Then what did you do for school?"

"Nothing," I said. "I didn't go to a school. I just read a lot of books. Hundreds that my father gave me."

"Hundreds of books?"

"Maybe two hundred? Two-fifty? I don't know," I said. "My father's read a lot more than that. Everything he can find or buy for cheap. He reads a book a day."

"Awesome," the first one said. "Just books. That's way better than school. And trust me, you didn't miss much in sixth to eighth grade."

But I did wonder.

I stayed a month with the climbers, sharing my food—running over the ridge to scrounge more from abandoned Tuolumne sites—eating their peanut butter and cheese. And at night, they gave me cans of beer.

It was late summer, then early fall. The first night of frost warning, at 8,000 feet, and the climbers left the high country the next day to return to jobs in Mountain View and San Jose. They all hugged me, left their food and beer at the door of my shelter. One of them said, "We love you, Jedi," then he hopped in his VW van and drove away.

I slept one night alone in their clearing, but all I could think of was returning to the Valley. Seeing my parents. So I hitchhiked down in the morning, put my thumb out on the Tioga road.

When I arrived at my parents' camp on the west side, Ribbon Creek, in August, my mother ran to me so hard that she stumbled and fell down. I helped her up, and she buried her face into my neck. I hugged her hair and cried with her.

My father walked up, his hands in his pockets, his head down. He kicked a cedar cone with the toe of his boot. "We thought you were gone," he said.

I wiped my face with the back of my forearm. "No. I'm sorry. Some things happened."

"Things?"

"Nothing really," I said. "Not important." I didn't explain more. I wouldn't tell them. I'd decided never to tell them about that morning on the boardwalk.

He tried again. He said, "What things?"

I said, "I just had to go for a while." I shook my head.

He nodded. For him, it was still 150 years ago, 1851, sleeping with the shadow of the 36th on the trail below, snow on their blue coats. I've read that some animals have the instinctual memory of their ancestors.

My mother kept hugging me and petting my hair. She picked pine needles out of my tangles.

I said, "I was hiking and climbing."

My father nodded and waited as my mother scanned back and forth across my eyes. She put her head down and wiped her nose. I kissed her on top of her head, smelling the oil on her scalp.

One evening, I watched my mother braille the grass, her eyes closed as she dropped into the V, dragonflies looping above the nests, landing blue on her head and shoulders.

I was running a trout line, fifty feet and trebles every five on a bite, eleven in all, with a grasshopper floating each. I'd tied no weights so the bugs struggled circles on the surface to make the fish rise as the day cooled to blue.

But I was watching my mother, down in the drop. I saw her closed eyes, and her hands the colors of shooting stars, pink to white, a palm-down dance like holding gravity against the top of the grass, the dragonflies landing, stay-winged prehistoric bugs on her shoulders.

Her mouth moved but she wasn't talking.

For five more years I lived in that camp with my parents, the camp of my childhood. We went back to our old jobs, my mother cooking and washing clothes, my father collecting wood and tending fires, me bringing back any food I could find.

We read books.

I went down to fish the eddies on the Merced. The dead pull of the whites and the quick slashes of rainbows at the turn, in the new day's light. I fished underneath the trees, away from the bridges and roads, where the rangers didn't go.

I cut firewood and collected deadfall for kindling to help my father. Built up the cord piles. Stitched holes in the tent with dental floss.

When there was nothing to do, I read books scored from the Curry lost-and-found or hiked above El Cap along the north rim and down the slabs descent. I slept sometimes in Camp 4, but always came back, always bringing fish when I returned to my parents' clearing.

I never heard any more about the superintendent. Nothing at all. And a year later, I often wondered if that morning had happened, if a man in a suit had ever smoked a cigar, if his suit compressed against my hands as I pushed him over. I carried that moment in a box in front of me, the rope digging into the back of my neck, the nylon frays like small wires cutting my skin.

I saw his face in the reeds. Saw his face on the body of a man at Curry, in the face of a man in a Merced rental raft. And then he was alive again.

I climbed the freestanding boulders on the Valley floor, rocks to thirty feet, gaining confidence in my climbing, my hands strong, my shoulders and arms building. I bouldered some evenings until my forearms gave out and my finger pads wore down. The granite edges cut flappers, and I sucked the iron from the slits in my fingers.

Then I hiked back in the dark along the Northside Drive, startling black-tail or peanut-butter-and-jelly coyotes with the thin fur even in winter, their fur like grease hair.

I tried not to think of the superintendent. I put his box on my shoulder. Tied him on my back. Bent with him. Bent as he breathed smoke into my ear.

Sometimes when I watched the rain, leaning against a pine tree, under its cover as the water came down around me, I wondered if he was watching me. Sometimes I turned around to look for him. And she was there too then, anytime I smelled the wet. Leaning at the granite as I bent over to land a fish, in the eddy swirl, the riffle, the turn like a water's exhale.

In camp, there were the three of us and little talk. My mother hummed as she ladled food into our blue aluminum bowls, and I recognized all her songs. But we ate to the sound of the wind gusting up-river in the evening, the cold air meeting the warm, the scrape of the low branches, and the tic tic tic of pinecones falling through.

Sometimes, after dinner, my father told stories, the two of us sitting side by side against the set log, watching the meteorites burn through the gaps in the trees. My mother walked away with the pot, toward the grit at the edge of the creek where she sand-cleaned dishes, and my father told me about Old Tenaya, The Prophet Wovoka, Captain John, everyone he'd read about. I chewed grass stalks, poking between teeth with the hard stems, memorizing what my father said.

"Sometimes we're stupid," he said. "Foolish. But even at our worst, there can be acts of honor."

I nodded. I wanted to ask if the superintendent was an act of honor. I said, "Have you ever done something in the moment and not known what was going to happen?"

My father picked up a flat chip of granite and spun it out in front of us as if he were skipping a rock on the river. He said, "We all do."

"But," I said, "do we all do bad things?"

He picked up another rock. Flipped it in the air above him and caught it with his other hand. He said, "They wanted everything.

They burned people out, caught the last few hiding, made this a plastic and gasoline world."

I said, "The soldiers made Old Tenaya lead them back up the Merced, right?"

"Yes," my father said. "But after that, they murdered his son. Even after that."

I was a teenage boy and it was just the tourist girls until Lucy. Girls with swimsuits like peach skins wet on their flesh, and I watched them at the El Cap bridge in summer, me coming down from the wall, and them standing at the bridge railing trying to decide whether or not to jump.

When I saw them, I didn't know what to do with my hands.

The bridge was not tall, never more than fifteen feet even at low water in August, but some people stood, waited, looked down at the height.

I heard a girl say, "Can't they regulate the flow out of the dam? The water's too low today." But this wasn't Hetch Hetchy. I watched the girl wait and wait, and never jump.

Another time, two girls in matching red suits and braids, and they were beautiful. I could see the wet pricking at the end of their swells.

I was at the end of the bridge. I wanted to do a back flip off the railing next to them. But somehow I couldn't make myself walk up there, and the girls in those suits the same red, thin and tight, and the legs and arms coming out of the red making me think of all of the skin on a girl's body.

There was no way for me to say hello. And what I would say after that? If they spoke to me?

A loud tourist boy yelled, "You afraid?" and shook his hips. He was down on the sandbank. He said, "Don't be scaredy little bitches, huh?"

I wanted to hold his throat for that. Shatter his teeth with my fist. But the girls jumped, first one, then the next, and swam over to him. They both kissed him on the mouth, one after the other as they stood up and walked onto the bank, and they smiled then and covered their shoulders with towels.

A tourist girl did kiss me once. When I was seventeen. Walking on the path near the bridge, she grabbed my forearm. Said, "Hey," and I turned. Then she kissed me on the mouth, smelling like beer cans warming in the sun. Her tongue touched my bottom lip, licking across.

I didn't do anything. It was my first kiss, and I didn't know what I could do.

The girl was gripping my forearm with her fingernails. Pink. I saw her nails as she pulled back. I looked at her, her smeared black lashes and blue eyes, flakes of chapped skin on her bottom lip like coconut.

Her friend said, "Whoa, slut," and pulled her away by her hair. "What were you thinking there?"

She tilted, leaning into her friend. I heard her say, "I had to. He just looked so wild."

In my tent that night, I thought of everything. Her eyes blinking. Her water-smeared mascara. The arch of her back and the bare expanse between the two pieces of her bikini. I wished I'd put my arms around her, put my hands on her skin, felt her hips, her rib cage, felt the droplets of water dripping down. I wished that I'd kissed her longer, asked her to come swim with me. I wished I'd done any of the things I'd read about in books.

I didn't sleep. I lay awake thinking about teenage girls I'd seen at the water. The bridge. Their bathing suits and bodies. I tried to remember each girl I'd ever seen. Then I wondered about hallways full of girls in the high schools in books. Beautiful girls sitting at desks, listening to teachers. I wanted to trade homework answers, help girls cheat on tests, ask girls to dances.

It was two full years until Lucy. So many girls at Sentinel, in Camp 4, the Lodge, Curry, and the Village. But none of them kissed me.

Nineteen years old the summer I worked slash on the Tioga road. I walked up to the crew chief and said, "Do you need people?" I'd been in Tuolumne, in the high country one week, sleeping in a shelter east of Tenaya Lake.

The crew chief said, "Are you a rock climber?"

I held up my hands, showed the flaking skin on my first finger pads. Torn callouses.

"Okay then," he said. "You'll do good."

I didn't know what to write on the address or social security lines, so I left those blank, and put the clipboard on the seat of the truck. Then I went to work.

At the end of the day, the crew chief called me over to his truck. "You do good work, kid. Piled a lot of slash." He tapped my application page with the back of his pen. "You don't have a social security number though, huh?"

"No," I said, "I don't think so."

He hocked a chunk of phlegm into his mouth and spat it over his truck. "No number at all? Or you can't remember?"

I shook my head.

He tapped the application page again. "I thought you looked maybe Mexican. Are you Mexican?"

"No," I said.

"Okay . . . " He rubbed his pen with his fingers. "But you're illegal anyways, huh?"

"Illegal?"

He smiled. "You know what I mean. You ain't exactly a citizen, right?"

I said, "I don't know about that."

He laughed. I didn't know what to do so I laughed too. We both stood and laughed.

"Well," he said, "whatever. It means shit to me. I'll just give you cash for what you do just like you were Mexican, okay?"

"Okay," I said.

He shrugged. He said, "Done it before."

I remembered my mother's hands in my hair. Washing. I was six years old. Half a year since that night on the Merced. I looked down at the meadows, heard her voice there, the crows'. Every morning when I heard them, I looked for her. That still tricked me.

My mother scrubbed my armpits, then my neck. Held my face in her hands that smelled like wax on the brown soap. I didn't say that I was cold. Sometimes I talked to her, and sometimes I didn't.

I looked back upstream, saw the water run the dips around the big boulder, like the hump of a submerged animal. My mother turned my face back toward her. Kissed my forehead, wiped it with the back of her hand. She pursed her lips.

I said, "I love you too."

The Tioga Road took two months, clearing slash all the way to the Meadows, like beaver dams piled above ground.

The other workers were college boys, here for summer employment. Joking with girls at Valley parties on the weekends. I'd seen those Housekeeping parties and wondered about the beach girls, their tight tank tops on cold evenings, red cups of beer, screaming for no reason. I wanted to be in the middle of one of those parties, hear the music from inside the house, smell the perfume and sweat and beer.

Our work crew was underneath Pywiack Dome in early August, off Lake Tenaya, the mosquitoes awake, waiting in the shade, sucking at the wets of our eyes. The sun turned around a grove of trees baking flakes of skin off the tops of our shoulders. I smelled the lake behind me, waiting to swim.

She came on a Thursday, two days before the weekend. The only girl ever. Too pretty for our crew.

I couldn't talk to her, but everyone else did, like the Village store lines. Every boy on the crew already there, shirtless, working close, talking and joking at her, throwing pinecones back and forth over her head.

After an hour, the crew chief yelled at them. He said, "All the brush doesn't lie in one spot, boys." He smiled and said, "Lucy." He motioned with his finger.

He talked to her about her paper forms. He leaned in close to point things out on the clipboard. She didn't seem to notice.

When she went back to work, I watched the way sweat dropped down from her forehead off the end of her nose, how she itched her face with the front of her shoulder, turning her neck. How her braids kept catching in her mouth as she leaned over the slash piles, her black hair like the finished burn.

I watched the neckline of her T-shirt where she'd cut the collar out, dropping it open. That was Thursday.

On Friday, I worked and tried not to look at her. She was too much to watch and everyone was staying near her.

I collected brush in the trees. Thought of finishing the day and getting to swim before dinner. I was the only one camping at the lake on the weekends, in one of the crew's wall tents, everyone else going back to the Valley to see friends, to drink, to buy food that they couldn't get in the Meadows store.

As soon as the group left each Friday, I climbed an easy route on Pywiack, feeling the granite on my palms and fingertips, the knobs on the lower dome, then the cracks, climbing past the chopped bolts into the systems up high.

On clear evenings, I liked to lie on top of the dome and watch the stars drop down. It was like submerging in the reed shallows above Mirror Lake, turning with the slow current until Half Dome disappeared, everything multiplying, pine needles, snags, blades of grass. The barely visible molecule circles in the air.

I was scraping moss off a boulder with my boot, early Friday afternoon. Lucy was out to my right. I'd worked back toward her.

She stood up. "Is anyone staying up here this weekend?"

I stopped scraping.

Other workers shook their heads.

"Nobody?" she said.

The crew chief picked up his water bottle and pointed at me. "The Valley kid is. Tenaya." He took a drink. "The one with long hair. He stays up here every weekend."

Lucy looked at me. "You're staying?"

"Yes."

She smiled, one dogtooth turned backward, like a river pearl. That tooth angled wrong. She said, "So I can stay up here with him?"

The crew chief shook his water bottle back and forth. "No, no," he said. "We don't really do that. The tents are for weeknights or emergencies. Nothing else. You can ride back down with me if you want to."

She took off one of her gloves and wiped her forehead. "I can't go down this weekend. Just can't."

All the other workers had stopped working. We all stood and listened.

The crew chief said, "What do you mean you can't?"

Lucy shook her head. "I just can't go down this weekend."

The chief flipped his water bottle and caught it. He cleared his throat. "Well," he said, "I mean, I guess you could stay up."

I smiled and turned away. Went back to scraping moss. Clearing the boulder wasn't part of my job but I did this sometimes at the end of the day so I could come back and climb a feature.

I heard one of the other boys say, "Lucky fucking bastard. And he doesn't even barely talk."

We used the group stove to warm up Nalley's Hot Chili out of cans. Lucy cut slices of cheddar cheese off the block. "Want some?" she said.

"Thanks."

She smiled, and I saw that crooked tooth again, so turned that it caught on her bottom lip.

I opened a bag of corn chips and held them out to her.

"Thanks," she said. The chili was warm, and she flipped off the stove. "Good enough, right?"

We ate.

She said, "You don't want to go down to the Valley on the weekends either?" She pointed her spoon at me.

"No, not really," I said.

She took a huge bite of chili and said, "Me either," with her mouth full.

I said, "Why not?"

She swallowed. "I've been there a lot before," she said.

"Me too."

After dinner, we cleaned our bowls with jug water, scrubbing with the pads of our fingers.

She said, "Want to go for a swim?"

It was almost dark and I'd gone swimming earlier. I'd planned on climbing after dinner. Venus was blinking in the west and I climbed every night now. But I looked at Lucy, a girl close to my age, prettier than granite. I said, "Yeah, I could swim."

At the edge of the lake, she stripped to her bra and underwear. Black and black with a small line of lace along the top. She was facing away, so I stared. Surprised by how strong she was. Big shoulders. She had a curve in her spine like a snake turning over stone, and scar lines across her left shoulder, two straight lines two inches across. Her skin there and down, I examined the space between her bra and underwear, that curve of her low back, then her backside, the half-circles of her butt, the muscles and the shadow between her legs. I held my breath.

She ran through the shallows and dove in. Swam out. I was still standing. Hadn't even undressed yet. She bobbed up and wiped her eyes. "Aren't you coming in?"

"Yeah, sorry," I said. I pulled off my shirt, then my jeans. Ran in. The water was cold, tightening my pores. I swam out to Lucy.

She was shorter than me, barely able to touch where we stood, and she kept kicking off her toes, bobbing like a small animal crossing a river. Her nostrils flared as she bobbed. She said, "Do you like it out here?"

"In the lake?"

"No, no," she laughed, "in the high country. In Tuolumne."

"Yeah, I like the Domes," I said. "That's why I came back this summer."

"The Domes?" she said. She looked up at Pywiack, mounded above the lake. She stared like she hadn't seen it until then. Then she turned and looked across the road at Polly Dome. "Oh yeah," she said, "the Domes are cool. I didn't think about them."

I cupped water over my hair. Dove down and grabbed a handful of the gritty silt from the bottom. Rubbed it all the way to the ends of my hair, the way my father had showed me.

"Did you just put mud in your hair?" she said.

"Yeah."

She laughed at me. "Nature's soap, huh?"

"The grit works," I said.

"Okay," she said. She flipped and went under. Came up with two handfuls. Scrubbed her armpits. She said, "It feels like sandpaper."

We both scrubbed like cleaning the dishes before. That first night, we cleaned together.

Lucy said, "Did you grow up near here?"

"Yes, in the Valley."

"In the Yosemite Valley?"

"Yes." I bent my knees and washed the mud out of my armpits. I didn't know why I was being so honest with her.

"Your family is park workers then?"

"No," I said. I leaned back and started to rinse out my hair.

When I came back up and wiped my eyes, Lucy said, "But I thought . . . "

I knew what she was asking but I didn't explain.

She did a backward roll, flipped, and came up next to my face. She spit water and swam away.

I cut my feet and swam in place, watching her swim out farther, toward the only deep part of the lake, where the water turned from gray to black.

My sleeping bag was already set out in one of the boys' designated pole tents, across from the stove. Lucy came in and laid her sleeping bag down, perpendicular like a T at the bottom of mine.

She said, "I didn't want to sleep alone in the girls' tent again. Since no one else is up here, is it all right if I sleep in here with you?"

I said, "Sure."

It got warmer in the tent. I tried to relax. Lucy was lying on top of her bag, breathing deeply, inhaling and exhaling. I'd started to read but couldn't follow the sentences with her breathing. She was just beyond my feet, six inches from the end of my sleeping bag. I kept thinking of her bra straps, the thin line of lace across the top, the way she looked before she ran into the lake, her near-naked body standing by the water in less than a swimsuit.

I flipped the page of my book and realized that I'd forgotten to read it. I went back a page. Then I sat up. I said, "I was just lying down for a minute, but I'm not really that tired. I'll be back, okay?"

"Okay," Lucy said, and turned over.

I stepped out of the tent and jogged up the road. Turned toward the dome, then into the stunted trees. I jogged down the short switchback and hopped across the creek. In the dark, up in front of me, the white granite glowed.

I found the south face. It's easy climbing. Knobs on 50-degree rock, then 60 degrees as the steepness increased. Up higher on the dome, hand jams in a long, arcing, more vertical crack, then laybacks on the left side of the crack system, stepping over a corner. The stone was bright even in the dark, and I climbed barefoot. My feet were calloused from climbing each night, bouldering near the lake on weekend mornings.

Half an hour later, on top of the granite dome, I was alone. No other climbers there at that time of night. I looked up at a waning crescent moon and millions of stars. I was facing south but Orion hadn't yet returned to the sky. I looked back at the Ursas. Cassiopeia. Polaris. I felt the stars drop down and prick my skin like droplets of water. The water thickened and covered me as I extended my arms and rose up, floating.

Lucy was in my tent, her sleeping bag touching the bottom edge of mine.

My father says, "Warriors."

I say, "What?" I'm twelve years old. We're fishing the logjam pool across from Housekeeping, fifteen feet deep where the river gouges on the north side.

"Yes," he says. "They don't care about now because they're always fighting the past."

I don't know what he's talking about. "So is that good or bad?"

My father looks at me like he looks at scrub jays when they tear apart a food bag in our cache. He says, "Good, of course. That's all we can do."

"Oh," I say.

"Never, never," he says. "We can't forget the old things, the old wrongs."

He pulls a three-pound whitefish out of the water, oily and fat. Unhooks it from his treble.

I cast into the pool again. Reel across the current line, and my rooster tail runs downstream.

He says, "You understand me, right?"

I don't, but I say, "Yes."

"The betrayal, right? Do you understand me?" he says.

He hooks his index finger in the squirming whitefish's mouth. Gains leverage. Lifts his elbow and his thumb pops a hole through the top of the skull. The whitefish jerks once then stops moving.

The stars like bugs on the water. Black on reflected white.

Lucy was in her sleeping bag when I came back. She turned over as I unzipped the door.

I said, "Sorry to wake you."

"You didn't," she said. "I was already awake."

"Good." I lay down on top of my bag, still hot from running back through the woods. Sweating.

She said, "I watched you climb."

"Huh?"

"The dome," she said, "I watched you climb it."

I touched my fingers together, the calluses like rubber caps, no feeling through that thick skin, and I couldn't see Lucy in the darkness.

She said, "I followed you, then stood off to the side at the base to see your profile." She shifted and I heard the rustle of her body against the sleeping bag's nylon. "You climbed pretty fast."

I was still sweaty, but cooling off now. I said, "It's not a really difficult route. Anyone could do it."

"Are you sure?" she said.

"Yes. And I've done it so many times."

I tried to think of something else to say after that but couldn't. And in a few minutes, I heard Lucy breathing loud and slow. I'd stopped sweating, and I slid my legs into my sleeping bag. I closed my eyes but couldn't sleep yet. I lay there and listened to Lucy's breathing. Then I held up my hands in the dark, saw them obscure the lighted tent walls on the moon side.

We made breakfast with the food from the group cooler again, a cooler that smelled like old fruit. I fried potatoes and eggs with milk and cheese. Lucy poured too much salt over the top of everything but it was still good.

The mosquitoes came in a black mist before the sun cut.

Lucy said, "Will you spray me with DEET?"

I grabbed the bottle from the gear bin.

She turned her back to me and held up her hair. I sprayed her neck. Then she slid up her shirt, showing the small of her back. She said, "Will you spray it up underneath my shirt so they don't bite through?" I was looking at the top of her black underwear, a small mole on the left side of her hip, at the top of her hipbone.

I sprayed.

She lifted her shirt further and I sprayed over the back of her crooked spine, over the strap of her bra. Across the lace.

Lucy turned around and lifted her shirt in front, to the bottom of her breasts.

I wanted to swim again. See her pull her shirt off. Watch the swell of her chest in her wet bra.

I tried not to think about that as I sprayed her stomach with DEET.

She said, "We grew up near each other."

I tried not to look at her chest as I sprayed her stomach. Then I bent down and got the fronts of her legs. I said, "Where?"

She turned around and I got the backs of her calves. The spray dripped down. She reached and caught the drip. Rubbed it in.

"In Mariposa. The park south," she said.

"South? Really?"

"Yes," she said. "Take off your shirt. I'll get you now."

Down by the water, children played in the shallows as their parents sat reading in camp chairs. Off to my left, Lucy lay out in the sun. Browning. Eyes closed, asleep, her eyelids twitching while I stared at her. I tried not to, but she didn't have a swimsuit on, just that bra and underwear again, what I wanted to see all day long. I watched her breasts rise and fall with her breathing, noticed the thin layer of sweat on her stomach, sparkling like salt.

I left the lake to get away from her. Mumbled to myself that I was going to climb the Polly slabs, maybe swim later. I hoped she'd be gone when I got back. I could barely be around her now. I was struggling to do anything. I felt sick to my stomach.

In the early evening, I didn't see Lucy by the water. I swam 50 yards out from the north shore. All the tourists gone, the water cold, and I turned down-lake, looking to the end, and the rise of the high-country peaks behind. Snow patches were still on the north slopes. I considered swimming all the way to the end of the lake.

Then something brushed my back in the water and I spun around. It was Lucy. She laughed and dropped underneath. Grabbed one of my ankles and turned me.

I rolled. Then came back toward her.

We wrestled in the water. She was stronger than she looked. And meaner. She bent my pinkie finger back, bit my forearm hard enough to leave indents from her teeth.

I pushed her down under the water and held her head. Shaking it. Then she jabbed me in the ribs with her thumb. She came to the surface spitting and laughing. Kicked me in the thigh and swam away like a frog.

I swam after her.

She turned and splashed me in the face. Said, "Where'd you go today?"

"When?" I said.

"This afternoon."

"Oh," I said, "the Polly slabs."

"More climbing, huh?" She reached out and tugged on my wrist, pulling my face into the water.

I came up and slapped the water to splash it into her eyes. Then I backstroked. "Yeah, more climbing, why?"

"Well, I was asleep, so thanks for ditching me." She faked one way then went the other.

I dove toward her but missed. Came up and turned around. She was smiling, happy with her dodge.

She splashed me again. I dove and missed her once more.

"Missed me twice," she said. She spit water straight up, then swam ten feet away. "Are you hungry?"

"Yes," I said. "Definitely."

She slapped the water one last time, and I turned to let it hit the back of my head.

She said, "Let's go eat then."

More chili and cheese and chips for dinner. The only dinner food we had in the bear box. I liked that Lucy didn't complain. We could've hitchhiked into the store and gotten different food if we'd wanted to. But she didn't say anything about that.

I filled both bowls and handed one to her.

She bumped into me with her elbow, almost knocking the bowl out of my hand. "Oh sorry," she smiled. "Real, real sorry about that."

I bumped her back.

She said, "Are you going to climb again tonight?"

I nodded.

"Really? I was kidding," she said.

I took a gulp of water from the jug.

"Same dome?" she said.

"Probably."

"Don't you get bored by it?"

"No," I said.

"It doesn't matter to you how many times you've done the same thing?"

"No," I said. "Not really."

"Huh. Okay." She poured water into her bowl and began cleaning the inside with the tips of her fingers. "Do you like climbing more than talking?"

I smiled. Poured a little water into my bowl and started to scrub. "Normally, yes," I said.

Lucy finished scrubbing her bowl with her fingers and dumped the cleaning water out onto the ground. She said, "I like that. I really do. Some guys just talk too much. Did you know that you were the only guy on the crew who didn't talk to me the first day I worked up here?"

"No," I said. I rubbed the ends of my fingers around in the bottom of my bowl, finished cleaning, then drank the dishwater.

Lucy shook her head. "That's nasty," she said. "Did you just drink your cleaning water?"

"Yes."

"That's sick. You should've dumped that out."

I said, "I always drink my dishwater." I grabbed a few pine needles to scrub a spot off the bottom of my bowl. Then I shook out my bowl and wiped it with the inside of my T-shirt.

Lucy pointed at the chili pot. She said, "You know, this would've been better with an apple for dessert. Or a carrot."

We walked into the trees. The hill slanting. Then the granite. I scrambled to an easy line I knew, only rated a 5.5, but a good line, up one of the southern ramps leading to a higher, easy crack system. When I started to climb, so did Lucy, just behind me.

I said, "Go slow. Keep as much contact as you can."

"Contact?"

"Two hands and two feet would be four points of contact on the rock," I said. "Keep three on the rock at all times and you'll be fine."

"Okay. Like two feet and one hand?"

"Right," I said. "Just move one thing at a time."

"Okay," she said.

We climbed together, one after the other, up the knobs, first, then the crack, following the weakness. The rock was never vertical, but a 50-degree slab leading to a 70-degree summit sequence. Each time I looked back, Lucy had three points of contact on the rock, reaching or stepping. She seemed comfortable, and that was good. We didn't have a rope.

The crack we were ascending ended and I stepped over a corner onto a 60-degree slope, slightly less vertical than before. There were little chicken-head knobs and divots there. Below us a few feet were blocks sticking out of two cracks.

I was moving right on the slick rock. Lucy was behind me. The granite felt wax-covered on my bare feet. I looked back just as Lucy slipped.

She didn't scream. Her foot caught and she over-corrected, stood up. Teetering. I reached for her and lost my balance. My foot popped off, and I slid past Lucy as she leaned in and grabbed a big knob.

The rock was angled, and I slid slowly. But as I went by Lucy, my foot hit one of those big knobs at the lower corner, one of those iron doorknobs that stuck out on that section of the climb. And that chunk popped me up, vertical, stopped me, made me weightless for a second, before I started to teeter again, my hands missing everything that I reached for.

Then there was Lucy's hand in front of my face. She was holding onto a big in-cut knob above her with her left hand and reaching down to me with her right.

I caught her index finger, just that one finger, and I didn't let go. Lucy was fully extended between that good hold she was gripping with her one hand above her head and the other hand reaching down to me. She screamed as I caught her finger, as I pulled myself into the rock using her one digit for leverage, and that finger popped, turning out of joint. The skin and tendons held even after the bone dislocated. Lucy sucked in a breath at the end of her scream like choking on sand.

I reached a good knob with my other hand and grabbed it. Pulled myself onto the rock the rest of the way, stood up solidly on the knob beneath my feet, and let go of Lucy's finger. There was no chance of me falling again then. We were both secure.

Lucy slid and stepped down to me, onto a knob near the one I was standing on, using her good hand on the knobs in front of her face. We stood there on that slab together, and she ducked her head into me. I couldn't see her other hand.

"Did you hurt anything else?" I said.

"No, just that finger."

The wind coughed twice against us, the only wind yet. The gust could mean a storm was coming. I was holding the in-cut in front of me, my other arm around Lucy. I said, "I want to look at your hand but I can't right here. It's too dark in this corner. I know an easy way up from here, though. We can traverse to the east and it'll get way easier."

"Okay," she said.

"Can you climb if I help you?"

"Yes," she said.

"Then step right there." I pointed.

I spotted her as she stepped over the corner, and we followed a low-angled wave of granite around the dome. I had her climb in front of me. The wave was a ramp for a hundred feet, with an easy scramble to the top from there. Each time Lucy had to use her right hand, she sucked in, breathing through her teeth like mint and cold air.

I held a fistful of her shirt in the back and helped her through the few moves where two hands were necessary.

We got to the summit of the dome, a rounded field of gray-white granite. And there, beneath 6,000 August stars, I snapped

Lucy's finger back into place. She didn't scream then, but gasped like I had played a bad trick on her. Then she set her forehead against my shoulder.

I put my arms around her and held her as she cried. I said, "It'll be better now. It'll hurt less now that it's in." I tucked her head underneath my chin. Smelled her hair.

After a couple minutes, she pulled her head back and looked at me. "I'm okay," she said.

"Good," I said, "and thank you for catching me. I would've gone all the way without you, a ground fall."

"Yeah, but I lost my balance first."

"But you held on," I said, "and you caught me."

We hiked off the back of the dome. Scrambled a few steps on the way down, but nothing like the southwest side, and hiking down didn't take too long.

At camp, I taped Lucy's index and middle fingers together with duct tape. I taped over the end of her fingernails hoping to push back the swelling, to keep the blood and the fluid dispersed in her hand.

"I've got something that might help," I said. I went and found half a fifth of Old Grand-Dad that a climber had left for me after we'd bouldered in Camp 4 together a few weeks back.

I unscrewed the cap and held it out to her.

Lucy read the label. "Eighty-six proof?"

"Yeah, I guess."

She smelled the opening. Shrugged. "Could be good."

"I don't know," I said. "I haven't had any yet."

She sipped and coughed. "Whoa."

"Strong?"

"Yeah." She took another swig and passed the bottle to me.

I drank a gulp. I said, "I thought your finger was going to come off in my hand."

Lucy laughed and took the bottle back. Drank another gulp of whiskey. "And then?"

I shook my head. "And then it didn't."

"Well you're lucky," she said.

I thought about that. The angle off the dome. The fall would have been 200 feet of tumbling down to sharp talus. I said, "You're right. I am lucky."

Lucy looked at her taped fingers. She said, "It's aching so bad."

"I'm sorry about that," I said. Other than the tape, there was nothing we could do.

We each took another swig. The alcohol was unraveling me, everything tight coming apart. I sighed.

"Are you okay?" Lucy said.

"Yeah, I'm okay," I said. "Just thinking about falling, and the rocks. Glad neither of us went."

She said, "If either of us had gone all the way down, that would've been it. We would've died."

"Probably," I said. "At the very least, we'd have been broken."

Both of us nodded. We were sitting on the picnic table, drinking our way through the bottle.

Lucy took another swig. She said, "Do you know people who've died?"

"Yeah," I said. "I watched a man die once after a little fall, a really little fall."

Lucy said, "Did you know him well?"

"No," I said. "I was just there."

She sipped the whiskey. "How far did he fall?"

"Just a few feet. But he was upside down, and he broke his neck."

"Oh wow," she said. "That must've been horrible." She handed me the bottle.

I took a swig. I said, "Yeah, I didn't expect it."

I thought of the newspaper reports, how the sheriff's department investigated for over a year, trying to figure out who had bled on the boardwalk. The *San Francisco Chronicle* kept updating the story, writing about the new superintendent and how he planned on carrying out all of the old superintendent's plans for the park. Concessions and advertising. But after a while, the stories stopped. The sheriff's department never found any leads on the person of interest, and I stopped reading.

"You just happened to be there at the time?" Lucy said. "That's weird."

"Yeah," I said. "It was weird."

We sat on the picnic table, passing the bottle, drinking until it was empty. And I didn't explain anything.

My father holds the oak chunk in his four-fingered hand, his left. Then the short ax in his right.

He says, "You have to keep the hand ax sharp. Or else it won't chop through."

His fingers splay over the top of the wedge. He chops down to splice off kindling. Short blows, and the wedges of oak come off in inch-wide shards.

He adjusts his hand, and the ax blade cuts through where his index finger would have been. "You know how I lost this?" he says.

"No."

"I was a little kid in Manteca. We got in a car accident and I wasn't wearing my seatbelt. The impact threw me forward and I hit the seat in front of me with my hand straight out." He puts his arm in front of him to act it out.

"And what happened?"

"That one finger caught and it ripped off. Strangest thing. But strange things happen. That was when I realized that. In real life, the strangest things really do happen."

In the tent, Lucy lay down first. She pulled her sleeping bag over the top of her. Face up. Protecting her hurt hand.

I watched her, saw her submerge inside of her bag and rustle around. I thought she was changing her clothes.

Buzzing from the whiskey, I stripped off my shirt and lay down on top of my bag.

Quiet then. Near dark. Wind moved the tent canvas behind my head and made a flapping sound. I looked into the corners of the tent, felt the canvas press against my hair. I scooted away.

Lucy crawled over to me, her clothes in her sleeping bag behind her. Crawling to me, wearing nothing.

I watched the lines of that nothing, the slopes of her shoulders, the rounded, hanging half-circles of her breasts, the dark nipples pointing down, nothing I could believe. Above me now. On her hands and knees. She kissed my chest and up to my neck.

I could smell her. The hair and skin smell of her scalp where she parted her braids. Her duct-taped fingers. Then we were kissing, and I smelled the clean smell of her cheek. Her whiskey breath. Tongue tip warm.

Her body over me, my hands on her hips, sliding on her skin, then down. All of that skin.

Her thumb hooked at the top of my shorts. She pulled them down, one side, then the other. Then she was against me. Wet slick. I kissed her chest. Felt her breasts against my skin. And that smell at her throat, the scent of animal fear.

CHAPTER 3

*They blame us twice. First for their own raids on miners'
camps. Second for the war. They are like the ground squirrels
in Camp 4. Bloated and conniving. Living on the infection of
tourism. Do you understand? This is as much us as anything.
But there was before that too.*

*I told you about Juarez in San Francisco, but you weren't
old enough to remember that.*

*Listen to me now: James Savage, the mining camp leader,
takes Juarez because he wants the Miwoks to be intimidated.
Juarez had spoken out, saying he did not believe the stories about
the whites, stories that they had become like foam on the water.*

*In the city, Juarez trades gold dust for whiskey. Drinks on
the street. Spits racial slurs. Calls Savage the name of a dog
that he had beaten to death for snarling at him.*

*Juarez says, "There is a war coming for you." He is not a
Yosemiti, but this speech leads them back to the Valley.*

*The Yosemiti are here, unknowing, like a bear that
wanders in front of a lifted rifle. Even the hunter is surprised
as he holds the gun, the groove of the trigger smooth behind his
index finger.*

I woke up early and felt her body against me. Her naked breasts
pressing against me, her nipples hard in the morning cool. Arm
draped over me. Her one duct-taped hand.

I shifted slowly, not wanting to wake her. Slid to the side of her
injured hand. Worked my body away, pushed up, and tried to slip
out of the sleeping bag.

But she reached and caught me with the fingertips of her injured hand. Winced. She woke up all the way. She said, "Tenaya?"

I had started to slide out of our sleeping bag.

"Come back," she said. She moved her hips over, underneath me. I was up above her, above all that naked skin. She shifted and centered herself.

I held there, my heart pumping the lake, Tenaya's blood. Running barefoot on the sand. The smell of water.

Lucy scraped the fingernails of her good hand down my chest, my stomach. I smelled the water and the shore. A man held the rock that killed Tenaya. I was above her and Lucy's legs were open.

I left the lake. Lowered, Tenaya moved away, lowered down, inside of her, tasted her neck, breathed her skin. And she did not know about the stories, and they were not her fault.

"We can't. Not all week," she said.

"Okay."

"So they won't know," she said. "Then they'll leave us up here."

"Okay," I said again.

We kept apart. Didn't talk. Hoped they wouldn't suspect us. I heard Lucy ask the crew chief the second Friday morning. "Can I stay up here again this weekend? I really don't have anything to do in the Valley."

He looked up from his time log. "Again?" he said.

"Yeah." Lucy pointed to the Domes. She said, "I just love this country. I don't want to go back down to the Valley or to Wawona. Mariposa."

The crew chief said, "Your hand though. Shouldn't we get that looked at?"

The finger was bruised black, one streak to Lucy's wrist like a line of ink.

"No," Lucy said. "It's getting better. And taped up, it barely hurts."

The crew chief spun his pen between his fingers. Squinted at her. "That Tenaya kid's going to be up here again though. Was that a problem last weekend?"

"No," Lucy shrugged. "It was fine. He leaves me alone."

The crew chief flipped his pen again. He said, "Well, I guess it doesn't matter. So whatever you want to do . . . "

I turned so the crew chief wouldn't see me smiling. I walked off to work a slash pile at the edge of the clearing.

At quitting time, I went straight to the tent. Pretended to be reading. I heard the first few trucks pull out, and I realized that my hands were shaking.

After the last person left, Lucy came over to the tents, and I met her at the tent door. She kissed me so hard that our teeth clicked. We kept kissing, and I pulled her head underneath the tent flap. I tore one of the seams of her T-shirt as I ripped it off. She fought with the shoelace that held my shorts up. Bit the knot loose with her teeth.

We didn't come out at dinnertime, not until after dark.

We were swimming in the afternoon the next day, Saturday, when we saw the rattlesnake. I had just gotten to the shallows and Lucy was behind me in the deep, near the rocks' slag. The snake slid off a split shelf and cut out.

Lucy was submerged to her eyes, saw the snake making S-curves toward her. She stayed where she was and the snake never veered. It swam right by her head, not more than a foot away.

When it was past her, I said, "Why didn't you move or at least go under?"

Lucy ducked her head, swam to me, and bobbed up. She said, "Why would I move?"

"Because a rattlesnake was coming right at you."

"It wasn't a big deal," she said. "I like rattlesnakes."

"Oh," I said.

She said, "I once saw a four-foot Northern Pacific Rattlesnake eat a chipmunk. The snake struck it, then sat back and watched the thing twitch. Then the snake swallowed it whole, unhinged its jaw and slid it in." Lucy leaned to the side and squeezed water out of her hair. "Incredible."

"But coming at you in the water?"

Lucy said, "I scared one off a log once, scared it toward me, on the Merced. I was downstream, and we kept zigzagging back and forth, trying to get out of each other's way. I just started laughing."

I said, "My mother kills them."

Lucy shook her head. "That's not good. We need rattlesnakes."

I said, "You sound like my father."

Lucy raised her eyebrows. "Then I like your father."

I said, "My mother once found a rattlesnake coiled under the outside corner of our tent. I heard her suck in breath and knew it was a snake because of the sound she made. She killed it with a shovel, and I saw the venom drops against the metal. Then she buried the head, skinned it out, battered and salted the meat. We fried it in butter and pepper, and it tasted good."

"You liked it?"

"Oh yeah. Gray and tender. It was pretty nice, but it was also something other than fish, which was good. My father was always talking about the treasure that we'd found when I was little, but he never wanted to buy meat."

"Treasure?" Lucy said.

"That's another long story."

Lucy opened the food bin and got out more Nalley's cans. "Chili burritos? What do you say? Instead of plain chili we can wrap it in something for variety."

"Sure," I said. I got out the tortillas and the block of cheese. Started cutting slices.

We warmed two cans on the Coleman stove, then glopped big scoops onto slices of cheese on top of tortillas. Then we wrapped them.

Lucy's burrito spilled and she rewrapped it. She said, "I don't like reptiles dying."

I took a big bite. Chewed and swallowed. I said, "I guess that's not my favorite thing either."

Lucy said, "My cousin caught an alligator lizard on the Vernal Trail when I was six years old, and it was about this long." She held her hands a foot apart. "He caught the lizard in a pile of leaves and needles, then started waving it around like it was a toy."

"And it was dying?"

"No, no. The lizard was fine. Healthy. But then he put it in my sister Anne's face, and she held up her hand, and the lizard bit onto her finger."

"Bit hard?" I said.

"Oh yeah. Wouldn't let go. Anne was screaming and trying to rip her finger back out, and my cousin was just laughing and laughing. Then Anne started cussing at him, so he took out his sheath knife and pried the point of the blade into the side of the lizard's head. He was still laughing as he popped the jaws open and tore the top of the lizard's head off."

"What was your sister doing then?"

"Still screaming," Lucy said. She took a bite of her burrito. Talked with her mouth full. "The lizard writhed and spun around, flipped upside down. Its blood was everywhere. It was sick." Lucy swallowed her bite. Took another.

The cheese hadn't melted in my burrito but I liked it like that. I was eating fast. I said, "So you were pretty mad at him?"

Lucy said, "I called him a murderer."

I laughed.

"But he was a murderer," she said. "That was murder. And I called him a murderer for a long time after that too."

"Well, it sounded pretty intense anyway."

"It was."

Lucy smiled. Touched her chili burrito to mine. "Cheers for more chili dinners, huh? Same old chili, but a new style of eating it."

I said, "People do terrible things sometimes. Much worse than killing lizards."

"I know," she said. "But I was six. And that sort of thing is worse when you're six."

"Right," I said. "That makes sense."

"But just the same, tell me a terrible thing you've done." Lucy ate the last bite of her burrito and tapped me with her index finger. "You go," she said.

"A terrible thing?"

"Yes," she said. "No, wait. Don't tell me a terrible thing. All terrible things are the same. Tell me something beautiful instead."

"Beautiful like what?"

"Beautiful like an image," she said. "Tell me something I can picture."

"Okay," I said, "let me think." I took a bite of my burrito. Chewed. I thought of the butterflies in August, how they came in great orange clouds when they were migrating, landing on me as I stood still. But then I remembered something I loved even more. I said, "Some nights in winter, when I was a kid, and it was cold, we'd go into our tent right after dinner, and I'd lay my head in my mother's lap and my feet in my father's, and we'd have these thick, wool blankets over all of us. My dad would read from this book of animal stories, where a rabbit was always getting in trouble and a coyote and a fox were always tricking each other, and there was a big bear and a family of deer, and I loved it. We read that book three, maybe four times all the way through, and I could look out the door of our tent at the stars and listen to my father read."

"Exactly," Lucy said. "That's exactly what I wanted to hear."

A tourist told us about the first wildfire that night, in the mountains to the southwest. Out of the park, but not far. Cabins burnt. Utility lines and 10,000 acres scorched.

The tourist said, "It's going to fill the Valley with smoke. And they're saying this season will be the worst fire season in a long, long time."

Lucy said, "Isn't it too late in the year for fires?"

"No," he shook his head. "Big Indian summer coming. They're saying lots of fires will go all fall."

I woke up to the smell of her in my sleeping bag. Didn't want to sleep anymore. Didn't want to lose the time with her. I could hear her measured breathing, the quiet pull of air. Water and the seasons. Geology.

I kissed her face.

"You awake?" she said.

"Yes."

She said, "I don't want it to be Sunday night."

"Me neither."

"Or Monday and the rest of the silent weekdays," she said.

"Weekdays like drought."

Lucy smiled. She said, "It's like drought without me?"

"Yes," I said.

Then the workweek again. The crew around us, and we worried that everyone would catch on to us. We never talked during the day, but in moments in the evenings, by the bathrooms or the lake, or if the group broke up after dinner. The other boys on the crew continued their attempts with Lucy, so I'd walk off to avoid watching that.

By Friday, I had trouble eating. I'd been waiting five days to be with her. Each night, sleeping with the ghost of Lucy. Her hair across my face. An elbow in my ribs. I'd smell for her as I listened to the other workers snore around me.

Midmorning on a Friday. Piling slash on a steep hill near Fairview Dome. Two of our crew members were over a small rise, in a ravine shaped like a question mark. They were talking loudly. They couldn't see each other so they yelled back and forth, the sounds slamming off the fractured granite, spilling out of the ravine to where I was working.

The first one said, ". . . with Lucy?"

I stopped when I heard her name.

The other one said, "Oh, hell yeah."

I thought they were talking about me, so I crept closer. I thought Lucy and I had been discovered.

The first one said, "I hear that."

I snuck up to the lip of the ravine. Looked down into the curve of the question. I was on my stomach, listening.

The one to my right, downhill, said, "She *is* fine."

There was a pause, then the left one yelled back. "Oh, yeah. Real fine, no joke except for that snaggle tooth."

Neither of them said anything for a minute while they worked their own sections of the cut. Then the left-side one said, "But that chest and ass?"

My stomach tightened. I wiped the sweat off my forehead.

The other one said, "Definitely."

"I mean, I'd fuck the hell out of her. I'd just lean her up against a tree and go to work."

The blood pounded in the front of my head. I picked up a fist-sized rock.

They kept talking but I couldn't hear words. Just the noises of them. One was to my right, but I was working uphill toward the other one, the one who'd said that thing about the tree and Lucy.

I slid down the embankment, behind a stand of white pine. Crouching. Waiting to move only when he was making enough noise to mask my footfalls. Then I got to him. He was on one knee, oiling the chain on his saw, yelling over his shoulder at the other worker, the other crew member in the ravine.

I came from the left side, his blind side. I hit him once with the rock. Put him down.

The crew chief called a meeting at lunch. "Guys, we need to talk a little bit about safety. This is dangerous, uneven terrain. What happened to Joey can happen to anyone. And imagine if he'd slipped while his saw was running. Believe you me, that wouldn't have been just a bloody knock on the back of his head. If one of you falls backwards with a saw running in his lap, you can damn well cut yourself in half. You understand?"

We nodded.

He looked at us and mimicked the motion of a chainsaw turning on him.

He said, "Joey's been transported down to the hospital in Bishop. EMTs said it's a bad contusion and a serious concussion, but he should be all right. Now you all need to watch yourselves for the rest of the day. Okay?"

People mumbled, "Okay."

I didn't tell Lucy.

That night, Lucy asked, "What are you thinking?"

I was remembering crawling back up out of the ravine and throwing the blood rock as far as I could into the trees. Thinking about my hands and the superintendent. Blood this time. Not from my tongue.

I said, "Nothing."

"Are you sure?"

"Yeah, I'm just tired," I said.

Lucy put her arms around my waist. "Too tired?"

I kissed her mouth. "No. Not too tired."

My father held his fist in the air. I imagined that he meant to put his finger up. He said, "There's a voice inside your head and you know." He tapped my forehead with his fist. "You know, Tenaya. And you can't ignore that voice. That is the Valley."

Fifteen then. I went to chapel services alone in the old Yosemite Chapel. Sunday mornings after sleeping away, hung over from the Camp 4 parties the night before. I thought the services could take away the ghosts.

I felt the repetition of the Lord's Prayer, my knees and shins flat on the cold floor. Forgive us our trespasses as we forgive those who trespass against us. Trespasses universal. Trespasses against the Valley, or my trespasses. But I could not forgive what I had already trespassed. Passed to judgment.

Dust caked like dry-cracked blood. Flaking. Remembering the petroglyphs I found near Sentinel: two men hunting mammoth and one man following. He who hunts men, the painting of the one who holds human bones.

Lucy came out sick. A Tuesday morning. She didn't look sick, but then she threw up.

The crew chief said, "Better get in bed. Take care of that flu."

Lucy shook her head, "I feel good now." And she didn't look too green. She looked flushed and pretty.

I watched her. Kept circling back by the water so I could check on her. And the funny thing was, she looked more healthy than anyone else on the crew. She looked beautiful.

The next morning, she threw up twice. Once, first off, straight out of her tent, then again after breakfast. The crew chief didn't see either one, and Lucy went to work. Worked all morning.

I met her by the Porta-Potties. "What's wrong?"

"Nothing," she said.

"Are you sick?"

"No," she said.

"No?"

"I mean, I feel fine now," she said.

I said, "That's weird."

"Yeah, well, we better get back to work."

In the afternoon, Lucy went to pile slash over the slope, and I didn't see her for the rest of the day. I didn't like that. I tried not to lose sight of her the next day or the day after, working on the periphery of her circles.

The crew chief came over to me on Friday. He said, "Hey, Tenaya, a word?"

I waited.

He said, "Now this is none of my business, none at all, but you know Lucy?"

I said, "Yes."

He pointed. "You know, the only girl here, that one right there?"

"Yes," I said.

"Well," he said, "she stays up here all weekend with you."

"Yeah," I said. "I know."

He put his hand on my shoulder like my father would. "Well, you should seriously think about making a move."

"A move?"

"Come on, son. You haven't seen her watch you? I mean, you're a good worker and all, but you're not worth watching all day." He pointed to Lucy. "And she keeps you on scout. She watches every damn thing you do all day long. Did you know that?"

I didn't want to give us away, so I said, "Huh."

"*Huh*." He mimicked me. "Is that all you got? This is your last weekend up here with a pretty girl. And she seems interested in you . . . " He tapped me on the shoulder with his fingers. "So you think about it. But not too long."

"Okay, thanks," I said.

"Thank me after you make a move, all right?" he said. He picked up two chainsaws, and carried them back to the bed of his truck.

"Tenaya?" Lucy and I were in the tent, in my sleeping bag. She dipped her nose against my chest. "Where do you live in the Valley?"

We hadn't talked about it. My parents always told me not to tell anyone, but I told her the truth. "Up Ribbon Creek. West of El Cap. Up a ways in the trees. My parents have a camp up there."

"And you've been there for a long time?" she said.

"My whole life."

"What?" she said.

"My family's been in the Valley forever."

She said, "Forever?" She lifted her head.

"Since the first Paiutes. All the way through. On my mother's side. And my father's been there a long time too now."

She moved her finger on my chest, starting to draw a picture. She said, "So you're a Yosemiti then?"

"Yes."

She put her finger on the knot of my collarbone, the old break there. Lucy made a slash across my throat.

I lifted my head and looked at her.

She said, "And a Miwok girl." She settled back onto my chest and kept tracing with her finger. Drew something like a bird.

I had my arm underneath her. The smooth skin of her back, the calluses on my fingers catching. I said, "Do you know the history?"

"I only know what my father told me."

"Oh," I said.

"And Carlos," she said.

"Carlos?"

"My cousin." She was still drawing the bird, adding feathers to the wings. She said, "We grew up together. He's older, and he always took care of me. He works for the Park Service, has for a while. Some kind of patrol officer or ranger or something."

I said, "And he taught you the history of the Yosemiti?"

"Yeah," she said. "His stories are different from everyone else's. He says it's always 1851. That there are new developments but nothing new."

"What does he mean?"

"I don't know," she said. "He just warned me about my father too. It was this spring, a few months ago. He said he wasn't sure what my father was doing."

Lucy drew something on my skin, beneath the bird, something hanging in the talons.

I tucked her hair behind her ear. I said, "Does your cousin know what he's talking about?"

"Huh?" Lucy stopped her drawing.

"Well, does he know something?" I said.

"I don't know. My father is always dealing with the Park Service because of the property lease at North Wawona, where we live, and I don't know what's going on right now."

I wondered what a deal meant. New development. I thought of my own father.

Lucy said, "Carlos kept trying to talk to me before I came up here this summer. He said I had to know some things. But I kind of avoided him. He gets sort of crazy sometimes."

I said, "Maybe it is 1851." I thought about the sign near Mirror Lake. The one posted by the National Park Service. Pictures of Paiutes labeled as "The Original Inhabitants: The Miwoks" and a similar sign in the museum. I'd scratched the signs with a stone, but the words wouldn't remove, the etchings too deep. I'd finally broken the plastic and buried what I could break off.

Saturday afternoon. The sun came through the trees like shards of yellow glass. My cheeks tight, singed at the corners. The strips of skin under Lucy's eyes burned pink-brown. She'd thrown up twice again that morning.

I said, "Are you hungry for anything?"

"No," she said. She sat and looked over the lake. No wind now, and the water black glass.

Children played in the shallows, blond and chasing each other, laughing, their mother scolding them in German.

We were sitting side by side, leaning against the trunk of a fat juniper pine.

Lucy turned her head. "Do you ever want to leave, Tenaya?"

"Here?" I said.

"Not just here," she said. "Yosemite."

"For a while or for good?"

"For good," she said, "to live somewhere else." She picked up a juniper berry. Put it between her teeth.

"I don't know."

She bit down on the berry and chewed. Made a face. Spit blue and turquoise. She said, "You don't just want to leave? Go anywhere?"

"No," I said. "I've never thought about it much. Why, do you want to leave?"

"Yes," she said.

"Really?"

"Yes. Definitely."

I said, "We're in Tuolumne, far enough. Up here, in the high country, I feel like I've already left."

"Here?" she said. "This is still in the park though."

I said, "To me it feels different." Under the high sun, I thought of the stones, the opposite, and the cool. The smell of the river. The eddy when I was six, and the granite slab there. The small body laid out in the evening. I wondered where my mother was that night.

Sunday was my birthday, September 17. Lucy sitting next to me when I woke up. She'd never gotten out of bed earlier than me, but she was sitting there with eggs waiting on a paper plate next to my sleeping bag. Eggs covered in pepper and too much salt.

I smiled. She used spices like smothering a fire.

She said, "Happy birthday."

"What is this?"

She pointed to the eggs. "Cooked them by headlamp. I know how early you like to get up."

I reached for her.

She leaned down and kissed me on the forehead. "Eat your eggs."

"Okay," I said.

She had a plate too but didn't eat. I pointed to them, my mouth full.

She shook her head. "Too nauseous."

When I finished eating, she said, "Want to walk?"

Outside the tent, a Steller's jay hopped sideways to us. Lucy said, "Here you go," and set down her plate of eggs for the bird. The jay hopped onto the plate, his beak dropping like a hammer drill. He ate so hard that he popped a hole in the paper.

"That's how I feel in the morning."

Lucy said, "That's how I used to feel."

Greazy puffs his joint across from me, pointing with his pinkie. The year I met him in Camp 4.

He says, "Like the '77 weed, man."

"Like the what?" I say.

"The 1977 weed. The big score. The Lockheed Lodestar."

I say, "That was the year I was born."

"Fucking star-blessed." He giggles and scratches his beard with both hands. He says, "No shit, huh? That makes you sixteen?"

"Yes."

He says, "You know the story?" He inhales and holds it. Exhales slowly. He says, "Okay. So the story. Sixteen years ago, in the spring of '77, early that year, we all start hearing this thing about a Fed raid on a plane up at the pass. Lower Merced Lake. Funny thing though: it was a ranger who told us that the full score wasn't recovered. A fucking law ranger said that, said 1,500 pounds of weed remained in the plane. And it's March, so it's frozen as shit up there. But we cut holes in the ice and go down with scuba gear rented in Fresno. And man if those duffel bags don't dry out in a tent right here, in this site, number 33, Camp 4." Greazy pats the ground, then makes circles, dirt angels with the flats of his hands.

I say, "Did you get a lot?"

He giggles. "Oh, fuck yes, man . . . you have no idea. People set themselves up forever with one quick trip into San Francisco." He puffs and holds his smoke. Exhales through his nose. "One quick trip to the city and people set for life. If you're a dirtbag camping in the Valley, it doesn't take much to be rich, you know? All sorts of people scored it too."

"Like who?" I say.

"Like anyone who heard about it and could get the scuba gear. Climbers. Dirtbags. Hikers. Some of them just people who scrounged around for a while, anyone who wanted to live long-term here, that's who really went for it. I know a lot of people who never needed to work again. Not even Search and Rescue."

Greazy puffs one, two, three. Waits to blow smoke. He says, "There was just too much damn money in that plane."

Out along Tenaya Lake, early morning, the sun showing layers and spangling the flat blade of green water.

Lucy said, "Do you know?"

"Know what?" I said.

She looked at me. Her eyes flint. She laced her fingers into mine. She said, "I didn't think about that. Did you?"

I kept looking at her. We stood there next to the lake.

"Yeah?" she said.

Then I understood. "No, wait. Really?" I said.

She nodded.

"No," I said, "I didn't think about that possibility."

"Me either," she said. "I'm a little scared."

We started walking again. We walked for a while, not speaking. The water lapped on the granite next to us, each wave like the sound of a person gulping.

Lucy shivered and leaned in to me. She said, "I came up here to work for a few months, to think about leaving the park. I used to be so close to my father."

I said. "But you're not now?"

"No. He's into other things. And I don't know all of them. I need to get closer to him again. He keeps saying that he'll 'bring me in on it,' but I don't know what that means. I'm trying to decide if I want to be brought in on everything he does. I'm thinking I do, but maybe I don't."

Lucy walked a little faster. The birds were moving now, and out on the water, an eagle hit for a fish.

She said, "Are you close to your father?"

"Yes," I said. "But not as close as we used to be either. I spend a lot of time away now."

"Why?" she said.

"I don't know." But I thought of the superintendent, my first summer away. I said, "I guess I didn't know how to tell my father everything anymore. And that mattered to me."

"But he still talks to you?" she said.

"Yeah, we still talk, and he still tells me to be a warrior."

Lucy said, "A warrior in what war?"

"The old one, I guess," I said. "Or the one he says is still going on. Either way, I want to make him happy, so I think about it."

When we got back to the tent site, the day was warming fast.

"Play me in checkers?" Lucy said, and pointed to the slab below the dome's headwall.

"Okay," I said.

She got out the board and we crossed the road. Walked up to find rocks. She leaned down and picked one up. "I'll be white," she said.

"All right," I said, "I've got dark then."

We found twelve stones each, sat down, and set up the game.

Lucy said, "You go first," and we started to play.

I watched her think. The way she scraped her teeth together, top and bottom, the way she touched her tongue to her one turned tooth.

I touched her ankle. "My parents will be interesting," I said. I slid a gray rock toward her front line.

She rotated a rock, spun it in a circle, and tapped it on the board. She said, "They won't be happy with this?"

"Well . . . " I said.

She said, "They won't be happy with me?" She slid a white rock to the left edge where she was protected by the sideline.

I slid a checker to back up my first. "Maybe not with this," I said. "Not with all of it."

She moved a piece on the opposite side of the board.

I said, "My parents are . . . it's tough to explain. You'll see when you meet them."

She nodded and looked at the board.

"They're interesting," I said. I moved a middle rock forward into an open space, a stupid move, but I wasn't thinking about checkers. I said, "My father told me stories growing up."

Lucy raised her eyebrows. Jumped my unprotected checker. We played back and forth for a moment. Lucy's teeth sounded like two pebbles, grating. I'd noticed the slight indent where they rubbed on her right incisor.

I said, "Old stories." I made another bad move.

Lucy leaned forward. Double-jumped me. "Old stories?"

I jumped her back, once, but I had to open up a back-line square.

Lucy said, "Have you dated many girls, Tenaya?"

"No," I said.

She slid another stone to the edge. "How many?"

"None," I said.

She said, "None at all?" She flicked my hand. "Are you kidding?"

I said, "I've hung out with girls, been around them in Camp 4 or at the bridge, but I never dated anyone."

Lucy smiled and nodded.

I moved a checker but with no game plan. Moving just to move. I said, "You'd have to understand my parents. What they believe and where we live. If you saw it, you'd understand."

Lucy tapped a rock on the slab, two beats. Three, then four.

I said, "How would I meet a girl?"

Lucy set up another double jump.

I moved to block her.

"You'd meet a girl in Tuolumne," she said.

"Right."

She leaned across the board and kissed me. "And you'd be so happy."

"Yes," I said.

Lucy was playing outside in, keeping my checkers in the middle. The game wasn't close.

She said, "You want to keep living like that?"

"No," I said, "I mean, maybe . . . " But I didn't know.

Lucy leaned across and kissed me again. She sat back and crossed her arms. "When will you know?"

I stared at the board. There was no way to win this checkers game. I was already down four.

Lucy said, "Your move."

I moved, but I had no strategy. Each play worse than the one before.

"Some of these things . . . " she said. "Some of these things are . . ." she jumped me again, "they are what they are."

I was losing by five now.

I looked at the board trying to think of something to do, but saw nothing there.

Lucy's arms were crossed, her biceps strong. I admired her shoulders. I looked at her face then, the way her lips were set as she stared at the board. Her eyes and dark eyelashes over her sunburned cheeks. The only girl.

I moved a checker and said, "We could get married."

She'd had her head down, following my moves, but her head popped up when I said that. She said, "Are you joking?" She put her fingers to her mouth and pinched her bottom lip.

I tapped one of my rocks on the board. Looked out at the camp and the lake. "No," I said. "Actually I'm not. Do you want to get married?"

She said, "Really?"

I looked right at her. The flush in her face. The way she held that lip with her finger and her thumb. She let go, and I saw her hand shake. "Really?" she said again.

"Yes."

Lucy folded her legs underneath her and sat back on her ankles. Closed her eyes.

I said, "What are you thinking?"

"Okay," she said. Her eyes were still closed. She nodded. "Okay," she said again. She opened her eyes, leaned across the board and kissed me. Then she stood up. She had my checkers in her hand, the rocks that she'd won. She took a rock and threw it at the road sign down below. And missed.

I stood up next to her. "So, yes?"

"Yes," she said. She threw a second rock, and that one hit the sign with a clank.

Lucy hopped forward and screamed.

I screamed too. Then I began to throw my checkers at the sign.

One by one, we threw the rocks out at the yellow road marker. A few of them hit the metal, clanking, and we screamed like lit gasoline.

I came into my parents' camp as the sun set on the bottom of the nimbus. Sky like the underbelly of a pink ocean.

The '46 Plymouth was in the high grass near the creek. Full gas can next to the tree. In winter, my parents slept on the bench seats, front and back, inside the car, but their summer tarp-tent was hung off to the side of camp now.

My father was sitting in front of the car, shaping a figurine out of a chunk of incense cedar, working ticks off with his sheath knife. The soft, straight-grained wood whittled off in dips.

I hadn't seen him in almost two months. He looked older than I remembered.

He smiled when he saw me. "Did you like the job?"

"Yes," I said, "and I met someone." I'd decided to tell my parents right away. Not wait. I said, "A girl named Lucy."

He turned his knife through the cedar at an eye, put pressure on the back of his knife with his thumb. A small chunk of bright came off. I could smell the sap.

He said, "So you like her?"

"Yes. We're getting married."

He stopped whittling. Butted the knife on his thigh, blade up.

I said, "Soon. At the end of this month."

He wiped the splinters off his knees. Used his thumb to feel for burrs on the knife. "This month?"

"Yes."

He said, "So you're serious."

"Yes," I said.

He found a small burr and examined it. Took granite granules from next to his chair and set them on the sideways blade. Ran them across with a pressed thumb. He said, "And you've thought this through? Thought about everything?"

I saw a loose rock at the fire ring. I squatted to wedge it back in, took a smaller granite piece and puzzled it tight. I said, "No. I probably haven't thought of everything."

I looked at him and he raised his eyebrows. Still working that burr with the granules across his knife blade.

I said, "But I will." I shimmed the loose rock with another flake. Wedged it tight. I said, "She and I will."

My father popped the burr. Held up his blade and looked across. Popped again. Then he scraped the knife sideways on a block of wood to see for catch. He said, "So you're willing to make a mistake."

I found another loose rock in the fire ring and worked that one. Shimmed with flakes.

My mother returned to camp with full water buckets, looking too thin to carry the weight. She set the buckets down and hugged me. I could feel her ribs.

My father pointed his knife at me. He said, "Tenaya says he's getting married."

My mother's fingers curled, made a fist. Her exhale sounded a note.

My father said, "This month."

I hugged my mother and she gripped my back. I felt the ten points of her fingertips.

CHAPTER 4

This is how the war starts. Miners shoot a Miwok trapper in the back and call him a "brave." They tell the newspaper that he's been a horse-thief Indian.

The next war party leaves the mangled bodies of Boden's four companions, one of the men skinned alive. These are true stories, your history.

The Miwoks are divided. Juarez and Jose Rey are preparing for war. Those leaders are in the mountains, waiting. Others are living in mining camps, forgetting former lives, their wives and children. Drinking whiskey in the daylight.

During the militia's first campaign into the mountains, twenty-two Indians are killed without a single death among the settlers. The soldiers light the wigwams with irons from the fire, and the panicked warriors run out without any organization. Jose Rey is one of the first to be shot down, and the soldiers believe he has died.

The Yosemiti hear everything through runners. They hear that the ghosts will never come to the Valley, and they believe the story.

Tenaya is up north in the high country. Watching past North Dome. He sees a great cloud come from the southwest and blow over Glacier Point, filling the U. It drops down and hangs like fog among the trees. But it is not fog.

My father said, "It's like 1850."

"No. It isn't," I said.

"Yes," he said. "It is now. There are new things going on."

I threw my water bottle on top of my day gear. Cinched my pack. Then I hiked out of camp.

The night of the mountain lion. Lion like winter storm, like the metal mirrors in the Camp 4 bathrooms, dull, reflecting, and scratched. Of the winter flood and flashes.

I took the path across Swinging Bridge. Saw the logjams left over from the swell in January when the Merced flowed a quarter-mile across, fifteen feet above the top of the bank. The bears come now to paw at the watermark, wondering about all the berry bushes lost downstream.

I hiked Four Mile Trail under Sentinel, Union, Moran, the granite dust puffing in the heat. The smell of every summer, the dust and the green acorns not ripe hanging on the trees, and the bitter taste of the soft, green nut that wicked the moisture from inside my cheeks.

Up in the pines I met the Pohono Trail near Glacier Point. Then I could run, had to run to catch her before dark. I wanted to talk to her, ask her about the New Parks Plan, hear that everything was okay. I wanted to see if she was still real.

To North Wawona, past Bridalveil, maybe North Wawona by eight or nine o'clock. Running hard above the meadow, I noticed the easy cool in the trees and the smell of the wind coming over the high stream. The half-light slant like mist filling. The new dew smell.

And I saw the lion.

Up on split granite, rock that sluffs old skin, the lion waiting, hoping for a short hunt. I ran underneath him. But I saw him too, saw him as his body tensed.

The lion jumped soft yellow above me as I stepped back. Then he hit me and we fell downhill toward the meadow. Both the same size. Both animals. It was like that in the meadow, and I gouged at his eyes and kept my forearm over my own throat. I'd watched lions kill deer in El Cap Meadow in the spring and I knew what he would do.

We were face to face, and I could smell the rotten meat smell of his breath. Then we rolled and I saw the patterns of the pines above us like woodcuts displayed along the lodge wall.

Each moment clipped, with a gap between to keep it slow, slow at the freeze, that slow.

The lion rolled and I rolled with him. Then he bit my hand. He was growling, thrashing and biting, and I was yelling, and I didn't know at first that my hand was caught. I didn't see it go into his mouth. But I felt the bones give, felt the bones crack with a wet sound, a dull wet like saplings, not dry sticks, not short and *pop pop* but a slow *clssst clssst* sound.

My hand turned in the lion's mouth, the pain striking up my wrist, up the sinews of my arm, and my shoulder twitched hard with the sudden shock of pain and the wrenching. Then I felt the Valley in me, everything tighten, down, close and close, and the Valley was with me, and the Valley was me. I was with the Valley in the meadow, and slow now. Slow again.

I felt my broken hand ball up inside and began to force it down, push and force it down the lion's throat, slow, catching and sliding, forcing until that fist was fifteen inches down, down to the elbow. I felt the choking of the whole animal, the lion seizing.

The lion was on top of me, over my legs, a blanket of rocks. I pushed it to sit up. Struggled and cleared my legs, but my arm was still inside. And I saw that the animal was not breathing, that he was dead, something inside him broken when I forced my fist down into the bottom of his throat.

I felt the lion on my right arm, his whole weight, 150 pounds, and I ripped at the mouth, punched his teeth and jaw. Punched myself too, my right arm that was fixed inside and my punching was nothing, and the skin nicked off my left fist's knuckles when I hit his yellow teeth, the backs of my knuckles turned red from the yellow sharps of his teeth, turned red and dripped.

I punched once more, and hit my own bicep. Pink to swell. I watched the colors.

My father says, "You'll do this to me?"

"To you?" I say. I don't know what he means.

"Yes, to me. My whole life. And yours. Everything I've told you about the history."

I say, "This has nothing to do with you."

He laughs. He is retying a double half hitch at the tent corner. "Is that right?" he says.

"That's right," I say. "It doesn't."

He looks at me. "I never touched you," he says. "Not one time. You've lived soft, Tenaya."

I look downhill at the dark trees. The slope where the granite scatters. "I don't think so," I say. "Maybe you've been good, but never soft. And I'm not."

He hooks his thumbs in the sides of his shirt, pulling the edges out into triangles. He says, "I don't ask much, but I'm asking now."

"What," I say. "What are you asking?"

I moved the lion between my legs, like a huge dog. The waxy scent of its hide and new urine. It'd let go on my legs and shoes when I choked it, the smell of acrid wet on my wool socks.

I made myself count to hold off panic, a trick I'd learned while climbing. Pause between each number. Count up slowly and count down.

My heart was two pieces, ore-heavy, an echo knocking into itself *da-duh, da-duh, da-duh.* I could feel the metal at my lungs. And it was darker now. Night coming. The blond hair of the lion beginning to glow in the last light, glowing like one tent in a meadow.

And she looked like that. Fifteen years ago. Her skin. Whiter on the riverbank, whiter against the gray rock. Pale-blue lips. She seemed to glow. I remembered the cold of her cheeks, the color of river stones.

I opened my eyes. My heart still thumping but my head slower now, and I could think. I used the point of my left elbow and my body weight to force the lower jaw of the lion. I leaned until the jaw snapped under the point of my elbow, until the jaw broke like a beer bottle inside a towel. With the jaw broken, the lion's mouth was not as tight, and I began to pry at the throat, pulling to retrieve my broken right hand.

Sweat dripping. Pulling and slow progress now. Big drops of sweat off my nose down onto the glowing fur. Prying and pulling, my sweat wetting the lion's head, and pulling still.

Then the hand came out. My hand. I saw the turned claw, the broken fingers rounded down and in, like a black bear's paw, my hand no longer human. All four bones behind the knuckles were fractured like the fingers in front of them, the fourth bone sticking out through the skin. I couldn't feel the pinky, or the small bone coming out behind it. I couldn't feel that side of my hand at all, and I used my left thumb to push the stick of bone back through the skin, back into place. Then I flattened my palm on the ground and straightened the other fingers against the dirt.

I knew I would feel the hand soon enough, when everything came in, when my heart slowed. But my heart was still beating like stones, pounding and pounding. And I couldn't stop that beat, even with my mind quiet.

I knew the pain could rush like a spring. Turn the cracked block of ice in the river until it hit the sweep at the top of the falls, and wait, edge heavy.

I couldn't make North Wawona now. Not in the dark. But I could pull together a drag pile, a debris shelter. So I scavenged. Kicked at things with my feet until I found one big stick that I pulled over to a split rock. Then I found cross boughs of deadfall, and laid them as tight as I could with one hand. I couldn't interlace them, so I covered them thick with whatever I could find, built up an insulation layer over the top. Then I scraped piles of needles with the insides of my feet, big piles of fresh needles, and smaller piles of loam, kicking them into the shelter before swimming in with my good arm.

Lucy would be gone in the morning. She was off to Merced with her aunt and I wouldn't catch her now. I tried to picture her face riding in a car.

Then it was all the way dark and the pain seized. Pulsing. Pain from my fingertips to my shoulder, down the back of my neck, the muscles next to my spine cramping with the ache. I closed my eyes to shut out the throbbing. Then I waited. Pounding and waiting. Waiting through the dark with my eyes open, for the first hint of morning light, waiting until I could begin walking toward North Wawona again.

At dawn, my hand was so swollen that I couldn't open or close my fingers. I used my shirt for a sling, pulled the knot tight with my teeth, and hiked all morning to the tourist camp. The first-aid tent there was staffed by Berkeley and Stanford medical students. A medical student came out to meet me, her clothes bright and clean.

She said, "Come here often?" She smiled. She was a little older than me but young. Pale and blue-eyed.

I tried to smile back. "No," I said. My hand looked like meat turning rancid, purpled and gray.

She saw the hand and my small bone poking through the skin, pushed out again by the pressure of the swelling. She said, "Well, that doesn't look good at all."

"No," I said. "It was a lion." I picked at the bone, touching where it stuck out. I traced the dark purple circle around the puncture.

"I don't understand," she said. "A mountain lion?"

I nodded. "Last night near Bridalveil Creek."

She tucked her blond hair behind her ear, then called back to the aid station. She said, "Guys, I think you'd better come see this."

As she examined my hand, the other medical students asked me to explain what happened. I told the story from when I first saw the lion above me on the rock. I told about rolling downhill, the fight, how the lion choked on my fist.

One of the students kicked at a hill of dirt. Another squinted his face and shook his head. I knew they didn't believe me.

The young woman who was inspecting my hand said, "Can a man really kill a mountain lion with his fist?" She looked at the other medical students.

No one said anything, but they all shook their heads.

She said, "If you wait until this afternoon, we'll have an orthopedic resident come in. He'll be able to reset your hand and cast you if it doesn't need surgery."

"Thanks," I said.

"No problem. Why don't you come in here and we'll make you more comfortable?"

I followed her into the medical tent. She pointed to a cot draped with a white sheet. "You can lie down there."

She left and came back a couple minutes later. She had a little white cup in one hand, two pills inside, and a Dixie cup of water.

I swallowed both pills. Drank the water.

She said, "That'll keep the pain down. You'll feel a little loopy, dreamy, but it'll help a lot."

I said, "Thank you," again. My hand felt like I was holding it in a fire.

"All right," she said, "I'll go see about some food for you."

The pills hit and my head floated. I lay back on the cot. Watched the tent's ceiling drop toward me and back up. When a wind gust came, the tent shivered like my father when he washed himself in Ribbon Creek.

I closed my eyes.

Following my father. Sneaking tree to tree, far enough back not to be noticed. Following him to the pool just down the creek from our camp. When he gets there, he takes off all his clothes and walks into the waist-deep water. Then he squats down and washes his armpits. Dunks and washes his hair as well, using the silt from the bottom of the creek near the bank.

When he comes up from rinsing, I think he's shivering from the cold water, like normal, but he's not shivering. The night is too hot, 80 degrees, and the water is only cool this time of year, not cold. Summer heat hangs above the surface.

My father has his hands over his face and he's rubbing his eyes. I watch his body shake.

I opened my eyes in the medical tent. Blinked. The girl doctor there. Her hand on my thigh. She says, "A mountain lion?"

"Yes."

She leans over and kisses me. Tongue like mint.

The lion's jaws on my hand. Crushing. The tight, wet slick of its throat. The weight of the whole animal again.

Her blond hair. Breath. Eyes pale as the tourists' bottled water.

She's not there or I'm not. An empty tent. And the flapping sound like birds' wings overhead.

"This should help," she said.

The pills died. The medical student came back again with soup, saltines, Sprite in a plastic bottle. More pills. She said, "I heard the orthopod's driving into the park soon. Here's two more Percocet."

I sat up. "Okay," I said. I watched her eyes as they did not look at me. Her hair across her face.

"Did you?" I said.

She wiped her hair out of her eyes. "Did I what?" she said.

I swallowed the Percocet, cracked the Sprite, and took a sip. Lay back down. Laughed that Lucy and I both hurt our right hands. Lucy's index finger still unhealed.

My hand itched. I looked at the bone there, peeking through like something on the road, car-crushed. I felt it with my left thumb, the end of the fracture where it stuck out.

The medical student was gone again. My head rolled, the pills weighting. Even when I touched, there was only a nudge of pain, back where the bones didn't connect.

In Tuolumne. Fourteen. I rest my face in my palms. The night smells like pine mold. No clouds, this clear night, even, the sky stretched like a child lying in a field of grass. I watch the stars, recognize their slow shift around Polaris, the Ursas, Draco, The Charioteer, and Perseus, their rotation around a point 2 degrees from perfection.

A coyote yips from my right and another answers from my left. I've seen them run dog-like in the morning, ferrying stolen food packaging, Ball Park Franks' wrappers and steak paper dripping at the corners of their mouths.

He didn't have to die. An accident like bruises beneath the skin of fruit.

I hoped that the superintendent would fall, but he flipped upside down and turned, curled underneath, headfirst and down.

I picture him off the end of the boardwalk, lying in the reeds, smoking his cigar. Alive again and he puts the cigar to his lips, drawing smoke into his mouth, holding it, then exhaling at the corners.

My bones flourish like grass. His worm will not die.

I wanted to fix my hand. There was no one else in the tent, not the medical student, not the other volunteers, no other patients. Rows of empty cots and white sheets.

The haze of the Percocet as my head fell forward and drool pooled in my mouth. I let it slide to the floor. I stared at my hand, then pushed the bone down, pushed the bone back toward the opening in the skin. The pain came but I let that slide like the drool. The drugs put it on the floor, and I kept pushing the bone down and in.

The river ran clear, a rainbow finning upstream. I flicked a grasshopper out in front, the bug on a single worm hook, struggling on the surface. The bridge, fifteen feet with ledges on the underside, and the bone slid under the skin.

Dark rose in the hole and seeped. I clenched my teeth and squinted my eyes. On the pills, heavy, I pushed. A second time. A third. Adjusting the bone underneath the skin. I whispered to myself, "Just need to . . . " and hooked my left thumb into the opening to gain leverage. The bone moved with the sound of a rainbow trout's skull crushing.

When the orthopedist came in, he felt the newly straightened bones in my hand. He said, "The med student told me this was a compound. But this looks good actually. There's a hole here, but somehow the bone popped back in."

"Yes," I said.

"Alrighty, let's see here," he said. "Hamate and pisiform don't feel turned, everything in the correct place here." He pinched to the ends of my fingers. "Lots of swelling out here, but nothing out of place which is good . . . " He dabbed antibiotic ointment onto a Q-tip and slathered it over the wound. "A few sutures at the exit, and we'll be ready for plaster."

He left and returned with a kit. Then he sewed the fracture hole closed with three black sutures. The medical student came in with plaster packets and a metal mixing bowl. The orthopedist said, "This will be an old-school cast, a bit heavy, but you seem like you can handle that since you fight lions, right?"

I wiggled my thumb.

The medical student mixed, then dipped the strips. Added more water.

The orthopedist said, "Keep this really still while I cast. I don't want any of those bones moving around."

He was quiet while he formed the first few layers. Then he turned to the medical student. He said, "From here you want to keep that hand up. The thumb still. Make sure nothing wiggles. You want to add from here?"

"Yes," she said. She wound wraps. Pressed gently, then wound more wraps. "Does that hurt?"

"No," I said.

"Good." She added more layers.

The orthopedist said, "And that should do it. Come back here and get this thing off in six to eight weeks, all right? They can call for a cast saw if they don't have one."

"All right," I said.

He smiled. Patted the new plaster. "You take care now."

I called Lucy on a borrowed cell phone. I explained what had happened.

"A mountain lion?" she said.

"Yes, it came down off a boulder. I thought it was going to kill me. Then it didn't."

She said, "And you killed it with your fist?"

"Yes," I said. "Down its throat."

Lucy whistled into the receiver.

"I know. I know. It sounds so crazy."

"Are you okay?" she said. Her voice was different over the phone. Not as strong.

"Yes," I said. "They gave me something for the pain."

"Good," she said. "I'll come pick you up."

When Lucy arrived, she put both hands on the cast. Kissed me. She said, "I'm glad you're okay."

"Me too," I said.

The blond medical student came out to the road. She had two cups of pills in her hand. "These are anti-inflammatories," she said. "Every six hours. And these are for pain." She handed both cups to me. "Every four hours. Don't overdo it, and keep up with the pain."

I said, "Thank you." I was thinking about the tent. About before. I looked at Lucy to see if she knew, but Lucy was looking at my cast, picking at the edge, then touching the ends of my swollen fingers. The medical student walked back to the tent.

In the car, Lucy said, "We're going to have successive days of wedding feasts. My father wants it."

I said, "Is that the tradition?"

"No," she said. "The old tradition is that you come into my house and live with me. There's an exchange of gifts. Whenever we have our first baby, we're officially married." Lucy laughed. "That would be the old way."

"Does your father know?" I asked.

"No," she said. "No way."

"Does anyone know?"

She shook her head no again. "They're too busy with some Park Service deal."

I said, "What Park Service deal?"

"I don't know," she said. "It doesn't matter to me."

"But it might matter," I said.

"Well, my father said he needs me in on it. Says that my support is 'essential.' So I'll know more about it soon. And I'm sure it's good."

CHAPTER 5

The thunderclouds come, white stacks pushing black underneath, the Valley shadowed as Tenaya watches from the top of Yosemite Falls. The storm twitches electricity, ready to draw lightning. But the clouds open. Water pours down. And the frogs come up. They hop into the thatched homes, squeeze between the sticks, underneath the walls, dropping from the roofs. The frogs are in the acorn flour, the dried meat, the woodpiles. The frogs live and die everywhere in the Valley that summer and fall. The smell of their dying is in the water and the air, on the people's skin. When men kiss women, they kiss with the smell of dead frogs.

Then winter comes and the soldiers increase in number, soldiers of the 36th Wisconsin. Major Savage leads them up from Mariposa, and Vow-Ches-Ter is with them.

Savage gives the order: "Wait for the first, big, spring storm before we march in. That way there will be no retreat over the mountains. No retreat to the Tuolumnes or the Monos. The Yosemiti will be trapped by the wet snow."

He is coming to the Valley in March. The newspapers will later report that it is in the month of May, but it is March. 1851.

I saw the press release on a signboard in the Yosemite Village three weeks later:

The National Park Service and American Indian Movement are proud to announce the return of the

original inhabitants of the Yosemite, Yosemite Valley, Hetch Hetchy, and Tuolumne. The NPS is designing and building a Miwok village at North Wawona, and another Miwok village to come soon to the Yosemite Valley. The new native villages will allow for further cultural competence and recognition by park visitors as the tribe members hunt, gather, craft, and perform ceremonies within the boundaries of the National Park. Visitor centers will showcase the wonderful basketry, blanket weaving, tanning, and stone-napping skills of these original inhabitants.

I read the sign twice.

Old Tenaya's blood, Mono Paiute. Further back, Aztecan. I stared at the sign. Opened and closed my broken hand.

I'd torn the cast off the night before. Cut it with my sheath knife, then ripped shreds with my other hand. Only thirty days, but I could feel the injury healed, the muscles strong and rested. I felt my fist pulling the bones tight once again, tendons correcting. This is how I'd healed my whole life, more quickly than possible, the Valley in me.

That night, I said, "You have to come with me."

My father shook his head.

My mother didn't seem to hear us. Sometimes it was like that.

"You're my parents," I said. "So you have to come."

My father picked at his thumbnail. He said, "Tenaya, this is something else."

I'd come to their camp at dinnertime but I wasn't hungry. My mother stirred the noodles and she didn't hum.

I said, "You won't come to the wedding, or you won't come to the feasts? Which one?"

My mother looked up from her stirring.

My father said, "If we come, you'll have to do something for us."

I said, "What?"

He said, "You'll have to embarrass them." He licked his front teeth. Yellow across the enamel. Brown lines between each tooth.

"No," I said.

"It wouldn't have to be anything big," he said. "Just a small embarrassment to show you understand. A little thing."

I took out my knife. Squatted down by the log, and dug the point into the wood. I turned the tip to make a hole. "I can't do that," I said.

My father picked at his cuticle. He said, "I don't think you ever understood it all. This new 'Original Inhabitants' thing, have you heard about that?"

"Yes," I said. "I read the sign. I know it's wrong."

"But you don't care?"

My mother handed me a bowl of noodles.

I said, "I care but that's not the only thing here. Lucy and I are something else."

"Do you know that for sure? Is she something else?"

"What do you mean?"

"I mean, is she involved with this?"

"No," I said, "I don't think so. Probably not."

"Probably not?" he said. "There's a lot more there than you think. And it still matters." My father pulled a string of skin and a drop of blood appeared. He smeared it with his finger. "You know what you could do?" he said.

I shook my head.

My mother spooned two more bowls of noodles. Handed one to my father and took one herself.

My father ignored his food. He said, "I know you could do this."

I carved into the log, deepening the hole. Turned the knife. Felt the indent widen, and cut at the edges.

My father said, "It's a small thing to ask." He took his fork and wound noodles around the tines. "You can do something. A small embarrassment. That's all."

We were headed to North Wawona before the first feast. We took two days to backpack together, up Pohono. My parents were not as fast as they used to be. We stopped the first evening just past the steeps, at the rim, in a meadow that reminded me of catching gopher snakes as a child. I always caught them tail first, then slowly dragged them back out of their holes or spun them flat until they hissed.

We stopped at the meadow and my father said, "This isn't good. We shouldn't be going."

I spit on the trail. "You can't say that now. We're already on our way."

He loosened his shoulder straps and shook his pack off. Thumped it on the ground and let it roll onto its side.

I said, "Come on. Let's keep going a little bit further."

"No," he said. "I think I'll stay here."

I worked my thumbs under my own backpack's straps. I said, "Put it back on. Let's go."

He sat down on his pack. "I said, 'I think I'll stay here.'"

My mother walked into the meadow and put her face to the last of the day's sun, the low-angle beams on her closed eyelids. She still had her pack on.

I said, "And then I just don't get married?"

"Well," my father said, "it seems a little rushed, doesn't it?" He wiped his forehead.

I wedged my thumbs underneath the straps of my pack. "Maybe. But Lucy is . . . " I didn't know how to explain a girl who wasn't afraid of rattlesnakes.

"Okay then," my father said. "And I'll probably stay right here if you don't mind."

"But I do mind," I said. I pointed back at the trail. "We're late to the halfway point."

My father got some peanuts out of his pack and started eating. "Are you going to do what I asked?"

I said, "The embarrassment thing?"

"Yes," he said.

I stared up at the line of trees around the meadow, the crowns like an uneven ridge, up and down, circling back to us. My mother was still standing out in the middle, eyes closed.

I said, "Will you go with me if I do it?"

"Yes," he said.

"And you'll push on a little farther tonight too?"

"Yes," he said again.

"Okay, if I think of something, I'll do it," I said. "So my answer is maybe."

"So you will?" he said.

"Maybe," I said again.

He licked the salt off a peanut shell. Cracked it with his teeth, and shook the two peanuts into his mouth. Threw the shell halves into the grass. "That sounds better," he said. "If you understand the history, then it matters. All of it."

I'm little, and I watch him go to the car. He never leaves the trunk unlocked. He has the key around his neck on a string, and when it isn't on his neck, when he goes swimming, he has that key hidden somewhere but I never know where.

The 1946 Plymouth Deluxe sits next to the big tree, green and rusting underneath. Good tires the only addition.

My father looks both ways before he opens the trunk. Leans in and moves his hands like he's checking cards. Then he shuts the lid and locks it. Looks both ways again. I've never seen inside the trunk, and don't know what's in there.

The next meadow a mile up the trail. I hadn't returned since the night of the lion, four and a half weeks earlier. I let my parents hike past. I said, "I have to pee. I'll catch up."

They nodded and kept hiking. Tired and breathing hard again. My father looked awkward underneath his pack. It was late day, but still hot, and the pack had shifted off to the side, one of his straps slipping.

I waited until they rounded over the next knoll. Then I went to look. I found the carcass where I'd left it.

Coyotes had scavenged the flesh off the legs and shoulders, cleaned to the bones. The hide was pulled back where it wasn't missing. The top of the rib cage. I heard the buzzing before I felt the vibrations.

Inside the cavity where the lower intestines used to coil, bees were working, building. The combs were thick already, layered and dripping with honey. It was not possible for bees to produce honey in that amount of time, and I knew that it was not possible. But this is how it was. Like my hand. I looked at the healed hole, an indent, light purple, only four and a half weeks. I flexed my fist, the knitted bones straight now past the muscles.

I reached inside with that hand. The bees stung me next to the scar as I broke off a piece of the honeycomb. Pulled it out. The comb dripped down past the bee stings that welted, the honey dripping to my elbow.

I took a bite. The comb was soft and waxy, capsules of sweet popping between my teeth. I sat in the meadow next to the lion and ate, listening to the bees buzzing all around me. Workers flew in and out of the carcass, their rattle-paper wings, windows humming in a windstorm.

I reached in and broke off a larger chunk of comb, bigger than the first. Yellow-white. I ignored the new stings and started to hike again. When I caught up to my parents, I offered each a piece of the comb, smiling. Feeding them out of the carcass but they wouldn't know that.

Both of them ate, crunching the golden, sugared sweet. Smiling. They ate and hiked, rejuvenated by the quick energy, the honey from the body of the lion. I thought of the favor that my father had asked, and knew something that might work. I thought it was a small thing.

That night, I tested the riddle on Lucy.

I said, "Can you tell me what this means: Out of the eater, something to eat; Out of the strong, something sweet?"

We were in her bathroom at North Wawona, next to the bedroom. "No," she said. "What is it?"

"Guess," I said.

Lucy began brushing her teeth. Brushed all around her mouth, then her tongue. Spit. She said, "No, tell me."

I said, "You have to guess." I wet my toothbrush. "So here it is again: Out of the eater, something to eat; Out of the strong, something sweet."

I brushed my teeth then. Waited to see if she'd guess it.

Lucy leaned on the counter. She filled a cup of water and took a drink. She said, "Does this have to do with your broken hand? How it healed so quickly?"

"Yes," I said. "Good guess."

She rinsed her toothbrush and tapped it against the counter. "Okay," she said, "I give up. Just tell me."

I spat toothpaste foam. "I can't," I said.

"What do you mean, Tenaya? You can tell me."

"No," I said. "I can't." I rinsed my toothbrush. "You have to guess this one."

Lucy walked into the bedroom and turned toward the wall. She unraveled a braid of her hair. From behind, I could see the way her spine almost made a full question mark.

My father met me outside my room. He had been waiting, leaning against the wall in the hallway.

"How long have you been here?" I said.

He picked at a chink. He said, "Let's walk."

We walked down to the big grove of trees. He said, "Do you remember everything I told you?"

"Yes," I said.

He held up his hand. His missing finger.

I said, "Trust me. I did. I listened."

"No," he said. "Sometimes you didn't listen. I know that. But that's okay. You were little. But we're here now, and it matters that you're a man."

The bark on the tree nearest to us was patterned like a rattlesnake, a diamondback to the sky. I said, "Do you know what Lucy is to me?"

My father said, "If you'd listened . . . "

"I did listen," I said, "but this is something else. Some things change people. I'm not who I was always."

I stood next to the trunk of the tree, to the scales of snakeskin. I reached out and felt the bark, the slight stick of sap in the seams between dry fibers.

"Tenaya," he said. "Everything is everything. And the Valley is yours. Did you think of something?"

I looked at my father's eyes and the wrinkles underneath. Semicircles of dark blue like bruises. I said, "I've got something I can do, and it should make you happy."

"Good," he said. "I appreciate that."

Lucy and I got married two days later. Lucy's father performed the ceremony. Lucy was in her mother's cotton wedding dress. I wore a borrowed pair of pants and dress shirt.

After the reception, there was the first feast. At the table, all of Lucy's relatives, aunts and uncles and cousins. My father sat to my right. He'd been quiet the last two days.

I stood up and tapped my glass. I said, "I have something for all of you. A riddle. For fun."

Lucy's father smiled. He was heavyset and his smile crowded his eyes.

I spoke the riddle as the table listened.

People began to guess at the answer. Yelling out. Everyone smiling.

When no one guessed the answer, I said, "We'll try again later. Don't worry."

Someone yelled, "No, tell us now."

Someone else said, "Yes, you have to."

I looked at my father. His coyote smile.

"Come," my father says. I am nine years old. It is earlier than he normally wakes me. No fire yet. The first snow a week old, and the ground creaking white.

I say, "I'm tired."

"Shhh," he says. He holds his fist to his lips, the ghost finger extended. He tosses my coat to me and leaves the tent.

I follow him downhill, watch the way his shoulders hitch with his short right step to a longer left, right to left, right to left, always the same short-to-long foot pattern when he walks downhill.

He stops and points. A coyote lying down. My father approaches it, then kneels. The coyote is dead.

My father lifts the tail. I see strands of something there.

I say, "What is that?"

My father says, "A plastic bag."

"What?"

"They eat the bags too," my father says. "When they find food in them, they eat so fast that they eat the bags along with whatever's inside."

"And it kills them?"

He nods. "The bags obstruct them. Animals can't get a bag all the way through." He points to a dark patch under the tail. "You can see where he chewed at himself, trying to get it free."

In our room, Lucy said. "Don't do that again. That was weird."
I said, "What?"
"You know what," she said.
I said, "It was just a riddle."
"It was more than that," she said. "I know."
I tried to laugh but it came out like a swallowing sound. I said, "It was just a riddle."
"Okay," she said, and kissed me. "If it's just a riddle, then tell me the answer." She kissed my neck, my shoulder, my chest.
But I didn't tell.

At the next night's feast, I stated my riddle again. I was making this a tradition after the main course. I stood up, tapped my glass, spoke the riddle and waited for people to guess.
Carlos was there. Lucy's cousin. His hair cropped with a black cowlick, reminding me of pictures I'd seen of matadors in Mexico. He stared at me from the other end of the table, face like a sheared rock.
I drank too much wine. My father was not drinking, and he watched each time I refilled my glass. My father raised his eyebrows.
My mother was drinking more than me. I saw her humming to herself. She looked tall even when she was seated. Thin and tall. Fragile. Earlier, she'd looked at me like she was standing at the edge of a cliff.
I'd said, "I'm okay," and she laughed. Swigged her wine.
My drink washed over me. I stood up and retold the riddle for a second time that night. My father nodded and smiled.
Lucy's father was not smiling.

We went back to our room. I was drunk. The floor settled under my feet at different angles. The wall flexed.

Lucy said, "I'm your *wife*, Tenaya. *Your wife*. You have to tell me."

I lay back on the bed. Into the night's spin. A bed of wine. "It's only a riddle," I said.

"Don't lie to me," she was taking off her clothes, her long braids undone over her shoulders. "Who asks the same riddle every night at a wedding feast? Who does that?"

"It's . . ."

"It's wrecking things," she said. "And it's weird."

The room turned once, and I steadied myself. I thought of all the faces at the dinner table.

Lucy said, "I'm not sleeping with you tonight." She slipped on a big T-shirt and went out.

The two-by-six floorboards for the upstairs made ceiling beams for this room. I looked at them and breathed. Wondered about my father staring at other floorboards.

I got up and walked to the door. Cracked it and looked to see if Lucy had really gone. I closed one eye to see out into the hallway, to see if she was standing there mad, ready to come back in.

Two people were at the other end of the hall. My eyes swam, but it looked like their heads were together. One was Lucy. I waited and listened but I couldn't hear what they were saying. I shut the door and got back into bed.

The ceiling boards warped. Lucy came back.

I said, "Who were you talking to out there?"

"Who?" she said.

"At the end of the hallway," I said. I pointed toward the door.

"Carlos," she said. "My cousin."

"Your cousin?"

"Yes," she said.

"What did he say?"

"Nothing really."

The room spun around me once. Then back again. I felt sick. "Nothing?"

"Well, he said everyone was mad about the riddle."

"Oh," I said. I laughed. Tasted bile in the back of my throat. Sat up.

"But he also said he didn't mind. He said he 'liked the battle.'"

"What does that mean?"

"I don't know," she said.

The riddle didn't seem to matter. I said, "It's a stupid riddle anyway. It's honey out of a lion."

Lucy was changing, her back to me. She said, "What?"

"Honey out of a lion," I said. "That's the answer to the riddle."

"Honey out of a lion?"

I said, "The bees built their combs inside the carcass of a mountain lion. I found it in a meadow and pulled out the honey."

My stomach tightened and my mouth filled with saliva. I stood up and lurched into the bathroom. I knelt down in front of the toilet.

Lucy said, "That's the answer?"

I vomited. Retched, and vomited again. Breathed and wiped at my mouth.

"The answer is honey from a lion?" she said.

I said. "That's it. But don't tell them." I was still kneeling in front of the toilet.

Lucy came into the bathroom. I was resting my head on the toilet seat and I looked up at her. She was smiling, her dogtooth glinting. I turned and vomited again, as she walked out.

The next night, I tapped my glass and told the riddle again. I stood at the head of the table. I didn't want to tell it, not anymore, but my father gave me the cue. He held up his glass and caught my attention. His lips were curled back from his yellow teeth. He licked them in the front. Said, "Please?" I was unsteady once more from wine. Never drunk like this before, days and days now.

After I told the riddle, Lucy's father smiled at me.

Someone else said, "Is it sweet meat? Have we guessed that?"

"No," I said, "but good guess." I took a sip from my glass. Red stain.

My mother got up and stumbled over her chair. Righted herself, then left the room. My father didn't follow her. He was looking at me. Waiting and smiling.

Someone said, "Is it 'man'? Like that old Sphinx riddle?"

"No. Good guess," I said. I finished the wine in my glass. Looked for an open bottle. Lucy sat next to me.

Lucy's cousin stood up. Carlos with his cowlick. He was at the other end of the table. I blinked and pictured him as a marmot looking for salt. He was wearing a Park Service shirt. He sipped at a wineglass. He cleared his throat and said something.

I said, "What?" I was still holding my empty glass. Still standing.

Carlos took a bite of bread. Chewed and swallowed, not in a hurry. Everyone stopped talking and looked at him.

We were the only two people standing.

Carlos said, "Honey?"

I looked right at him.

Someone said, "What did he say?"

Carlos took another sip of wine, tilted his head back, and looked up at the ceiling. Then he swallowed and looked directly at me. "Is it honey from the inside of a lion?" he said.

I held my empty glass. Looked at Carlos. His smile.

I said, "How did you . . . " then I looked at Lucy.

Lucy was sitting with her head down. She was not eating.

Carlos put his wineglass on the table, next to his plate. "What is sweeter than honey?" he said. "And what is stronger than a lion?"

I said, "Lucy," but she didn't look at me. She didn't lift her head.

The candles flicked light off the wineglasses. Coals pressed to both sides of my head. Jose Rey ran doubled over. He straightened and showed the blood smear.

I grabbed a bottle of wine and poured it out onto the tablecloth. Piling red. People screamed and slid back their chairs.

Lucy stood and said, "He said he'd kill me. He said he'd kill me if I didn't tell him the answer."

"Who?" I said.

"He wasn't joking," she said. "He gets crazy sometimes."

"Carlos?"

"No," she said. "Not Carlos."

"But Carlos knew the riddle."

"Let that go," Lucy said. "Carlos said there's more to this."

"What?" I said.

Everyone looked back and forth between us. Carlos was still standing at the far end of the table.

I turned the wine bottle around in my hand. Broke it on the edge of the oak leaf.

Someone yelled at me.

Lucy grabbed my shirt, but I stepped away.

I flexed the lion hand on the neck of the broken bottle, long shards extending out of my fist. I stepped around the chairs, walking toward Carlos. He stood there, waiting, not knowing that he should have run.

I built a lean-to that night, in the small trees opposite the mariposa grove, knowing that no one would look there.

After dark, I dumped five gallons of gasoline over the half-built Miwok village. The government gear, the compressors and backhoe, nail guns, staple guns, a Bobcat, beams and Simpson ties. The burning of the framed-out longhouses was like a kindling fire. Kiln-dried Doug fir, an orange tracing of the old-style dwelling. Strings of pitch shearing, burnt globs.

Everything burned like standing grain, like a field of wheat.

I didn't see Lucy for a week. Her family was looking for me, the rangers too, and I snuck back to North Wawona, in through her bedroom window.

I put my hand over her mouth.

Her eyes opened as she screamed into the muffle of my hand.

"It's me," I said. "Tenaya." I leaned in. Took my hand away.

She sat and pulled the sheet up to cover herself. She said, "Why are you here?"

"To see you," I said.

"You've wrecked everything," she said. "This won't work now." She gripped the sheet in her fists. Even in the dark, I could see the bright nail polish she'd painted on for the wedding.

"Lucy," I said, "we can still work this out."

"After that?" she said. "After whatever the fuck all of that was?"

I put my hand on one of her fists. I said, "It was stupid. All of it. I can explain it though."

"No," she said. "You can't explain some of those things. And you burned the new village site too."

"What?" I said.

"Don't lie to me." She pulled her knees to her chest. She said, "I know it was you."

"Someone burned it?"

"Tenaya," she said, "you're the only person who would do that."

"No," I said. "You don't know my father. And there are other people who still care about that. About the truth."

"What truth?" she said.

"The truth about everything. About 1851. The Miwoks. The real history."

"The real history? Are you serious? That was 150 years ago. That's over," she said.

I said, "It's not. It should be, but it's not. I should've talked to you about it before. I'm sorry about that." I leaned in and kissed her.

She stopped me. "I know it was you," she said. "We all know it was you."

"You don't know that," I said, and I tried to kiss her again.

"My family knows," she said. "My father told the Park Service and the County Sheriff too. They'll find you."

I held her face and kissed her hard. She kissed me back for a moment, rain splashing. Then she pushed me away.

She said, "I had to tell him too."

"Him?" I said. "You mean Carlos?"

"What?" she said. "No, I told my father. I didn't tell Carlos."

I stood up. "That doesn't make any sense. And if that's true, I would've killed your father first."

"Don't say that about my father. Don't ever say that. And you're . . . "

"Capable." I said.

"Fuck you," Lucy said. "They're going to catch you. You can't burn federal property. You can't hurt people like that."

I was standing watching her.

Lucy closed her eyes. She said, "Carlos is not . . . "

"Fuck Carlos," I said.

"But his face," Lucy said. "That cut is huge."

I looked at her, huddled there on the bed, younger seeming than before.

I said, "If you didn't want Carlos hurt, you shouldn't have told him anything."

Lucy started to cry. She said, "I didn't tell him anything. I told you that."

I walked to the window.

Lucy said, "Are you leaving? So that's it?"

I cracked the window and stepped over the sill.

Lucy said, "Tenaya?" but I had already dropped down onto the loam.

* * *

Ten years old, my mother and I go into the bear-proofed dumpster. She slides the box top over, then lowers herself into the hole. I follow her down. Dark inside, that one square shaft of light heating the middle, the food rotting beneath us. Half of a broom. Used diapers. Dirty paper plates. Old chili. Plastic trash bags filled with leaking camp garbage. My mother digs.

I say, "What are we looking for?"

She hears me but she doesn't make a sign.

"Mom?" I say, and snap my fingers in front of her face, my habit to get her attention.

She still doesn't make a sign.

She finds an oil paint set. Pulls each piece out, takes off the tops and smells them. Cadmium red. Azure blue. Paint thinner.

She leaves the colors.

I follow her back out of the hole, push the bear door back in place, click the snap link gate.

My mother holds the paint thinner.

After North Wawona, I didn't know where to go. I slept under the El Cap Bridge on the north end where the flood debris piled. It was too dark to see there and the rangers would never look.

I heard her voice. Fifteen years back. Child's hands around a river frog. "See a biggy?"

"Good catch," I said. She could catch anything. And she held frogs soft enough. They looked to be asleep.

She said, "See a biggy frog?"

"Yes," I said, "that's a nice froggy, huh?"

I heard her little voice as the ducks reset their wings, the feathers rustling and the gurgles of their bills. The ducks piled next to my feet. Her voice was what made me leave.

I was careful not to go near my parents' camp. Nowhere near the creek. When I passed over the El Cap Bridge, I hiked east on the road so people might see me moving away from Ribbon. Then into the meadows, low areas. Sedge to pack up my shirt for sleeping insulation. Flower puffs.

I went to live in the Ahwahnee caves. The boulders stacked lean-tos from thousands of years of rockfall off the Arches. Dirtbag hotels. I'd grown up around the dirtbags in Camp 4.

It was quiet when I got to the caves. I passed three men reading dog-eared paperbacks, leaning against granite blocks. Greazy was scrambling near them on the slag. He hopped down. Said, "How is it, bro?"

"Good," I said. "You?"

"Not too bad. Not too bad at all." His arms were long for his height, weasel-muscled. He pointed to the backpack I was carrying. He said, "You going to crash up here in the caves, huh?"

I said, "For a while if that's okay."

"God's green earth, man. God's green earth."

"Thanks."

He said. "Kenny's cave is open actually."

"Kenny's?"

"Yeah, you know Kenny?"

"No," I said.

"Dirty adventure hippy? Dude who disappears, then comes back two or three months later." Greazy said, "He walks to Canada and shit with no money."

"That's cool," I said.

"Yeah, crazy. He's gone right now, so you can crash up in his place as long as you want."

I said, "Thanks."

Greazy showed me the cave. North-facing, opening uphill, so the back of the cave was bigger than the mouth. A barrel stove pushed against the rear wall, the pipe bent crooked to fit a gap between the boulders, and a molding mattress in one corner.

Greazy said, "It's like a hotel, huh? Posh. And I got an old down bag too, if you want to borrow. Not going to lie though, it smells kind of shitty."

I looked at the mattress. "Thank you," I said. "I'd love that."

Greazy fetched the bag, duct-taped at two seams.

"I appreciate it," I said.

For the next week, I hid out in the cave, ate the loaf of bread and half of a jar of Nutella that a climber dropped off before leaving for a month in the Tenderloin. I read four books I'd found in the Curry lost and found, then traded copies with another dirtbag.

At the end of the week, I snuck west, down the Valley to my parents' camp. When I walked up, my mother was cooking oatmeal on the fire-ring grate. She hugged me, smelling like burned wood. She pointed up the creek.

"He's up there?" I said.

She nodded.

I said, "I'll stay and eat with you two." I sat down.

She stirred the pot in front of her.

"I tried to talk to Lucy," I said.

She raised her eyebrows. Blew on the spoon and tasted the oatmeal. She waved her fingers in front of her mouth. Then she scooped another spoonful and held it out to me.

I took a bite, tasting the brown sugar she'd put in with the oats. I said, "It's good."

She touched my shoulder.

I nodded. I said, "I'll try again."

She put the spoon back in the pot and turned the meal.

I went to see Lucy. Hiked south across the Valley in the late evening, up to Pohono in the dark. I slept in the meadow by the remains of the lion, slept warm in Greazy's duct-taped sleeping bag, under the high-country stars. In the morning, I ate the honey, the capsuled combs.

I waited through the next day outside Wawona in the woods. When it got dark, I knocked on the front door of Lucy's parents' house. Her father opened the door.

I said, "I need to see Lucy."

He looked at me and didn't say anything.

I said, "I need to see her."

He licked the top row of his teeth, reminding me of my own father.

I said, "I want to apologize to her."

He opened the door all the way and said, "Wait here." He pointed to the wall by the door. He disappeared for a long time, then came back.

We walked down the hallway, him leading. There was no light on in the room. He flipped the light switch and closed the door behind me.

I looked at the window. Big enough to crawl through. I turned the light off and looked out the window. It was dark, but I could see a far-off light and woods behind the house. I stood between the bed and the window. The room smelled like the artificial cinnamon candles they sold in the Yosemite Village.

I heard something thump upstairs. Two people arguing. I couldn't tell if one of them was Lucy. No one came to the door.

I looked out of the window and thought I saw someone step behind one of the far trees, a pine at the edge of the house clearing. I waited but didn't see anyone else.

I tried the window. Opened it. Slid over the sill and down to the ground. Crept ten feet, hunched over. I saw movement out by the tree, somebody off to my right. Voices came from the side of the house. Quick steps.

I knew then, and I ran toward a dark section of trees to my left. Someone yelled, "That's him."

I was almost to the trees when I heard the crack of the rifle and the *shhrrtt* sound of the bullet going past me. Then three more shots. I was in the thicker woods then. A bullet thwacked against a trunk near me, but not close, the other bullets hitting nothing as they passed in the dark.

I ran downhill on the loam, dark forest but no slash, nothing to trip me, and I covered a quarter-mile in two minutes. I knew they couldn't catch me. I slowed my pace, kept running but not as hard now, steady to the rim, telling myself to get to the rim before first light.

Another week of hiding in the caves. Scrounging with Greazy. Half a loaf of moldy bread, picking off the green crust. A jug of warm milk not yet turned. A new Snickers bar that must've fallen out of a hiker's pocket.

Greazy said, "This life's your choice, you know?"

I was licking the inside of the candy bar wrapper. "Huh?"

"Well," he said, "it's either this or the rest of the real world, right?"

I nodded like I knew the rest of the real world.

Greazy laughed. "But that's one of the reasons I like you. That whole rest of the real world thing doesn't exist for you. Y-N-P. Am I right?"

"I guess so," I said. "I'm trying not to think about that right now."

Greazy said, "Do you think we choose our lives though?"

"Sort of," I said. I peeled the last part of the wrapper, found melted chocolate in the seam. "A little yes and a little no."

"No," Greazy said, "I don't think so. I used to think so. I used to think we were people with a million variables, so many choices that nothing could be predicted. But I don't think that anymore. Did I choose thirty-seven years here? Did I make that conscious choice? Or is this where I was when I found my true self?" he said. "I wonder now if everything led me to here, to this place, if all choices put us where we are. The great myth of free will."

I was finished with the Snickers wrapper. I folded it and put it in my pocket. I said, "You think there's a myth of free will? Everything we choose comes to right where we are?"

He said, "Yes. I think that now."

"But I could leave," I said. "I could go somewhere else. I could do something else."

Greazy handed me a bread middle. No mold. He said, "I don't think you could. Not at all. But you could try."

I scrambled up the talus to a natural bench. Stared southwest at the Sentinel. Drank from my water bottle and looked into the shadow of the North Face. I tried to imagine people in the crack systems up there, so small that they could fit inside the chimneys. I knew what I had to do.

I didn't realize it was a fire. I approached North Wawona in the evening, and the smoke was subtle until the wind shifted. Then I coughed on the thick smoke. I couldn't see any flames, just the heavy gusts of smoke blown from the south. I circled around.

At Wawona, people were running in front of me, Forest Service and Park Service vehicles lining the road. A huge group of men and women were digging a fire line on the south side, protecting Mariposa. They were spaced every five feet, picking and shoveling, yelling to each other.

Four houses were on fire still. Houses of the old settlement, the cabin-houses the government had given to the Miwoks years ago before the new settlement plan. I couldn't see it until I got all the way around. Then there was Lucy's house, black with the others. Because it was on the edge of that northeast line, it looked like it was one of the first to catch fire.

It hadn't burned down though. Her house still stood, upright, extinguished before the interior had burned. Someone had foamed and wet it down from the outside. The upstairs looked destroyed, but not the downstairs, and only one corner of the roof had collapsed. No one was by that house now, the fire crews moved further along the line, hurrying, only spending enough time to extinguish flames and move on.

I kicked the front door open and it fell off its hinges. Smoke billowed out and I stepped aside to breathe. Then the house pulled air, and I went inside. The hallway was so dark I had to walk slowly to avoid running into things. I bent over to see below the smoke. I ran into a coat rack, then a table. I went deeper into the hallway where the late evening light didn't penetrate the hanging gray and the flecks of ash. I started coughing.

I searched through the lower house, putting my hands in front of me to feel around. There was nobody in the kitchen or the first bedroom. Nobody in the living room. I threw a dictionary through a window for air. Then I went back into the hallway.

I found a big body on the stairs. A man. I turned him over and saw Lucy's father. He was not burned but he was dead. I knew how thick the smoke must have been then. Even now, with the door open and the living room window smashed out, it was hard to breathe.

I crawled up the stairs, not sure if they'd hold underneath me. The landing was lit by a small window at the end of the hall. On the wall there, I saw black streaks like swaths of dark paint. I went into the bedroom on the right and she was there, lying on the floor.

I said, "Lucy?" Shook her. Said, "Lucy" again.

I stood up and threw a lamp through the window. Felt the air rush in.

Her right arm was straight out, fingertips touching the wall. I folded that arm in and pulled her onto my lap. "Lucy," I said again. Her head lolled.

Only her right hand, the one that had touched the wall, was burned, the fingertips blistered, discolored. I touched her index finger, felt the swell of the previously injured joint. I kissed that finger at its knuckle.

I carried her down the stairs, not worrying about a collapse. I stepped over her father, down the hall, and out the front door. There was still nobody else near the house, everyone busy fighting the spread of the fire. I carried Lucy around the back, into the woods. I could hear the people yelling at the fire line a few hundred yards away.

Lucy's head tilted and her mouth opened. I saw her teeth then, the turned canine on the right like someone had flipped it with a wrench. I kissed her open mouth, her lips.

I hiked on. My biceps began to ache, then my shoulders, my forearms, and my elbows. I set Lucy down. Sat next to her but tried not to look at her lying on the ground. I looked up at the trunks of trees, at a meadow through a gap. Rested. It was getting dark. I picked her up once again and carried her as far as I could go. My arms gave out a second time. I set her down. I lay next to her and looked at the sky, our arms touching.

I said, "I'm sorry, Lucy. I shouldn't have done that."

There was starlight above us.

I said, "I was so stupid before."

I got to my knees and pulled her into me. Pine needles gathered in the back of her hair. As I stood and adjusted her body against me, I could feel the clutter stuck to her back as well.

We walked again. We walked the deer trail to the meadow and I talked to her about the northern constellations, about the trees we passed, about what we could smell. I carried Lucy close and never dropped her, even when I stumbled. But I had to set her down over and over again.

I got her to the meadow in the middle of the night, and I knew I would bury her there, next to the lion. I lay with her until it was light. I didn't sleep. And in the morning, I dug, breaking the ground with a green stick and scooping with my hands. When the hole was deep enough, I laid her in the bottom, her hair tangled around her face, full of sticks. I leaned into the grave and picked them out. Patted her hair behind her ears.

Lightning walked across the Valley in front of me. No rain, only the blue-bottomed clouds and the white hairs of electricity. White-stacked cumulus above. Light and dark at five o'clock in the evening as I stood on the rim, dark now to the Valley floor like a gray blanket strung in front of the sun. Then the inverted dark, the snow under, white to the river, and the river black as a line of charcoal after a forest fire.

PART II
The Caves

CHAPTER 6

Millions of years ago the surrounding domes were the
underground magma chambers of active volcanoes waiting to
cool. So this is the middle. The year before you are born.

In June of 1976, the Jeffrey pine on the summit of Sentinel
begins to wither. Park rangers and tourists carry buckets of
water to the summit slab to bathe the trunk and roots. But
the tree does not survive. After 400 years of living as a scrag
penitent, the Jeffrey pine dies in the heat of the next summer,
a summer of no water.

The six spring streams underneath the Arches become
one. Then none. Mirror Lake disappears. Finally the Great
Yosemite Falls dries up, and there is no Lower or Upper Falls.

Coyotes steal water from the Camp 4 bathrooms, edging
past people like domesticated dogs. Nervous, they drink from the
slew behind the lodges. Gulp algae and mosquito larvae, vomit
on the Falls path. The coyotes weave the Loop Road and stagger
through the campgrounds. They are labeled as "overly social."
Two coyotes per week are euthanized by Predation Control
officers, and the population does not stabilize for twenty years.

The blade of a knife. Flat water. I waited through the winter of the
coyote, a male with a white patch on his left flank. I saw him in
the gap down the Merced, under the El Cap slabs, the open woods
beneath the talus. He was sitting on his haunches with his head
tipped sideways.

I was hiking through and stopped to watch. He was only a hundred feet off the road, like the coyotes that hop into cars to steal

food when drivers pull over to view wildlife. But no cars came, and he waited, sitting on a rise.

He was watching me too. His head cocked, his one eye turned. I sat down and we watched each other.

The wind came with the smell of snow, the vertical push down into the Valley, the smell of the wet cold, the inversion of the Valley, white on the cliffs above camp that morning, and now the cold air at the bottom of the U.

The coyote sat. I had another mile to go to my parents' camp, my father sitting on the front seat of the old Plymouth, smoking, and my mother in the back with a book, leaning against the wall and side window, her legs crossed at the ankles.

They spent all day in the car in the fall, with the windows open, transitioning to winter when my father strung a wind barrier on the down-river hillside to protect against the up-Valley blow. December to March, they burned their campfire all afternoon and evening, ran through cords of wood that they'd built up behind the moss boulder. Needing ten cords, my father always stacked eleven going into season.

I told myself that I did not expect that life with Lucy. Not my parents' life. I did not expect anything.

A pinecone fell near me and the coyote turned all the way around. Didn't hide his watching me. I clicked my teeth at him, but he didn't yelp either. I hiked past where he sat, and he let me go.

My father said, "I don't know."

"I don't know either, but I can't let that be. This thing," I said, "other things too, I guess."

My father was holding the newspaper I'd handed him. "What was it like?" he said.

I drew it in the dirt. "It burned straight out from the back three houses. Straight, straight out."

"So you think it was arson?"

"Yes," I said.

"And who lit it then?"

I drew a circle. Fire lines and an arrow. I said, "I don't know. Who would?"

"Well," my father said, "they're going to think it was you."

"Me?"

"Yes," he said. He reached and touched the end of the paper to my knee. "If they suspected you on the Miwok forms fire, they'll suspect you on this one too. That's just simple logic."

"But Lucy?" I said. I picked up a rock, stood, and threw it into the trees. "Fuck them."

My father stood too. He said, "I'm just letting you know. That's what they'll think, so you've got to be real careful. I'm sure they're looking for you already."

"But what if I find out who really did it? What if I find out who actually lit the houses?"

"You can try," he said, "and maybe you should try. But it won't mean much. Whatever people think, that's the truth."

I went and got three pieces of wood and stacked them next to the fire circle.

My father said, "This is where we're supposed to be, but no one wants us here. You understand that? We didn't use to exist, but we do now. Or sort of. Because of all of this, you exist." My father closed one nostril and blew snot out of the other side. "So you're going to have to hide for a long time, right?"

November wet snow that didn't stick, and I watched from the eaves of the Camp 4 bathroom, hat low over my face, snowflakes flecking and melting behind the Big Columbia Boulder on the worn path. Smelling the old dishes and the food slop in the bottom of the sink. I thought of Lucy. Her telling of rattlesnakes. The way she threw rocks at signs.

Then the big snows, two feet overnight to start December, and I dug a hole down into the Bachar Cracker cave, put a pad and sleeping bag there, decided to winter out the way the black bears and the 1970s Camp 4 drunks used to. Nobody would think of a man returning to this obvious a place.

No rangers came in. The tourists were gone as well, the Valley abandoned. Badger Pass was the only part of the park that was active, and the Yosemite store, but not here. A few scientists and small groups crossed the meadows on snowshoes. Herds of mule deer, sixty or more, stood before them steaming in the midday sun.

I sat on a downed log and watched a fox hunt for mice in the middle of Stoneman Meadow, creeping on his toes before leaping high in the air and turning nose down, plunging face first into the drifts, thrashing with his jaws, clacking at the mice.

I turned around and there was the coyote again. Same white flank, him sitting behind me in the woods on his haunches. He watched me as I watched the fox.

That was the day I first saw Carlos again. He got out of a park ranger patrol car at the recycling dumpsters past sites 4 and 6, shuffled on the crusty snow.

There was no mistaking his face. The new scar ran vertically from his left eyebrow to his jaw, like a worm stretched against his skin. I watched from the slack-line tree fifty feet away, saw his scar twitch as he checked the bear locks on the dumpsters. One of the steel links was loose and he went back to the patrol car to grab pliers. I watched as he tightened down the wire clasp, fixing gear while the bears hibernated.

I went south again and tried to see the burn line once more, but the snow obscured the evidence. I followed the banded trees, black to eight feet, touched the trunks, felt the crumble marking the pads of my fingers.

I built a quinzee on the fire line, heaped snow and dug out an upside-down L on the inside to crawl in. I wanted to sleep where the fire jumped the line, turned from a house burn to a big burn. In the middle of the night, I woke up and left the shelter. It was 10 degrees then and I watched the fog of my breath puff in front of me while I followed the moon over the snow. I walked up to the charred skeletons of the houses, back to Lucy's and her father's. The house was wrapped in yellow caution tape, the front door still open. I thought about going inside, but there was nothing else to see in there.

I'd read the newspaper report in the *San Francisco Chronicle*: "One Dead, One Missing in Mysterious Yosemite Fire."

When it jumped the fire line, the fire had burned 10,000 acres to the southeast, wrapping around the Mariposa Grove, and exiting the park. I walked out to the last burned tree on the south side, above the road, a half-mile south of the houses. I leaned against the first healthy tree and looked back, watched the sun come up over the hill to my right, the sun burning the snow light-blue to white, and the burned tree bands staying dark even in the full glare.

That winter back in Camp 4, there were days when I did nothing. Never left the Bachar Cracker cave. Watched the midday melt refreeze on the inside of the crack along the ceiling, the lichen and granite behind like Coke-bottle glass, greenish, opaque with grit, and I touched it to see if it was as hard as it looked.

I saw the evidence of old warming fires in the bottom right corner of the cave, fifteen feet back, and I picked at the dirt to reveal the oldest fire stains. I wondered how many people had slept where I was. I knew this had been a hunting stop for hundreds of years.

My father told me about the disappearance of the Anasazi in the Southwest. He said, "They lived on the cliffs, hundreds of feet up. They had elaborate steps and ladders and rope systems."

"How long did they live there?"

"Oh," he said, "a long, long time. Maybe 2,000 years. Maybe more."

"Then what happened?"

"No one knows," he said. "They just disappeared. No evidence of a great war, nobody taking over and claiming their land. They just went away."

"To where?"

"Like I said, nobody knows. Maybe they became dust. Maybe they became birds. Maybe they became the Colorado and Green Rivers." He smiled and said, "They didn't really become rivers."

"I know," I said.

He said, "Their petroglyphs could give clues to the disappearance though. Blowing out a candle on a ledge. Then they were no more."

I thought of Lucy.

My parents and I used to read all winter, sitting in the car or around the fire at night. I read now too. In the mornings, when I couldn't go back to sleep, I read books with my back to the opening of my cave for light. Two Louis L'Amour westerns I found abandoned on the Lodge porch in December. Then three books I found outside the store a couple of weeks later. A copy of *The Grapes of Wrath*, with pencil-written rhyming poems to a girl in the page margins, *One Flew Over the Cuckoo's Nest,* and *Indian Creek Chronicles*. I liked the last one, by Pete Fromm. An inexperienced college boy in the Selway-Bitterroot Wilderness. I couldn't imagine not knowing the land, not knowing how to tie a half hitch, leaving a coat behind in the cold.

I found a box of books left out in Curry while scoring free coffee in the registration hut. They were cheap paperbacks, mysteries and thrillers, and I took them back to my Bachar Cracker cave and read through the pile during the rest of the winter.

The Yosemite winter of deep snow, four-foot drifts November to March, and I ate little. There wasn't much to scrounge, just the leftovers in the bear boxes from the late climber season in November: More Krusteaz pancake mix with water, Top Ramen, Nalley chili, and one huge tub of Adams peanut butter that I rationed, two tablespoons each day. I got thin.

In January, when only the peanut butter was left, I hiked past Church Bowl and opened kitchen bags behind the Ahwahnee Hotel, a place where tourists stayed all year for $400 a night.

I ate day-old fettuccini Alfredo out of the dumpster bags, frozen to white cream icicles, crunchy, and wondered if Lucy would've eaten this with me, wondered if she ever scrounged food in the park as a child, wondered if her parents sat up late by the fire and waited for her to come in.

Lucy and I would be in Mariposa now, in the fake longhouse with geothermal floor heating, weaving baskets for tourist entertainment. Or would we be in the high country, building our own hidden camp? Avoiding the rangers. A hut out of deadfall, then countersinking a true cabin in the ground, using the below-ground insulation to half-wall height that I'd read about in the LeConte Memorial Sierra books, the cabin I'd always planned.

I'd wanted my father to build a cabin like that, but he'd said, "No, as soon as those cabins are finished, the rangers find them. Those backcountry projects invite them in."

I thought of our camp at Ribbon Creek and wondered what he was talking about. The rangers never came in. Rangers stayed where tourists stayed.

I sat at the turn of the Merced below Housekeeping, where the logs jam and the suckers swerve in schools of thirty at the bottom of the fifteen-foot-deep, green-black pools.

I used to come here when I was small, with my father, drop treble hooks baited with mice. Pull up the hand lines quivering.

Big, bottom fish with no fight in them, and they lay on the ground gasping, not even flapping their tails at death.

We spent days away from camp the year I was seven, the year after my mother stopped talking, the silence with her like watching a rock grow.

My father told me the same stories over and over. Three times he told me the story of my conception. At first, I was too young to understand.

He said, "Summer and the heat. No rain July. Two thunderstorms of dry lightning over the Book Cliffs but no rain for a month." He said, "The details matter.

"That was back when your mother still spoke. 'Manoah?' she asked me.

"I felt her there, close, but I did not try. When you are older, you will understand what I mean. I had not tried for a long time. I closed my eyes, pretending to be asleep.

"Ribbon Creek ran down the border of our camp, and I listened to the water. I could hear the individual notes of each boulder deflecting the flow of water from above. It was late summer and the mosquitoes were no longer hungry. I'd left the tent door open so I could see the stars as I lay sleepless next to your mother. Through the trees to the southeast, I looked at the three stars of Orion's Belt just risen, the first constellation I'd ever learned as a child.

"I fell asleep. Woke to the sound of the creek once more and got up. I looked at your mother lying there, then left the tent.

"I made a fire and started coffee in the old kettle. I splashed cold water to make the grounds settle, then poured myself a cup. The mug was too hot to touch and I waited for it to cool. I hated to burn my tongue.

"The light expanded without the appearance of the sun, El Capitan softening the lines to the east. I walked to the creek and washed my face. When I got back to the fire, your mother was up. She was staring into the fire, her hair tangled. She said, 'Good morning.'

"'Good morning,' I said.

"That was how it normally was. When your mother drank coffee, she never minded burning her tongue.

"Then we were away from camp the whole day. Your mother to the store and me to fish, and when I returned to camp, I found that a bear had torn a hole in the side of the tent.

"That night, I sat on top of the bedding in the dark.

"'Manoah?' she said, 'you didn't see the bear?'

"'No,' I said. 'The bear was already gone.'

"She touched my hand. She said, 'And there was no reason for it to come in?'

"'No. Bears are bears,' I said. I had my hands resting on my knees.

"Your mother slid over and touched my hair. 'Manoah?' she said. 'Are you afraid?'

"I rocked forward and pushed on my knees with the palms of my hands. I began to say no but it would have been a lie.

"But your mother kissed me. She kissed my eyes, my cheeks, kissed my head until her mouth found mine and we touched for the first time in many, many months. We kissed each other like we were lapping cold water in summer.

"And that was the beginning of you."

We were fishing browns the last time my father told me that story. I looked at him and wondered at the meaning of touching. My parents did not touch each other. They did not kiss each other. They were like closed links of two separate chains, chains that could never connect.

One time, when I was little, I drew their circles in camp, in the clearing, by scraping my heels in arcs of dirt and loam. Where the lines intersected I made deeper Xs with each heel, careful to show that their lines did touch, even if I never saw it.

I met the coyote again, and this time I called him Pete Fromm, after the character in the book, the author who had wintered alone.

Pete Fromm was sitting on a snow plane in a gap between the trees, his white flank toward me. He didn't trust me, but he followed me, or so it seemed, because he was around me, many days, looking and waiting.

I tried sitting with him. I sat five or six feet away, sat next to him, and he turned his head but did not run away. I imagined that he was a domesticated dog then, and wondered if the national park had ruined him, wondered if other coyotes sat with humans and looked out on the expanse of the Valley's white snowfields in front of them.

The snow sprinkled down on us, turning helixes with each gust of wind, and the day was cold, not more than 5 degrees Fahrenheit at two o'clock.

Finally, he left. Pete turned and ran. Someone up the Valley yelled, and he jumped at the sound. He turned and looked at me once from the trees, then jogged away, lowering his head the way coyotes do when they're trotting through a gap.

Then it was February. A few days of bright sun and the snow melted off the tree branches. Dripping all around, then hard crust in the evenings, and colder than before. The wet hid in the cold like glass in the shallows, and I snuck a stick fire on the old remains in the corner of my Camp 4 cave. Dense, white smoke with the wet, and I worried about rangers seeing. But no one came and I burned three days in a row to keep warm.

Then the real snowmelt. The early spring rains splattered the road mud, and the foxes trotted through Camp 4 like small dogs. March rain, and I saw Pete Fromm at the falls creek, eyes turning as he lapped creek water. He was more skittish now, and he cut left when he saw me.

There was something on his side, across that white patch. I thought it was blood, at first, the mark, but it was graffiti. Somebody had caught him and spray-painted his side. Not the biologists' yellow number tags, but bright red letters that said "MY DOG" on his flank.

I could see where Pete had bitten at the marks, chewed the fur. I saw the breaks in the letters, still wet with saliva. I knew then that he was too socialized, that he'd come in on other campers, begging for food. When the big groups visited over the next month, he'd be relocated by the Park Service, and at some point, he'd come back, Predation Control officers with rifles and metal litters waiting.

March. California Spring Break. More tourists in the Valley and the Park Service patrol vehicles wound the loop. I crossed the road and didn't see two patrol cars pulled over at the turn. The officers were standing by the back bumper of the first car, and when I stepped out, they turned and saw me. One was Carlos.

I ran and they chased me. I'd crossed near the Lower Falls access, and I sprinted left toward Swan Slabs. Stayed along the wall there and tried to decide where I'd go. This was not the direction I wanted them to follow me, past my camp and toward my parents'. I ran through Camp 4 East, Central, and West. I hit the open oaks section, the wide gaps between the trees, and looked back over my shoulder. The two of them were still chasing me, but far back, slowed by their army boots and the bulletproof vests under their shirts.

When I got a gap of a hundred yards, I turned south, toward the river, hoping they wouldn't follow me. By the time I reached the water, a mile later, they weren't chasing anymore. I waited for them. Watched until dark, but never saw anyone.

I snuck back to Camp 4 around midnight. Then it was spring.

CHAPTER 7

*They hold a foot race to see which of the enlisted soldiers
are most fit to hike into the Valley. Those who can run a
hundred yards quickly will hike up the Merced River. Those
who lose the sprint will stay and guard the existing camp. The
losers of the foot race complain that a sprint does not take into
account a man's intelligence or experience. But that logic is
disregarded. It is the quick who are chosen.*

*Tenaya is with the 36th Wisconsin as a show of good faith.
He is hiking up toward his own valley, following the Merced.*

*But Tenaya's men do not come to him. He waits with the
soldiers, in the Merced narrows, but the Yosemiti are wise
and know that they should not come to him. Even the Miwok
scouts are afraid to enter the Valley where ambushes are so easy
along the river.*

So the Yosemiti keep their advantage.

*And the soldiers wait among the boulders at the mouth of
the Valley.*

I remember being seven years old. My parents in the meadow
across the road. My mother hadn't spoken in the past year, her eyes
dull black like the mud on the banks of the Tuolumne.

I climbed over the Plymouth's front seat on the passenger
side, put my feet down in the bucket, slid up to the glove box,
and hesitated. Looked both ways for my parents like checking
for cars on the Merced road. I couldn't see them out in the field,
which meant they were lying down. The velvet grass was two feet

tall that time of year. I looked once more, then I popped open the glove box.

Nine of the letters fell into the bucket where my feet were. I picked them up and organized them in my lap. Three from my mother. Big, looped handwriting. Six from my father. His short lines like broken grass stems.

There were fifty or sixty more letters in the glove box. Tight packed, reminding me of the saltine crackers we found in the Lower Pines bear boxes at the end of the summer.

I slid the first letter out of its envelope. From my mother. I read all the words I could make out. I did not put the words together because there were too many I could not decipher. Then I opened the next one. One of my father's, the handwriting even more difficult. He wrote the letter to my mother, "Love" at the bottom, same as hers.

I looked up and saw my parents walking back toward me, the car. They were not holding hands now. Their hands were like two dried animals shrinking, skins curving and turning away from each other.

I stuffed all the letters back into the glove box, closed it, and climbed over the seat. Then I lay down on the bench and pretended to be asleep with my face turned away.

That was a year afterward.

My father read aloud to me in the tent that night. *The Old Man and the Sea* by Hemingway. An old man fishing alone through days and nights on the Gulf Stream off Cuba. I was piled in wool blankets against the cold. Seven years old and I couldn't imagine an ocean or warm water.

My father put a snow-cracked finger in the book to hold his place. He said, "This is our story."

I said, "What?" I was picturing the great marlin dragging the old man's boat. And sharks. I didn't know what they looked like other than the drawings my father had made on the brown paper grocery bags the night before.

"This is *our* story," he said again.

The harpoon had gone down into the shark's brain at the criss-cross mark of the skull. There was the night and the darkness, the old man alone on an ocean. When I asked my father, he described it: "An ocean is endless water," and to me, endless water sounded like innumerable drownings.

My father was holding the book. He pointed to me and then to himself. He made circles with his hands. "This is our story. Every-one's. We're all alone on the ocean."

I pulled my blanket up to my ears.

He said, "That night at the river?" He never said her name. He pointed with that no-index-finger fist. Not pointing at all.

The winter of the acorns. The winter of the old ways. There is no food my seventh year. My mother pretends to find grind holes on the nearby boulder, but I know she'd found them years ago. She raises her eyebrows.

"Oh?" I force my voice into a question to play along.

We brush the wet pine needles off the top. Blow hard to clean out each of the dozen grinding holes, then dry them with the hems of our T-shirts. My mother pours out the acorns on top of the boulder. Sweeps them into the holes with the flats of her hands.

I've been playing pretend. My fingers are two men running across a granite sweep. Falling off a ledge.

My mother rolls her pestle and starts to crush the pile. Her flour always comes out even. She hands me the other pestle. I crush, then rock in the mortar hole to remove lumps. Rotate outside in like my mother has taught me.

We grind until our holes are half-full, then scoop with our hands to put the flour in the big bowl. My mother makes three times as much as me. I lick the dust on my hand. Bitter from the tannin. Unsoaked and unsalted. Not edible yet. My mother licks too, and smiles.

My father takes one deer late in the fall with a pit trap, a large doe. The venison and the acorn bread keep us through early March. But there is still snow on the ground up and down the creek.

My parents argue. My father says something and waits. My mother doesn't make eye contact with him. My father says something else. "I have to. If I make a big deal, one deal, then that's all, then we'll be finished with it."

My mother looks right at him.

"I don't see any other way." He picks at a callus on his palm. "I'll go into the city for a couple days tops. Get it done, and come back. Then we'll be set."

I am supposed to be adding water to soak more meal, stirring the last of the grinds, but I am watching my mother's eyes.

My father says, "It's not right, I agree with you, but neither is this. In Camp 4, right now, two miles away, campers are eating hot dogs and washing their throats with Coca-Colas. They're waiting for their coals to settle for s'mores. But we're eating acorn bread and running out of three-month-old venison. So I'm going to sell the rest and be done with it. No little by little this time. One big deal and we'll be set."

My mother's face drops and she turns to get something from the tent.

My father is gone five days. When he returns, we never eat acorn meal again. Whatever we need at the store, we buy.

My father made me study literature and history. I didn't know that children studied math. I could only add things together and take things away. I had never done anything more than that, and until Lucy told me, I didn't know that other math existed. But I read. Every book my father gave me, and every book I found abandoned by campers. I spoke to the characters I read about in books. I spoke to them on walks, while I hunted mushrooms, while I scrambled over rocks and climbed trees. Joe Hardy and Napolean Bonaparte. Leatherhand, Abraham Lincoln, and Robert Jordan.

I spoke to my sister too. I told her stories that I'd read, places I'd found, the baby squirrel I'd caught underneath a basket and hand-fed for a month until it ran away.

The August that I was eleven, my father handed me three new books. He held them out: *For Whom the Bell Tolls*, *At First Light*, and *La Salle and the Discovery of the Great West*. They were hardbacks with jacket covers, and I read the backs, starting with Hemingway because I already knew him from his book about the old man and the sea.

I read the Parkman jacket last. I said, "Discovery?" My father didn't believe in that concept. He'd told me.

He said, "First you have to read what is best, the best writers, then worry about truth."

I said, "But I already know the truth."

My father laughed. He said, "You're eleven years old."

We were collecting wood two days later. Up the creek, west. My father said that his father hit him with that same copy of *For Whom the Bell Tolls*, the one that he gave to me.

He said, "My father stole it, along with a Coleman stove, a lantern, two sleeping bags, and a case of beer from a campsite in Tuolumne Meadows. I remember him coming into our camp with that jumble in his arms.

"He drank the beer, and I fell asleep. Later, when he came into the tent, he threw the book and it hit me in the face."

"While you were sleeping?"

"Yes. I woke up and my eyelid was cut. Bleeding. He hit me with *For Whom the Bell Tolls*. Something symbolic in that."

I looked at my father who would never hit me. I said, "How bad was the cut?"

"Just bleeding a little. And I kept the book. I hid it underneath my pillow right then and there. Read it every day after that until I finished. It took a month to get through."

I began to read the book. I read it while I sat against a tree on a downhill slope, my favorite reading spot in the afternoon, when the sun came in from my right, and I could see all the way to the river.

The book didn't make sense to me. I didn't understand who the fascists were. I asked my father. "Who are they fighting?"

"The fascists."

"Yes, but who are those people?"

He was splitting kindling off larger rounds. Fingers spread, he stroked with the hatchet through the gap between his middle finger and thumb. This was his kindling technique. He said, "They are the people who do not believe that humans are equal. They want a hierarchy."

I was thinking about the scene that Pilar described, when the fascists were thrown into the gorge at Ronda. "Why do they want the fascists to die though?"

"The republicans?" My father chipped off a wedge of pine. "They want the fascists to die because the fascists want the republicans to die."

"So they both want the other ones to die?"

He scraped the pile of kindling to the side and looked at me. "Exactly."

I still held the book. I was about to go back up to my tree to keep reading. "Wait," I said, "would we be the fascists or would we be the republicans?"

My father held up a sliver of wood, pinching it between his middle finger and his thumb. He wiggled the wood. He said,

"Tenaya, we would be neither. We would be the peasants. In the middle. Always."

The next day, my father told me the story of my birth. We were collecting crawdads at the mouth of the creek. My father chummed the shallows with mouse entrails. He held a crawdad out to me, its red pinchers flailing. He said, "I waved to your mother from the rail of El Capitan Bridge."

"When? The other day?"

"No, no," he said. "This is the story of your birth. Just listen."

"Okay."

"I waved and she waved back. She was sitting with her arms behind her, her large pregnant belly in front of her, and her black hair hanging long. She was wearing the tortoiseshell sunglasses that she found earlier that day on the sidewalk in front of the Village store. I remember all the little things. Those glasses were too big for her, and they made her look like a child wearing her mother's glasses. It didn't seem possible that she was already forty years old.

"The drought had shrunk the river. I jumped off the bridge into one of the only remaining holes, maybe seven feet of water. I let myself drift in the wind current. Felt the sun and the cold water, holding my breath. Then I swam up.

"I looked over but your mother wasn't on the beach anymore. I couldn't see her. I looked back and forth from the beach to the bridge, and still nothing.

"I put my head down and swam. Forty feet around a dried snag, crawling to the shore and standing up, jogging to the top of the bank. She was there, leaning against a road sign at the north end of the bridge, clutching the post. Her sunglasses had slipped down.

"I said, 'Let's get to the car.' We hurried to the south side of the bridge, to the car, and I popped the backseat forward and helped her slide in. She scooched against the far side, her legs open, her right knee up and her left foot down in the scoop behind the seat.

"I could smell the vinyl, the rubber, and your mother's forehead sweat like old sugar and wet clothes. And there was the copper scent of the blood too, the baby coming. That was you.

"I didn't close the passenger door and we did not drive. I helped her get her underwear off and then I held her hand.

"No one stopped to help. No one called a doctor. People left us alone. The Valley left us alone.

"Maybe an hour later, you were coming, and your mother's back was against the inside of the car and I was still crouching in the bucket behind the seat, and your mother screamed as your head pushed through. Your head stopped then, face-down. You were black-haired like a wire-covered grapefruit. Your shoulders would not go through and your mother screamed more and more.

"I tried to pull a little, and I told her to push. I said, 'Push, just push,' over and over, but you were stuck and your mother was screaming.

"This went on for maybe two or three minutes. Then a new contraction came and I did pull. I pulled and turned, and my thumb hit your collarbone, and your collarbone broke underneath my thumb. Your mother pushed one final time and you slid out blue and strong and slick, followed by a short gush of watery blood.

"That's how it was," my father said. He was still holding the crawdad.

I held the bag with the rest of the crawdads squirming on top of each other, ripping each other's pincher-arms off. I felt the little knot on my collarbone.

My father dropped his crawdad into the bag and it went to war with the ones underneath. My father said, "A boy with a collarbone already beginning to mend. So fast. I cut your umbilical cord with a pair of sewing shears I found wedged in the middle of a flattened roll of duct tape underneath the front seat. Your mother pulled her legs up, curling around you. I slid in and closed the car door behind me, and we fell asleep like that, for an hour, then I drove us back to camp. When I stopped the car at our tent, I realized what I needed to name you. I looked at your mother and said, 'Tenaya. You know? We'll name him Tenaya.'"

CHAPTER 8

First snow too early. She looks at the sky as if betrayed.

The people have moved to the far end of the Valley, near Mirror Lake. They constructed new lodges in the trees, more camouflaged than the ones that came before. There are rumors of what is to happen, blue men with guns, pale, unlike any animal they've seen. Not like the brown bears or the lions. Not like the Miwoks to the south.

She catches a squirrel raiding the acorn stores. Bludgeons it with a six-inch shard of granite. She hangs the squirrel from a low branch by its tail, an upside-down warning to the others.

Later, while cooking dinner, she notices a spot of blood on the back of her hand, but does not wipe it off. Behind her, they are coming up the river. Coming in their dark boots. Marching. Camping wherever night catches them.

My childhood and Lucy's mixed. I didn't want to sleep because of the nightmares. Sometimes I was at the river again, five years old, looking into my sister's eyes. Only Lucy now, her face whitened by smoke. I kissed her cheek but there was no smell of her.

I lay back on top of Greazy's sleeping bag. Closed my eyes. Lucy wrestled with me in the water. Sucked her teeth at the cold. Pursed wind-chapped lips. Arched her back against me. Nothing but skin.

I opened my eyes and saw a dimple in the rock. Two lines lateral from the roof crack. Where the lichen touched at the lip.

Greazy gave me a pint of Southern Comfort. He was working Cocaine Corner, a boulder in the middle of Camp 4, by himself. Shirtless, he had a fist-size bruise above his left kidney. He said,

"You want that bottle?" He pointed to his open backpack. "Dude gave it to me but I can't drink SC. Too damn sweet."

"Thanks," I said. I uncapped it. Drank. A small sip at first. Then a couple bigger swigs.

Greazy said, "Like it, huh? Shit makes me puke every time."

"No," I said, "it's fine."

Greazy climbed the opening moves on the corner and slipped. Fell back and missed hitting his head on a rock by six inches. He looked at the rock and laughed. Rubbed his head.

I said, "Hey, Greazy. How many people got in on that weed score?"

Greazy stood and brushed the dirt off his butt, then the bottoms of his shoes. "You mean up at the lake, the one I told you about?"

"Yeah, the Lower Merced crash. The Lodestar."

"Fuck. Let me see. How many people . . . let me think about it . . . " Greazy put his hands on the corner of the boulder again. He rolled forward onto his feet and started climbing. He exhaled. "Fifteen or twenty?" he said. "All dirtbags pretty much." He moved higher on the arête, and I set down my bottle to spot him.

He fell from halfway up the boulder and I checked him, keeping him from landing on the big, triangular rock below the crux.

"Thanks," Greazy said. "I never get this shit. Never. And I've fucked myself up on that big rock too, a few times."

"Sure," I said. I picked up the Southern Comfort. Each swallow was a sugar-dipped ember. I'd drunk so fast that it rushed. I said, "After this spot, I'm going to go walk around. I'll catch you later, okay, Greazy?"

"Cool, man, cool. Take care of yourself." Greazy slapped my shoulder.

I walked south into the boulderless gap. I kept sipping on the bottle, going for drunk. At Site 37, I stopped when I saw Carlos. He wasn't in uniform. He was wearing a flannel shirt, standing ten feet away.

Someone behind me said, "Stay where you are."

I turned around and saw a man with a pistol.

"Just relax," he said.

Carlos said, "I'm not with another officer right now. Understand?"

"No," I said.

"Well, you will," he said. "I'm not arresting you."

I looked at the other man. The gun he was holding was one of those porcelain ones, not metal.

Carlos said, "We're not riding in the patrol vehicle and I'm not in uniform. Right?"

"I don't understand," I said.

"You will," Carlos said. "Let's walk down here." He led the way along the path to the parking lot. I followed with the other man behind me. We passed the culvert and the ranger's kiosk.

"Here's our vehicle," Carlos said. He pointed to an old Buick, blue and dented. "Get in."

He opened the driver's door and popped the seat forward. I ducked and got in back. The other man walked around the truck and got in the passenger side. He didn't turn around and point the gun at me. He held the gun in his lap and sat, facing forward.

Carlos settled into his seat and started the car. Then he drove up the north side of the loop, heading east. He stopped the car in front of the Delaware North Company's offices near the store.

Carlos pointed. "Watch."

I watched as men moved a couch out of the first office and walked it down the road to a truck. Then a woman followed with a big box.

I said, "Are they moving offices?"

"No." Carlos pointed each time someone came out or returned from the moving truck. We watched the people go back and forth.

I swigged on the bottle. There wasn't much left. My tongue felt thick and I needed water. The liquor was like silt in my brain. I said, "Is the Park Service giving them a new office?"

"No," Carlos said. "DNC's leaving for good."

I felt too relaxed to understand. I said, "So what?" but that wasn't the question I was trying to ask.

Carlos laughed. He said, "So you'll see." He turned the key and drove us back to Camp 4.

The other man got out. Then Carlos opened his door, stood, and popped the seat forward. I hunched to slide through the space, turning my head, and didn't see Carlos jab. He punched me with his right hand, and I fell back into the bucket, my face split next to my eye. Squinting, then opening my eyes again, I saw the ring-knife, the one-inch-serrated mini as it flashed between Carlos's index and middle fingers.

Blood ran down to my jaw. I wiped my face and smeared it to the corner of my mouth. I said, "What the fuck?" The liquor was waving. I touched my face and closed my eye.

Carlos laughed. He said, "What the fuck, or why?" He reached into the cab and grabbed my face, stuck his thumb in the split and pulled it sideways.

I screamed and punched, hit his hands and the back of the seat. Then his forearm. I was punching from a seated position. Carlos dug his thumb in and pulled the slit sideways until it tore. Then he stepped back.

I pressed the zigzag closed with my palm. Sat and watched him with one eye.

Carlos said, "That's for even. Nothing more, nothing less. Just let that be."

"Fuck you," I said.

He said. "It's not as bad as mine. Not nearly." He fingered the long, pink line down his face.

Blood seeped past my pressed palm, dripping onto my shirt.

Carlos said, "You better get that stitched."

The other man walked around the car and stood next to Carlos. He'd put the pistol in his pocket, the handle sticking out. He tapped his thumb on the butt.

Carlos stepped back and made a motion for me to get out.

I was still looking out of one eye.

"Go ahead and get out," he said. "We'll let you leave now. Let you think."

My palm was starting to slide around on the blood.

Carlos took another step back. "Come on," he said.

I ducked my head and got out of the back of the car. Stood up full, still holding my face.

Carlos said, "There's a lot more going on than you think. So I'll let you know."

"Let me know?"

"Yeah," he said, "I'll let you know."

I pulled my hand away and the blood drizzled down my face.

"Then you'll see," he said. "And you'll trust me then."

"Trust you?"

"Like I said, there's a lot going on." Carlos folded the blade of the mini-knife, and slid the ring back onto his key chain. "See you soon."

I walked to the caves by the Ahwahnee and got Super Glue and duct tape from Greazy's stash. Greazy wasn't there, but I knew he wouldn't mind. Then I went to patch myself in the Curry shower building where the mirrors are clean.

The cut went down an inch next to my left eye then turned at the bottom toward my ear. I filled the torn run with glue first, then up, sealing and pressing as I went.

I hit the hand dryers with my elbows over and over as I used both hands to press the edges closed in the warm air. Then I duct-taped a thin crisscross, laid a wide strip over, to the corner of my eye. The smell of Super Glue reminded me of my mother.

I didn't see Carlos or anyone else for days. In the spring, during the week, the world of people broke apart like leaves falling across a stretch of river. Only a few cars looped the Valley road, elderly people checking off Yosemite National Park in their Park Service passports, their car heaters set on high.

Camp 4 was quiet. A cougar walked through, head down, hoping for an over-fat ground squirrel. The cat leaped the boulder in front of me and moved uphill.

I slept as much as I could. Woke to sip water and eat a tablespoon of peanut butter, then continued with hibernation. I had to re-glue the bottom of my cut twice, but the split was healing.

Warm air came in one night as the seasons wrestled. Then all of the snow disappeared from the Valley floor, and the high country went to patches.

I hiked back up to Wawona, to the burn site. I walked around the house twice. Looked at it from every angle. I walked back and forth from the house to the woods until I saw something. Out by the trees, where the snow had disappeared, I found a patch of ground with no pine needles. The dirt was a mound there, soft. I dug the earth with my hands.

The gas can was not deep, only a foot down. I pulled it up and scraped the mud off the sides. It was a five-gallon can, red, not small or plastic like the one I'd used to burn the forms. It was metal and heavy, and I kept it. I hiked that can back across the high country and down the slot. I buried it off the Cathedral Trail, near the Valley loop junction. I built a three-rock cairn to mark the spot.

I wandered Camp 4 West that evening, watched the layering of the sky.

I climbed the boulders, grabbed an edge, and cut a flap of skin back from the pad of my index finger. I pushed and picked until the flap came off and a droplet of blood filled the divot. Then I sucked and tasted the sweet iron. I felt the cut next to my eye, but the tape and glue had held.

The rocks dotted white and gray, runs of quartzite like snakes hanging on the boulders in the late evening. Graphic granite.

A hiker walked by on the Falls Trail, his headlamp already turned on. He yelled back in Japanese to a woman behind him. She didn't answer.

I sat and let the night come. Squeezed blood out of the end of my finger and tasted some more. Then I began climbing in the dark. Easy routes at first, then harder. I don't know what I was trying to do. I made four moves up Yabo, on the corner, bouldering in the dark, when my foot slipped. I fell and hit my knee, heard the bone thwack against the rock, the deep bruise filling with blood. I limped over to the base of an oak tree, its branches snarling through the stars above me.

I thought of Lucy again. Our checkers game. I tried my knee but it would not bend. Saliva pooled in my mouth and I spit. Then I limped back to the face of the boulder, touched the rock in front of me, cool now in the dark, cool and white, glowing, the river and the story of the Yosemiti's river treasure. But there was only one thing I wanted back from that water.

My father said, "When the soldiers came in, all the gold was hidden in a woven box with no opening." My father pretended to hold a heavy box in front of him. He said, "It took four men to carry it."

He stood, and I watched him stumble around with the imaginary box.

I was nine years old.

My father reached down to pick up his coffee cup. He took a sip and said, "They dug out the bank at the turn, cutting down into the soft soil underneath the water. Then they lowered the box and placed rocks on top. Many rocks."

"Then what?" I said. "Did someone dig it up?"

"No," my father said. He took another sip of his coffee. "Not then. I wasn't there then."

"But later?" I said. "You found it later?"

"Yes," he said, "I found treasure later. But that's a different story."

"Wait, can you tell me?" I said. "Please?"

"Maybe when you're older." He finished his coffee and turned his mug upside down. Tapped the grounds out of the bottom of the cup, then wiped with the three fingers on his left hand.

I stayed in my sleeping bag for days. The bruise on my knee went from red to blue to purple-black, dripping yellow lines off the bottom, down my leg. I got up and limped around. I hadn't been this hungry in a long time. I'd been out of everything but peanut butter for a few days.

I limped through the campground to find leftovers, the climbers' camps best for lost food, and found a third of a loaf of wheat bread. The heel had greened from mold. I ate two pieces and tried to pinch the mold off the rest without wasting. I limped back to my cave and slept well with the bread in my stomach.

Three days later, I limped down to the northeast side of the Big Columbia Boulder. There were climbers there that I didn't know. It was misting, spray floating from the south side around the boulder. The overhang kept us dry.

A climber walked up and threw each of us a Budweiser pounder. He said, "Beer in Camp 4, stays in Camp 4."

I was eating white hamburger buns I'd found that morning. Almost a full pack and no mold. Not even stale.

A French climber tried to move off the lightning hold on Midnight. His friends said, "*Allez! Allez!*" Then he fell.

I cracked my can and took a sip. The beer was warm but still tasted good.

The French climber sat and stared up at the rock. He and his friends discussed the moves that were difficult. Acted them out and shouted at each other in French.

A young, dreadlocked man walked up and sat down next to me against the tree. He was a little older than me, wore a down jacket repaired with duct tape in many places. He hadn't shaved, and his beard was like the hair on the underside of a blond elk. He was wet from the mist. Smiling.

The cut steps in the old tree bark were above our heads, and we sat next to each other. I held out half of a hamburger bun. "Want some?"

"Oh yeah," he said. "Thanks. I'm Kenny." He took the bun and shoved the whole thing in his mouth, chewing slowly and breathing through his nose.

I nodded and drank my warm beer. We watched the French climber try Midnight Lightning again. When he fell off a second time, Kenny spoke with his mouth full. He said, "He'll get it."

I said, "It's pretty hard actually."

"No, he'll get it," Kenny said, and held out his hand. "What was your name?"

"Tenaya."

"Like the Indian chief?" he said.

"Yes," I said. "Like the Indian chief."

"Okay. Cool."

The French climber had started to climb again. He'd pulled off the ground and climbed through the first two moves. Then he lunged and stuck the lightning hold with his right hand. *"Allez! Bien!"* His friends were underneath him, hands up, ready to catch him if he fell.

Kenny stood up. "Go, man! *Allez*, man!"

The French climber pulled to the lip. I stood and joined the group underneath him, raising my hands as well. Then he lunged and caught the final big hold, pulling up and over, topping the boulder in the mist as everyone cheered. Kenny turned and bear-hugged me. I could smell the wet nylon of his jacket and the molding down underneath. That smell mixed with body odor was like hugging a drowned animal.

He yelled in my ear. "Awesome, man! Awesome! Climbing Midnight Lightning in the rain!"

The French climbers were jumping up and down, chanting what sounded like a nursery rhyme, clapping in unison. Kenny joined their rhythm and faked the words. I started to clap as well.

One of the French climbers turned to us. He said, "You would like to join us at our camp for wine and fire?"

"Wine and fire?" Kenny said. "Why yes."

I nodded too. My one beer was gone.

At their camp, the French climbers handed out metal coffee mugs, coffee rings brown in the bottom. I took my index finger and scraped the circle. Then a climber poured wine from bottles of Two-Buck Chuck.

Kenny smiled and took a sip. "Cheaply delicious."

The French climbers didn't speak much to us. They told animated climbing stories in French, pantomiming the moves with their whole bodies.

Kenny and I drank our wine together. He said, "So you live here in the Valley, huh?"

I took a gulp. "Yes, at Bachar Cracker caves right now. And the Ahwahnee caves before that. Maybe again soon."

"The Ahwahnee caves?"

"Yes," I said.

Kenny said, "Me too." He took a ball of hair out of his pocket and dropped it in the fire, watching it crackle. He said, "But I only live there sometimes. I've been roaming for a while."

"Roaming?" I said.

"Wherever. Just got back from Canada. Squamish. Colorado before that. Met so many good people." He took a sip of his wine. "So many."

I said, "So you're *that* Kenny."

He raised his eyebrows. "That Kenny?"

I said, "I think I was sleeping in your cave a while back. Greazy set me up."

"That's perfect," he said. "Did it have a stove and a crooked pipe?"

"Yes," I said.

He patted his chest. "That's me. I put that thing in myself. Works well, huh?"

I said, "I didn't use it because it wasn't cold when I was staying there. But it looked good."

"Makes sense," he said, "and it does work well when it's cold." He swirled his wine, then gargled a little in his mouth. Swallowed and sucked his teeth.

I fingered a rock in my pocket, a trade from a visiting climber out of Monument Valley. Red sandstone.

A French climber held a newly opened bottle toward us. "*Vous voulez?*"

Kenny said, "Yes, please. I *voulez*," and held out his cup.

The climber refilled both of our cups.

One of the Frenchmen was taking big, exaggerated steps, acting out running from something. Then he tripped and hit the ground right next to the fire. One of the others helped him up.

Kenny smiled. "I noticed you're limping."

"Yeah," I said. "Bad, bad bruise." I pointed to my leg. "I took a boulder fall off Yabo's. Cracked my knee pretty hard."

Kenny said, "Were you drunk?"

"No," I said, "just tired. It was late at night, and it was dark, and I was tired."

"The dark'll do that to you." Kenny laughed again. He seemed to laugh at most things. He said, "I was camping at the rim of the Grand Canyon once, April, near Toroweap. Way out there, and it was cold, and I didn't think I'd see anybody for weeks. Have you ever been out there?"

"No," I said.

"Oh, it's beautiful. You really should go. It's wilderness there, real wild, man, lonely and remote. And anyway, this BLM truck shows up out of nowhere. And I'm disappointed because I think they might hassle me about not having a camping permit or some crap like that but it turns out they're just two old college buddies hanging out, camping for the weekend somewhere pretty."

Kenny paused to take a gulp of wine. "Yeah," he said, "they just flat-out proceeded to get drunk. Hammered. I mean obliterated." He made big sweeping motions with his hands. "Then they went and pulled a juniper tree out of the back of their truck, an entire juniper tree, a young one, but an entire tree, maybe twelve feet tall or so, tall enough in fact that it hung out of the side of their truck by four feet, and it had a root ball and all. Then they started a fire underneath it."

I said, "The BLM guys burned an entire tree?"

"Yeah, weird, huh? Big fire. They invited me over too. Then one of the guys started telling a story about high school prom, and in the middle of imitating someone else's dancing, he just fell into the fire, right into the middle of it. I reached and grabbed him out, but this was the strange part: When I pulled him out, he rolled into a fetal position and started shaking, and I thought, *Oh, man, he's messed up.* Burned bad. I couldn't see his face or his hands, but I imagined that they were pretty bad. Then he fell onto his side and I realized he was laughing super hard." Kenny shook his head. "This guy was laughing like falling into a huge fire was the funniest thing he'd ever done in his life. His buddy was laughing too, fell down laughing, and spilled his beer in his lap."

"Was the guy burned?"

Kenny scratched his beard. "Probably," he said. "I don't know. He didn't seem too bad that night, but he was drunk, so you never know. I went and slept in the shelter I'd built a quarter-mile away, and they left in their truck before I got back to their spot in the morning. So that's all I know."

"Weird," I said.

"Yeah, weird." Kenny pointed to my right hand. "What's with the rock?"

I'd pulled it out of my pocket and was rubbing it with my fingers. I said, "Sandstone. I got it from another climber. An old habit."

"Collecting rocks?"

"No," I said, "not just rocks. Rocks from other places. Places I've never been."

"So it's like traveling?" Kenny said.

"Right. Like traveling."

He took a sip of wine and sucked his teeth again. "Well, why don't you just travel for real? Sandstone and pumice and obsidian can all be found in this great state of California." He squatted down and patted the ground with his palm. He said, "This state right here."

"Yeah," I said, "I've just never left the Valley."

"What do you mean never? Never at all?"

"No," I said. "Never at all."

"So you were born and raised here?" he said.

"Yes."

"Hmm," Kenny said. Then he clinked his metal cup against mine. "Well, okay then. A true, born-and-raised Yosemite man. That doesn't happen much, at least not anymore."

"Nope."

"But I like that," Kenny said. "I like that a lot."

Two weeks later, I ran into Kenny again. I was in the Yosemite Lodge bathroom. Kenny came out of a stall while I was at the urinal.

"Yosemite Valley Man?" he said. His hair was matted together in clumps of dreadlocks. He had a thick layer of dust on his down jacket as if he'd been rolling in dirt all night. Rings of mud around his wrists looked like rubber seals. But he washed his hands with soap.

He said, "Are you scrounging in here too?" He meant the cafeteria.

"Yes," I said. "I always do when the tourists start to come back."

"That's what I like to hear," he said.

We walked back into the dining room and waited for a family of four to get up and leave their breakfast trays. Then we sat down and finished the rest of their food. Half-links of sausage, a few bites of hash browns with ketchup, some scrambled eggs. Two mugs of lukewarm hot chocolate.

"Delicious."

"Yep," Kenny said. He smiled with his mouth full, hash browns in his teeth.

I took a tray off the table next to us. Two and a half pieces of white toast with jam already spread. Kenny traded me a deserted mug of coffee for one piece of toast.

"Still warm, huh?" he giggled.

"Still good," I said.

We ate quickly and left before a cafeteria worker could bother us. As we walked through the door, Kenny said, "I've found that I can do that every other day during tourist season. Less often in the fall. But you look a little better than I do. So maybe you could do it more than me without being hassled?"

"I don't know," I said. "My hair's long. They probably look at that."

"But your hair's in braids," he said. "Looks good enough. You could blend in." We were across from Camp 4 in the parking lot. He said, "Are you still staying over there?"

"Yep," I said. "Another couple weeks maybe. Then back to the Ahwahnee caves again."

We passed a crew of climbers racking up for a big wall.

I said, "Do you climb some, Kenny?"

"Yeah," he said, "I like to go up on El Cap."

The Three Brothers blocked my view of El Cap from there. I couldn't even see the far edge of the East Buttress. "Big wall climbing, huh?"

"Kind of big wall climbing," he said. "I like to go up there and just hang out. I like to stay as long as I can."

"As long as you can?"

"Yeah," he said. "The opposite of speed climbing. I like to just hang out and wait for weather, the best entertainment God gives us." Kenny squatted down and picked up a handful of gravel. "Weather and this landscape. The one we're losing right now to cement and gravel."

I said, "Or already lost."

Kenny dropped the gravel pebble by pebble. He looked up at me. Smiled. "Exactly," he said.

We walked across the street into Camp 4. I said, "They're trying to reallocate land to the Miwoks now. A tourism stunt."

"Really?"

"Yeah. People would come into the park and get to see real Indians. This is how they lived. This is how they gathered berries. This is how they wove baskets."

Kenny shook his head. He said, "That's fucked up. You know they're also trying to bring in a strip mall? Well, we already have one strip mall—the Yosemite Village—but they're trying to add fast-food restaurants and everything."

"Fast food?" I said.

"Burger places," Kenny said. "You know?"

I didn't know.

"Fries, shakes, and a drive-through?" he said. "Right. You've never been to a fast-food joint, have you?"

"No," I said. "Are they bad?" I rolled up my pants and checked my leg. The final yellow of the bruise had dripped down the shin, and I wondered if I hadn't cracked the bone. But I could walk, and almost run now.

Kenny was grinning and nodding at me. "It's kind of awesome that you've never been to one."

"Yeah, well . . . "

"It's kind of awesome and kind of scary."

"Scary why?"

"Well," he said, "you don't know the difference between any-thing, between the good and the bad. And you have no idea what they're trying to bring into this place."

I saw this on a Curry signboard:

The National Park Service is pleased to announce a new food services contract for Yosemite National Park. Twin Burgers, in partnership with Thompson Inc., will be the food contractor for Yosemite Lodge, the Yosemite Village Store, the Ahwahnee Hotel, Curry Village, Housekeeping, and Tuolumne. Twin Burgers has made a worldwide commitment to selecting, transporting, and cooking only the healthiest and highest-quality food, and will now be serving the greater Yosemite area with over sixty years of customer service experience.

The day after I read the sign, Twin Burgers' semis came into the Valley. I was at Curry when they started cooking their fries, the line of tourists backed to the parking lot. The smell was incredible. I stood on the pizza deck and breathed in and out. I'd never smelled anything so good in my life.

I waited for a group to leave some unfinished food, and I didn't have to wait long. The first table of customers left a few fries in the bottoms of their bags on the table. I picked them up. Lukewarm but still crunchy, fried to a yellow-brown and coated in salt. It reminded me of the first time I'd tried bacon, in the Tuolumne climbers' camp when I was fourteen. Too unreal for food.

I didn't know if Thompson Inc. could be wrong if their fries tasted this good.

A *San Francisco Chronicle* article said that a Twin Burgers restaurant was going to be built on the road at Housekeeping, next to the LeConte Memorial. A big, Golden T.

In Camp 4, I heard a climber say, "Dude, they just gouged a backhoe into the ground near the Pathways. Ripping huge chunks out of the earth."

I walked to the construction site. A crowd had already gathered, some of them jeering the construction workers. Three deputy sheriffs stood off to the side, watching the protesters.

Kenny was there, sitting on a moss-covered boulder, his arms wrapped around his knees. I went and sat next to him.

He shook his head. "Architectural plans must have been drawn, discussed, and ratified before the release of the new food contract, because this was all way too fast."

The moss we were sitting on was like the thick carpet squares boulderers carry around to scrub off their shoes.

Kenny said, "If they had this all set up, there's no way to stop it now."

We watched as the backhoe scraped and stopped on a slab of granite. Scraped and stopped again.

Kenny said, "Too many rocks to dig straight through though."

"They'll blast a hole," I said, "like the CCC making the step paths. My father told me the stories." We weren't far from the LeConte's structure. "The granite here never stopped anything," I said. "But I burned the Miwok forms."

Kenny said, "Burned what?"

"I burned the forms for the fake longhouses they were going to build for the tourist Indians in North Wawona."

"Really?" he said.

"Yeah." I told Kenny the story, how the longhouses were planned and forms set up, how I piled the gear, dumped gasoline, and lit it in the middle of the night.

"Like Monkey Wrench style?"

I said, "I don't know."

"The Monkey Wrench Gang? Ed Abbey? The ELF?"

"I don't know what you're talking about."

"Oh man," he said, "you don't even know what you're part of."

"I'm not part of anything," I said. "I just don't want this." I pointed to the backhoe in front of us.

"Neither do I," Kenny said. "Neither do I."

The backhoe driver had turned the vehicle and moved over to a far corner of the hole to try to pry a chunk of granite from the ground. The bucket was wedging underneath the slab.

Kenny said, "Did burning it stop development?"

I nodded. "As far as I know they haven't started to rebuild yet, and I haven't seen anything written about it since. But maybe they're just waiting for next summer."

"Probably," Kenny said. "They don't give up easily. But still, you stopped them for a whole year. That's better than nothing. And you might be able to stop them again."

I fingered the scar next to my eye.

Kenny said, "How'd you get that thing there. That scar's kind of new, huh?"

I said, "It's a long story."

"Okay," Kenny said.

"Maybe another time."

The backhoe wrenched a four-foot-wide slab out of the ground, tilting it vertically. A worker jogged over and slid a large cable around its lower half. The cable ran to a huge winch. With the winch and the bucket, they pushed and pulled the rock out of the way.

Kenny said, "There are prophets and there are judges."

"What?" I said.

"Prophets and judges. Both are holy, but they have different jobs."

The backhoe was digging at another rock now, the bucket wiggling as it snapped off the slab.

I said, "What if a person isn't holy at all?"

"I'm not," Kenny looked at me. "Or maybe not. And maybe not you either. I don't know."

We couldn't do anything about that Golden T in the center of the Valley, right across from Housekeeping. We talked about sabotage but the construction company left a sheriff and a ranger in rotation. Men with guns watching over the site. And we left it alone as they laid the foundation, then set up the frame.

A week later, they broke ground on the second Miwok Village. The article in the *Chronicle* said: "In the beautiful splendor of the Yosemite Valley, a strange reclamation is taking place underneath the shadow of Half Dome . . . "

The new village was at the east end, near Mirror Lake, underneath the belly of the dome, in the creek meadow. I wondered about the flood line.

This was easy for me. I found Kenny in Camp 4, under the Thriller Boulder oak tree where so many people like to read.

I said, "Kenny, do you want to wreck it with me?"

"It?" he said. He folded the page he was reading in his book.

"The new Miwok Village. Do you want to wreck it? Burn the forms?"

Kenny stood up, paused, then slid his feet around and did a little dance, tapping his right foot twice, then his left, and back to his right. "Oh yeah," he said, danced some more, "I'm in." He tossed his book to me and hopped off the ledge. "I thought you were a judge."

We retrieved the gas can, then Kenny siphoned from a Park Service vehicle. "It really makes the most sense," he said. He sucked four times on the hose, caught gasoline, and spit. "Damn that tastes good," he said, and giggled.

We watched from the Death Slabs approach, a thousand feet up, under the northwest face of Half Dome. They cut the earth with a Caterpillar D9 like it was road repair on the 120. The workers set concrete forms down, wood-framed with two-by-twelves, rebar reinforced. It looked like the foundation would be an underlay, run with solar heating tubes, warm beneath the faux dirt floor of the "original style" structure. I'd read about that design for the first Miwok longhouse.

Kenny said, "They're going to pour concrete there."

"Yeah, concrete right next to Tenaya Creek. Next to Mirror Lake. It's crazy."

"Concrete anywhere is fucked up," he said, "but we've got to stop it because of your name."

"Right," I said, "but it's also going to be a Miwok longhouse which is just as wrong."

Kenny looked at me and said, "One hundred and fifty years, and you still don't like the Miwoks, huh?"

"Well," I said, "if they'd leave us alone, stay south . . . " I started sliding down on my butt, the gas can catching and clanking on the rocks. We moved quickly until we got to the trees.

We drank water and ate homemade oatmeal–peanut butter bars Kenny kept in his pocket. Waited until dark. A security guard was stationed at the site, but he wasn't a sheriff's deputy and he wasn't a Park Ranger. The security guard was reading a paperback by Maglite. I tried not to slosh the gas in the half-full, five-gallon can as I stopped at the edge of the trees. We didn't make much noise and the guard didn't look up. He was focused on his book. I sat down and waited. Kenny sat down next to me.

Kenny said, "He'll fall asleep soon."

"Yeah," I said.

But he didn't. He kept on reading.

The security guard was to our left. The CAT D9 was to our right, off in the trees, one hundred yards from the forms, as if the company was trying to hide it. The security guard and the machine made a large triangle with the tree we were hiding behind.

Kenny whispered to me. "Watch this."

He picked up a couple palm-sized rocks. He threw them as far as he could, over the top of the CAT, making thumping sounds in the woods behind.

The guard's head came up out of the book. He swept back and forth with his flashlight. He stayed on his chair but he didn't read anymore. He scanned the woods in the direction of the CAT.

Five minutes passed. We watched the guard. The guard watched the trees.

Kenny picked up two more rocks and threw them in the same direction. The first one made a small sound in the woods, but the second rock hit the side of the CAT, producing an enormous clank.

The security guard stood up, aimed his light in the direction of the machine, pulled his baton, and started walking toward the sound.

As soon as he'd passed us, Kenny whispered, "Let's go."

The half-full gas can weighed twenty pounds, and I had trouble jogging with it. But I went as fast as I could. When we got to the forms, I unscrewed the lid and poured gas on the two-by-twelves, walking along the outline of the wall. I looked up only once, to see if the guard's flashlight was still searching in the woods by the machine, and it was. I could see zigzags of light in the trees behind the CAT.

Kenny was piling gear as quietly as he could. He made a signal to dump gas there. I started to pour, and he whispered, "Save some."

"What?"

"Save some for the CAT. We've got to burn that too."

I stopped pouring. There was maybe an eighth of a can left. "How are we going to do that?"

Kenny said, "Give me the can and wait for me to get to the trees." He pointed. "That guard'll come running when you light this. If you wait for me to get over there before you start it, when he's running back here, I'll get to the CAT and already be dumping gas by the time he's here. We'll get him going two different directions, and I'll circle around."

"I like it," I said. "Go."

Kenny took the can and jogged back to the trees.

I lit the pile with my lighter and the forms exploded like a blast of wind. Then I lit the gear pile.

The security guard yelled and I saw his outline running back across the clearing, straight toward me as I circled behind the burn. I couldn't see Kenny going to the machine, but I knew he was.

I went straight back, then north, away from the trail. When I looked over my shoulder, I saw the CAT go up like a huge animal lit and burning. The security guard's flashlight swept back and forth between the two burns.

Kenny met me on the north side of the clearing. He had the gas can in his hand and he was laughing so hard that he was wheezing. We watched the security guard's flashlight bounce up and down through the field.

The creek was rushing with snowmelt, and Kenny had to spin around and throw the can high and far to get it across. Then we swam after. I found the can in the reeds.

We hiked southwest in the trees, moving slowly now, avoiding the moss on tops of rocks, wet grass, dry tree branches. We tried not to hit anything that would scuff or imprint, anything that would leave an easy trail for people to follow the next day. We walked ten feet apart. Quiet for half an hour. Watching our feet.

Kenny kept giggling.

We cut west underneath North Dome, then the Arches, and arrived at the east end of the Ahwahnee property in less than half an hour. While it was still dark, I dug a grave for the gas can and buried it.

He said, "Are you really worried someone will find it?"

"Well, I might have to use it again."

"More arson?" he said.

"Maybe," I said. "Not sure what I'll need to do."

"Okay, then. You sift needles over that dirt. I'll make an arrow and a small cairn over here to mark the direction." He counted paces and made the marks.

CHAPTER 9

Jose Rey does not die on the battlefield. He is carried off the field by his warriors and survives in a grove hut.

The elders talk about his bravery against the grizzly, when he fought the animal alone in the dark with a sheath knife. There is a scar down Jose Rey's back like a river running next to his spine. He says that the scar is from his dance with the bear, when he cut around the heart, his fist doubling in size, when he left the knife inside the bear and pulled out the animal's heart.

Jose Rey releases venom in his last days and there are many who listen. They say that his venom is truth. He says that the ghosts are tearing through the blackberry patch, rending the roots from the ground. If they can, they will find a way to take the very ground itself.

Carlos walked up to me near the Upper Falls path. He surprised me because he didn't sneak. He knew where I lived.

I grabbed a rock.

He held out his hands. He said, "It's not like that. We're even now, one to one. Or actually—" he touched his scar—"mine's worse."

I said, "What do you want?"

He smiled. "I know you burned the new Miwok forms."

"You don't know anything, Carlos."

"Look," he said, "I don't mind. That's fine with me."

I laughed at him. "I didn't ask you. And you're a ranger anyway. I know you care about that."

"I do?" he said. "Is that right?"

I was holding the rock and he was standing with his hands up. He said, "We need to talk about some things." He dropped his hands and put them in his pockets.

The rock I held was heavy enough to crush his skull, a Chief Tenaya rock. I said, "Maybe I don't want to talk to you about things."

"Maybe you don't," he said, "but we should talk anyway. Then you'll understand what's going on."

I waited. I didn't go toward him or away.

"For example," he said, "Twin Burgers is paying private investigators to supplement the FBI's investigation of what the Park Service calls 'The Yosemite Arsons.' Three burns in one year. Twin Burgers doesn't want similar trouble with its Valley locations. The security guard from the night of the third arson saw two men, but he didn't have good descriptions. Young and athletic. Long, dirty hair. The FBI and the investigators are pursuing those descriptions."

I hoped Kenny hadn't talked to anyone about anything. I said, "What does that have to do with me?"

"You and I both know what that has to do with you, Tenaya." Carlos turned and walked off down the trail. I watched him until he reached the Camp 4 entrance path. Then I went back to my cave and found my sheath knife. I ran cordelette through the belt loop and tied it so the knife hung behind my right hip.

I moved out of the Bachar Cracker cave. I took my sleeping bag and gear further up on the north side to a lean-to of gray boulders, not even rainproof. But the sky was clear, and I slept near the bear hollows.

"Not to anybody, right?"

"Right," Kenny said.

"I know you wouldn't brag about it."

"No," he said. "I thought it was funny, but I didn't tell anyone."

"Good."

Kenny and I walked into Curry, around the back of the shower building. It was early morning, before anyone was up. Kenny said, "My parents probably wanted something different for my life. I'm thirty-one now." We got to the lost-and-found boxes. Most of the things I owned were from those boxes.

"Look at this puffy." Kenny held up a bright orange jacket, waiting on top of the first box, clean and bright compared to the one he normally wore.

"That'll work," I said. I pulled out a pair of long underwear and smelled them. They were rank, but I could wash them in the free showers with the pump soap.

He said, "My parents are cool though."

I found a North Face fleece. Checked the size and tried it on. It was big but close enough.

Kenny said, "They really are. And they want me to be happy."

I nodded, started sorting through the second box. Mostly T-shirts.

"You know what I hate?" Kenny held up a Yosemite Sam T-shirt. "Junk drawers."

I smelled a polypro shirt, body odor like rotting onions. I waited for Kenny to explain.

"You know what I mean," he said, "the drawer in the kitchen, next to the phone, full of rubber bands, pennies, pliers, old pencils, golf tees, string, tape, wire, everything?" He was making a pile next to his lost-and-found box, mugs and hats and T-shirts. "Most houses have them," he said. "Then again, I guess you wouldn't know about that."

"No," I said.

"Do you miss that?" he said. "Houses and everything?"

"I don't think I miss them, but I sometimes wonder. Houses or the ocean. Or my father taught me to drive a car, but I've never driven a car anywhere but the Valley Loop Road. And what would anything else be like?"

"Right," Kenny said. "Right."

We were finished with the boxes. We each had a couple items.

Kenny said, "Want to score free cups of coffee before the rangers and tourists come around at the kiosk?"

We went to the rentals center. The employees glared at us but didn't say anything. Kenny poured the first cup of coffee and handed it to me. He said, "My parents wouldn't want my life, and I wouldn't want a junk drawer." He poured himself a cup. "But they're good people. Probably yours too."

I added cream to the rim. Took a sip. We walked to the amphitheater and sat down on one of the wooden benches. I said, "Sometimes I feel like I'm less me and more everything around me. You know?"

"That makes sense," Kenny said. "Like you have no control?"

"Right," I said. "I'm angry about it. I know that. Like I'm trying to live a life that doesn't exist, or like everything's fighting me, and I can't make things work the way I want them to."

Kenny sipped at his coffee and looked at the empty amphitheater's stage in front of us. We were the only people sitting in the rows of benches. He said, "I think most people feel that a little bit. And that's why I go on my long adventures. It's true. I just try to push and push, go by myself to see how far I can go in any direction, to see what I'm capable of."

I nodded and sipped at my coffee.

Kenny said, "We've got a little time, but that's all. We've got to live these little moments."

My mother could improvise with newspaper, putting the glue in the middle, then catching the corners of the square and pulling those four corners in until they met in her hand. When she blew, the newspaper ballooned in front of her as she waited to take that first big inhale. I watched her hands shake at that moment, right before, putting the fist of newsprint to her mouth, closing her eyes, and her hands shaking, anticipating that first big suck.

I was in Camp 4, under the Thriller oak tree, reading a book. The pages kept flipping in the wind, and I had trouble concentrating. I kept thinking about the FBI and Twin Burgers.

A little girl was there. Her parents were bouldering, and she was playing make-believe with a pile of pinecones and a stick wand. She kept spinning around in circles, casting spells at invisible monsters. Dark and curly haired. Kid dreadlocks like tree roots coming out of her head. Maybe five years old.

The little girl whispered, "*A la muerte,*" as her mother attempted Thriller.

The little girl had a centimeter gap between her two front teeth. She balanced on her right leg, swinging the left, then hopped. Her arm shot out and she waved the wand in the air.

I tried to see her face better. Her eyes. It had been so long.

She spun again. Turned on something with the wand in her right hand. Facing away, and I sat forward.

Then she spun around and pointed her wand right at me. Her hair was wild as matted weeds, a clump of hair stuck off to the side. She looked right at me, and I knew she was someone else. So I looked away.

That night, Kenny said that he wanted to walk to Truckee.

"Walk there?" I said. "How far is that?"

"Two hundred miles," he said. "Maybe 250 walking, or maybe less. I'm not really sure. I want to see Lovers' Leap though, look at the place where they jumped."

"Yeah," I said, "my father told me that legend when I was little, the one about the suicide pact."

"Did he call it a legend?" Kenny said.

"Yeah, the legend of them jumping while holding hands."

He shook his head. "That's not a legend, man. Not if you mean legend as untrue. Most stories like that are more true than anything else we hear."

I was starting to understand Kenny. He'd laughed at the idea of a newspaper when I'd showed him the last *San Francisco Chronicle* article. He'd said, "You believe anything in that thing? It's probably secretly owned by Rupert Murdoch too."

I didn't know who that was.

Kenny said, "So you want to walk with me to Truckee or what?"

We were under the Book Cliffs near the Lower Falls Path. We'd just climbed up Munginella, down the broken trail, and now we were sliding on the loose pack.

"Walk to Truckee?" I said. "I'm not sure."

He said, "To the Leap," and made a cliff edge with his left hand, someone jumping off with his right, two fingers kicking in the air.

"No," I said, "probably not."

Kenny tied his shoes together and hung them on his neck. He said, "Is that 'cause you always stay here in the park or what?"

"Maybe," I said. "I don't know."

"No, seriously," he said, "are you ever going to leave here or what? Even for a little bit?"

We turned a corner on the trail, and there was a longer steep straight below us. I said, "I don't think so. Well, maybe. I don't really know."

"You never just want to go? Just leave?" he said. "Just take off somewhere?"

"Yeah, I did want that. I wanted that last year for a while. And I've been up in Tuolumne . . . twice now. Two different summers up there in the high country, and I wanted to keep going then."

"And?" he said.

"And I didn't. I didn't have the opportunity," I said.

"The opportunity? But you have the opportunity all the time. Just start walking, then keep walking."

"I don't know. I guess it didn't feel right. I didn't want to go farther than Tuolumne. Or at least it didn't feel like I could," I said. "It's hard to explain."

Kenny's feet slipped on the trail and he fell onto his butt. He laughed and stood back up. He said, "So that's it? You're never going to leave?"

"Last year I sort of started to, at least in my mind. I made a decision that I was going, that I was leaving, but . . . " I was talking about Lucy, but I didn't want to talk about Lucy. I said, "It just didn't work out."

Kenny waited, but I didn't say anything else. He looked at me as we hiked down to the end of the steep, then back into a zigzag turn. I hiked off the trail there, to stomp steps, and Kenny followed me. We scrambled over and under fallen trees.

Kenny said, "There's still time, you know. You're not going to die tomorrow."

The Lower Falls was blasting mist to our left, snowmelt surging from the high country. There were hot days coming.

My father says, "Think like Tenaya." He taps my forehead.

I'm eight years old. I don't know what he means.

He says, "Nothing less than that. Do you understand me?"

I say, "Yes," but I don't.

"The Great One. Like you?" he says.

I say, "Yes," again.

The fox has stolen both packages of meat, the white-wrapped hamburger from the cache.

My father says, "He could only do that if he came through twice. You know that?"

I don't want to admit that I missed him twice, that I didn't protect our food stores.

"Think," my father says. "A third time through and you catch him, okay? So what are you going to do?"

"Catch him," I say. "Set a good trap."

"Right," he says. "You have to know these things. Learn everything. This is where you'll live forever, in this place, in this Valley, Tenaya."

I slept underneath a log near one of the Arches streams. The cool air came off the water and I lay down. Turned and slept all night. Some days, after climbing hard, the tiredness comes in like a wool blanket pulled to the chin.

Morning then, and I smelled the familiar smell of pine loam. Dew smoke. Childhood in my nostrils, and the camp up Ribbon Creek. I stepped over to the Arches stream and took two cupped hands of water and drank. This stream didn't have any giardia. I'd walked it up to the wall dozens of times, climbed Royal's routes above, jammed through splitters and seams, corners of waterfall that made my bare feet slip until they dried. I'd seen the purifying granite. Washed my head in the 38-degree water that dizzies.

Everything visits me in the morning smoke. The superintendent keeps his cigar, his back straight, his neck, black-and-white clothes pressed. No body in the bushes. No turned face.

I tapped my index fingers and thumbs, a beautiful day cracking from the east like freeze-water splitting loose granite. The loam smoked as the sunlight scratched toward me like a thousand forest fires at their beginnings.

She was there too. Water droplets on her temples. The green slash of one blade of cutgrass stuck to her cheek.

At the hotel dumpster, Kenny was foraging like a blond bear. He had the door tilted down, shoulder deep in the box, and he pulled out a garbage bag. Ripped it open. Shook his head and threw it back in. Then he went for another bag.

When he had what he wanted, a bag full of dinner leftovers from the hotel restaurant, he smiled. Tore the bag and found mixed pasta and sauces from the night before.

Kenny took a fistful out, then passed it to me.

He said, "You all right, man? Your face doesn't look good."

I pulled out some of the pasta. Linguini in a cheese sauce. Cold. I said, "Yeah, I'm okay."

"You sure?"

I shrugged.

He said, "I'll tell you a bad story. Trade mine for your trouble."

"Okay," I said. I grabbed a second handful of noodles. One in each palm now, I started to eat.

"You know how much I like animals?" he said.

I didn't really know, but I could guess.

He said, "Here's a story about one animal that I loved."

Kenny squatted down with his pasta. I squatted next to him, leaned back against the dumpster, my palms full of the cold noodles. I ate out of the edges of my hands.

Kenny said, "Our family friends had a dog named Beau. A big old boxer. Beautiful. Brown coat and square face, muscled chest, strong. And every time I came into town, I'd hang out at their house and play with that dog Beau.

"So one time, I was going on this camping trip with a couple of my friends, going out into the woods near the Sand Dunes National Rec Area in Oregon, and my friend said, 'Why don't you take Beau?' He knew Beau would love it.

"So I went and picked him up. That's back when I had a truck, a house, all that. Different lifetime for me." Kenny held up a handful of pasta and laughed. Squished the noodles through his fingers and ate the falling pieces off the back of his knuckles. "Way different lifetime."

I ate my noodles and nodded.

"Anyway," he said, "I went and picked up my two friends, and they threw their stuff into the back of the truck with Beau. Then we hit up a store for food. Beau jumped out like he was going to walk into the store with me and I laughed and said, 'I love you, man, but you can't go in.'

"So I got him back in the truck, and clipped him to one of my old climbing ropes. I didn't short-rope him though, so he'd feel okay about being tied. I just clipped him to a big old length of tatty rope tied off to a corner of the truck bed. I knew Beau was a good dog, and that he would stay in if I tied him to anything.

"Anyway, I went into the store, bought a little food, and came back out. A couple of us threw Beau a treat before we started up again, and then we drove for an hour while we told fishing and backpacking stories in the front of the truck. I didn't worry about Beau. I didn't even think about him.

"And when we got to the coast, we headed south. I cut west on a Forest Service road toward the beach, and I remember looking back right at that turn and seeing Beau sitting in the back, over my shoulder, smiling the way boxers always do. He was really great, that dog. So content. So mellow.

"Well, the road got twisty and beat-up. Unimproved since they finished logging it a decade before, and I focused on the driving, on not grounding out or missing a turn. We bounced all over the place in the truck. It was a rough couple miles from there.

"And when I stopped the truck, and looked over my shoulder, Beau wasn't there. He wasn't behind me. I figured he'd laid down in the truck bed. That, or he'd gotten sick, and I hoped he hadn't puked on our packs.

"I hopped out to see what he was up to, but he wasn't in the bed. He wasn't there at all. Just the rope. And it was stretched pretty tight over the back end of the tailgate. I realized right then. I remember yelling, 'No, no, no . . .' as I ran back.

"And fifty feet off the back of the truck, there was Beau, all drug around and missing most of the skin on both sides of his body. His right leg was broken upward, and he was real dead. Just like that. Just, finished."

I looked at Kenny's face, now bright pink. He was crying a little, and he ducked his head and wiped his face on his shoulder.

I said, "I'm really sorry, Kenny."

He nodded and took a bite of noodles. Choked on his bite and coughed.

I said, "I'm really sorry, man," again. I still had two handfuls of noodles, so I patted him on his back with my forearm.

Kenny cleared his throat. Spit noodles and phlegm onto the asphalt. Sniffed. He said, "I buried him. I carried Beau way out into the woods and dug a deep hole so no coyotes would get to him. I added some rocks, and pissed all over the top of those so the coyotes wouldn't like the smell of it. I waited a while and pissed again to be sure. And Beau stayed down there. I went back a year later to check and see that nothing had messed with him."

Kenny cried while he ate a bite. Wiped his nose on the back of his hand.

I said, "I'm really sorry," again.

"Yeah, me too," he said. "Nothing should have to drag and kick itself to death, or break its own leg trying to stand up. Nothing should die like that."

We crouched next to the dumpster, each holding the rest of our pasta.

Kenny picked a hair out of his food and took another bite.

I said, "You sold your truck after that, huh?"

"Yep," he said. "Didn't ever want to drive it again. Couldn't really stand to look at it. And I've never had a car since."

"Never?"

"Not in ten years," he said. "You?"

"Had a car? No. Not unless you count the car I was born in."

Kenny tipped his head back and scraped noodles off his palm with his teeth. Then he shook out that hand. Wiped it on the blacktop.

I ate my handful until I tasted something bitter and spat it out. Then I tossed the remainder of my handful.

Kenny reached in the garbage bag and pulled out red noodles. He looked at them from both sides and smiled. He said, "These look better."

I grabbed some of those too, and they were good. Long, flat noodles with marinara soaked into them.

Kenny said, "What was bothering you this morning?"

I said, "It's not important."

Kenny held one long noodle above his mouth and sucked it in. He smiled, red sauce in his beard. "I don't believe you," he said, and wiped his face with his sleeve. "But that's cool. Maybe another time."

"Yeah," I said, "another time."

Kenny said, "You know what happened right after that thing with Beau? It's kind of funny. I was hitchhiking in Northern California, near Crescent City, the redwoods at Jedediah, when this huge Chevy Suburban I was hitchhiking in hit a deer. The Suburban broke that deer, and the deer barely made a mark on the vehicle. Just one busted-out headlight, that's all, and the deer's neck was snapped, head turned all the way around backwards.

"We were standing there on the side of the road, staring at the deer when I realized she was connected to Beau, and I needed to make something of her, of her death, something I couldn't do with Beau.

"So I got my backpack out of the car and thanked the people for the ride. They were nice enough. The man said, 'Sorry about that. Didn't mean to hit a deer, you know?'" Kenny took a bite of noodles and chewed slowly. He talked with his mouth full. "So after they drove away, I dragged that doe into the woods, built a smoke pit, and cut a few hundred thin strips of meat off her. Then I smoked it all and lived off it for a month."

"A full month?"

"Yeah," he said, "a full month. One moon. I watched the sky at night. I ate that deer and whatever else I could find out there, some berries and roots, a couple snakes for variety. And I stayed in the woods and thought about a lot of things. Felt like Beau wasn't being wasted then. That he was in the ground, and had been killed by a car, drug to death, a pretty fucking evil thing altogether, but that the deer had redeemed him. I don't know why the doe was given to me, but she put a bookend on Beau's life. Put it all into a circle. That doe gave me a new way of being."

I said, "The doe redeemed Beau because you ate her?"

"No, no," Kenny said. "It wasn't because I ate her. It was because she gave me time, an entire month to be alone, a month to think about Beau, to think about cars and houses and jobs and food and video games and junk drawers and everything else that I think about now, everything I gave up. Everything you . . . " he stopped and tapped me with his elbow " . . . everything that you know nothing about. That's what she did for me."

I said, "Honestly, Kenny, I don't know that I didn't miss some things being here. You know how lonely I was?"

Kenny looked straight up at the sky as if the blue was about to fall on us. He said, "Yeah, I bet you were."

"No," I said. "Really, really lonely. So many days of nothing, and I'd see kids my age in the camps in spring and summer and I'd wonder what their lives were like, what they did when they drove out of this Valley, if they were happier than me, having friends and schools and whatever else."

"Well," Kenny said, "I don't think so. There's this whole world of nothing out there. Completely valueless. Kids not really living, never being outside, hooked to wires, to computers and TVs and video games for hours every day. Kids who are afraid of bugs and spiders and wild animals, afraid of the dark and of camping, those who have never even been camping. And you had this Valley. This one." Kenny made a circle with his finger. "You have no idea."

I looked up at the black water streaks on the Arches above us, 1,500 feet up the granite wall. "I know I like what's here," I said. "I do love this Valley. But I had no people to be with. Or not enough people."

Kenny laughed. He said, "People are the worst. That's something I kept coming back to when I was alone out there for a month. People are selfish and wreck things. I'm selfish and wreck things. We don't care about anything but ourselves. But you, living in this Valley? You made the best choice."

"But I didn't choose this," I said. "I didn't choose this at all."

"Are you kidding?" Kenny said. "You're choosing this right now."

I stayed with the Valley, the park. I walked with Kenny as far as the Vernal Falls path. Then I stopped and watched him hike along the river.

He'd packed bread and some peanut butter I'd given him. A couple hundred feet away, he turned around and yelled, "Hang out in a few weeks?"

"Okay," I yelled back. "Sure."

He flipped around and hiked again, his head swinging back and forth looking at everything he was passing. He lifted a hand and waved.

I waved back, then walked back to camp. Filled my water bottle at the dish rinse station and slung it on a cord over my shoulder. Then I headed for the slabs, the west end of Swan Slabs, where the beginner rock routes led to loose, fourth-class climbing, loose but easy. I cruised a few hundred feet in the next half-hour, traversing across to Selaginella and the top-outs in the trees above the Books. I climbed this sometimes, west along the rim, looking back across the Valley at Sentinel.

When I found the in-cut, the shallow cave, I stopped and sat down at the corner where the cave met the open air. The cliff opened beneath my feet, at an overhang, then the wall dropped vertically for a few hundred feet. A thousand feet above the treetops, the trees didn't look like trees at all but a dark-green mat, arcing in a half circle below.

I waited.

Nine years old, in a place I called the Moss Drop, a green gap in the ground near our camp. My eyes itched and the dry moss beneath me compressed. I slept there one night, sitting first, watching the dark until my head fell forward, and I lay down on my side, curled like a coyote pup.

Before I fell asleep, I could hear my father calling to me, his flashlight beam sweeping across the surface of the forest. But there was no way for him to see into this hole, and I didn't reply. I sank deeper into the summer moss. The smell of old dirt around me. I hid. Then he went the other way and I fell asleep.

In the morning, the sunlight was above me. I sat up.

My mother was there. Ten feet away. She'd found me in the night, and she was leaning against the boulder to my left, sitting, eyes open, forearms across her knees. She was staring at me when I woke.

From the cave above the Books, the Valley was uninhabited. I saw the buildings abandoned, no one outside or in, no one in the store buying Popsicles or in the Ahwahnee Hotel watching television. Was this better? My father would say so. And Kenny maybe.

The white glints of motor-home tops and the silver curls of cars showed movement then. More trees from here though, the open meadows green and wide in the expanses, the animals hidden down there, deer and elk, bear and cougar, rattlesnakes lying on snags in the river, gathering sun, warming their cold blood.

I waited.

Kenny was off to Truckee, walking now. Lucy was in the ground, underneath the aging carcass of a lion, a layer from loam. The superintendent had waited six years with his eyes. I'd circled hundreds of times around that meadow, but I hadn't crossed that boardwalk since.

My parents were up Ribbon Creek, stacking wood and cooking, forty years now.

I was not hungry. I would not let hunger come to me. There were times as a child when I realized that hunger was not something real but a thought that could be suppressed for a long, long time, for hours first, then days. From reading the *San Francisco Chronicle*, I knew that some people learn this when they're young. I thought of stories I'd read about Central Africa and U.S. Indian reservations. Calcutta, India. Eastern Russia and rural China. None of those places sounding anything like my Valley. So maybe Kenny was right.

I flexed the muscles of my arms, my hands, let them relax, my body. Middle of the afternoon. More white and silver below, the traffic lines of the late afternoon, the Valley Loop Road filling with lines of painted metal.

Evening now, the sun passing the nose of El Capitan like a guard burning his watch. Then down. I sat in the late shadows on my ledge above the expanse. I did not pile sticks and brush. No shelter. I let the night come, and the cool. More than cool, the cold after. I pulled on my wool hat, the only extra clothing I'd brought, a hat that I'd stuffed in my pocket.

In the night, I began to shiver, but I flexed my stomach muscles and chest, pulled myself tight the way my father had taught me when I was little. Tightened away from the cave wall to hold my heat. And the cold went away.

In the morning, I woke up cramped. Slumped sideways, having slept against the wall, the granite pulling my heat, and I was cold again. The dew dropped, a little water, misty, and the sun followed, glancing off the white granite like sparks from an ax head hitting stone.

I stayed through the day. No other humans, nobody passing. I stood and stretched. Walked in a circle until I was warm, then waited again. Sat down. Waited through the day and it was long. Ants crawled a line over my bare right foot. I let them. They carried the body of a yellow jacket an hour later, the insect's armor plates tilting as the ants climbed the side of my heel.

Ravens fought in front of me, a physical argument, not loud with squawking, not like the crows on the Valley floor. I saw one raven drop and slam the body of another from behind, the second one rolling.

Another night, and I argued with my stomach. Kept hunger away. Sipped water from my bottle. A second dark. I didn't know what I was waiting for. Same as childhood. Alone, and that was enough.

My mother's last words to me. To us:

"Go play," she says.

We both stand.

"You two need to go play," she says again. "Or go swim. I'll be there in a little while."

We walk away. I reach out my hands like wings, fly until I pass the bark of trees. I like the feel of them, each tree different to touch, varied patterns. I close my eyes and imagine that I am blind, and she follows the sightless me. When I pick up my foot, she sets her smaller foot in its place. I can hear her right behind me, the way she breathes through her nose.

The heat and then the cool. I can feel the change even with my eyes closed, the way the river holds cool air. I stop when my toes stub a rock. I open my eyes. We're at the edge of the river and our father isn't there yet.

That night, he whispers to me, "It is not your fault. I promise that. It's not your fault."

I walked a circle to get warm, then sat down and fell asleep again. Fitful with no food. In and out of the dark.

Then the third day. Bright and too clear, as if a sheen of glass cut in the light before my eyes, a refraction of the daylight's colors, the sun's spectrum, elements splitting the world. I watched the sun move across the new sky, the slow swell of the arc and back down. The ants came again but carried no yellow jackets.

Evening of the third full day.

And the ravens. I thought they were vultures this time, circling a few hundred feet above me, in slow arcs like black charcoal etchings on the cave wall. But these birds moved like hawks, and their wings did not tilt on the turn as vultures' wings do. No wavering tilt, and I saw that they were ravens once more, even before they came close.

They gathered on my ledge and did not squawk. Three of them. No noises but the dragging of their talons on the granite crystals. Their heads turned as they resettled their wings. Hopped and resettled again.

I said, "Hello," and my voice cracked, not used to working after the last two days.

The ravens scraped their claws, moved away, flew off. Then they came back. Settled on the ledge with me, and when I fell asleep, they were still there. Scraping and watching.

This is true:

They brought me food. The ravens. In the morning, when I woke up, they were there once again, close to my hands, holding the meat like wet newspaper, the putrid gray-brown strands. Their black beaks gripping the fermented meat. I ate.

Teachers bring schoolchildren into the Valley from Merced, from Fresno, from Manteca, Sacramento, and San Francisco. They sit at the other end of the long picnic table. Four of them. Eating bacon and swinging their legs. Talking with their mouths full. Giggling.

CHAPTER 10

I have read that some animals wage war. I have also read that humans are animals, but I do not believe that lie. No animals are like us.

The army comes into the Valley for the first time. Not the whole army but a small part of the 36th Regiment. They are soft and pale, with heavy shoes, walking as if their feet have been burned in a fire.

We let them pass by twice. They have the Miwok scouts with them, the diggers who crawl on all fours like the bears they will become in the next life as penance. The Miwoks have given their own wives to the regiment's leader like stringing meat for wolves.

Yes, in this war, the soldiers of the 36th Wisconsin will burn acorn stores, starve the young, torture and murder, attack women while they are sleeping. But this is nothing new. This is true of all wars.

The Yosemiti live in the Valley and the Valley is beautiful, and no people can live somewhere beautiful forever. It is like holding water in your hands.

I set three fish lines on short sticks and waited behind a tree. Treble hooks are illegal in the Valley, and the squirrel entrails I used as bait, but no one ever fished there and the rangers stayed in the campgrounds.

After an hour, I checked the lines. The first had a brown, the second nothing, and the third held a white. I killed both fish with a rock, gutted them, then looped my lines. I rolled the fish in the bottom of a plastic bag, tied the top, and stuffed it into my back-pack. My mother would cook anything. Even the white.

I hid my fishing sticks in the usual spot between the split rocks.

I walked on the Merced side of the road until I got to Ribbon Creek. Then I crossed the road and headed up into the trees. It was early afternoon and hot. I followed the creek boulders, hopping from rock to rock to avoid wearing more of a path on the bank. My father told me that he had seen the rangers pass by twice that sum-mer already. And one visit would end my parents' camp forever.

When I got to their clearing, I saw the tent between the boul-ders, the fire ring, the clothesline to the left in the woods. But the car wasn't in the gully. It was next to the rocks. The nose of the '46 Plymouth stood out like a rusted grizzly. My father must have driven it up there somehow, not by the path, winding it slowly between the trees.

I walked over. He was in the car. My father's face pressed against the rolled-up window, lips smeared down. His face like burned meat, bloodshot, dark bruises on his forehead between the streaks of red.

I pulled open the door and he fell against me, breathing through his teeth, making *sss, sss* sounds.

"No, no," I said. "Fuck."

I squatted down and held his weight against my shoulder, breathed into my ear, and I saw my mother then, over his shoulder, in the passenger seat, the glove box open like a throat. She held the scissors in her left hand, and she was cutting pieces of paper, put-ting them in her mouth, chewing and swallowing.

"Mom, what the . . . "

She was humming and cutting as my father was breathing those S-sounds into my shoulder, and I pulled him out, his armpits wet, a bad smell there, and I popped the seat forward, then pushed my father back into the car, slid him in, then picked up his feet and tucked them in.

I hopped into the driver's seat, closed the door, and turned the key. The engine caught. My mother was still cutting.

I backed the car slowly between the boulders, backed it into the gap, turned, and drove downhill, weaving between trees. When I got to the Loop Road, I sped across the bridge and drove fast toward the Village. My father made scraping sounds through his teeth.

At the Meadows, I wove in and out of slow-moving cars, zigzagging through tourists gawking at their first views of the Valley. I almost hit a man who was standing in the road, staring at a waterfall. I pressed on the horn but it hadn't worked for years, and he jumped as I swerved around him, my front end a foot from taking off his legs.

I turned at the bridge, cut back west, and pulled in at the clinic in the Village. I jumped out of the car and said, "I'll be right back."

I ran inside and found EMTs eating sandwiches. One of them stood up. He said, "Can we help you?"

The EMTs ran out with me.

Both car doors were open now, the one I'd left open and the passenger's side door. My mother wasn't in the car now. My father was still in the back. The first EMT saw my father's face and ran for the ambulance. The other EMT put his head into the backseat.

They put an oxygen mask on my father's face and he blinked a few times.

He said, "Tenaya?"

They were running an IV in one arm.

I grabbed his other hand. "Yes?"

He opened his mouth and struggled to make more words.

I said, "They're taking you to a hospital."

"Don't," he said.

"What?"

He said, "Don't leave."

"Don't worry," I said. "I'll stay with you."

"No," he said. He squeezed his eyes shut. Opened them. Breathed in and out on the oxygen. "Don't leave the park. They want you to." He closed his eyes.

The EMTs were hooking the fluids to the IV line.

"Who wants me to leave?"

He still had his eyes shut. He said, "Promise me."

An EMT patted me on the back. He said, "We've got to go. In a situation like this, every minute counts. Are you coming?"

I looked at my father.

"No," he said, "he's not."

I turned around to see if my mother was near the building, along the road, anywhere in sight. I said, "I don't know."

The EMT pushed my father forward, into the bay. He said, "We've got to go now, okay?"

"Okay," I said. "You go ahead. I have to find my mother."

He motioned to the driver. "We'll do everything we can. Go back inside and fill out the paperwork. They can fax it over to the hospital in Merced."

He closed the ambulance doors, and I took a step back. I watched the ambulance drive to the stop sign, then turn west on the Loop Road. I turned around. The Plymouth was still empty.

I closed the passenger-side door. Looked at the entrance of the clinic and thought about going in to fill out the paperwork, but I didn't know what I would write. Beyond my father's first name, I didn't know anything.

I drove across the street and slowly looped through the parking lot at the store. My mother wasn't there. I drove past Church Bowl, up the Ahwahnee drive, looked in the trees. I pulled over and hopped out, hiking through the boulders. Then I went back to the car and drove to Curry. A few women looked like her from afar, but when I slowed down and passed them, they smiled at me with faces that were not my mother's. I parked and walked through the tent cabins, out along the tiny run off next to the Lower Pines campground. I jogged through to the Merced, down its south bank, then back to the car.

I drove back to the El Cap bridge and parked. Then I got out and looked there, on foot. I searched the nearby woods, and down at the river too, through to the clearings, and up the other side. I walked in and out of the trees, all the way to Sentinel Beach. But by then it was evening, and I came across the paved meadow path as it got dark. I looked in the Lodge dining area, the laundry facility, and the bathrooms, but it was getting too late, too dark to see much of anything that wasn't lit by bathroom lights.

The white sand of the Swan Slabs made it light enough to search there, but I didn't think I'd find her in the slabs. And I didn't.

When I was eleven, I followed my mother past El Cap meadow, followed her to the bridge where everyone was pointing up at the climbers on The Nose. We walked past binoculars and cameras, Japanese tourists, beyond the bridge, up the road into the trees. She'd motioned for me to follow.

I walked behind her as she hopped down onto a deer trail in the trees south of the bridge, and I followed her into the woods. I didn't ask. It had been five years since the night at the river, and I didn't think about her not talking anymore.

She walked in front of me, and I followed her through a grove of incense cedar, my shins brushing the mariposa lilies in the sun gaps. We came to a small clearing, protected on one side by a crescent of white boulders. My mother stopped and pointed. Held her arm out straight.

In front of her, a cinnamon-colored bear was digging the ground, and next to her, two cubs wrestled. The mother bear smelled us and raised her head. She weighed more than three hundred pounds and the muscles in her shoulders rolled as she moved her head to look at us.

I looked at my mother, but she still had her arm up, pointing, and she didn't move.

The mother bear stared at us as the cubs continued to wrestle next to her. They were not Curry Village bears. They didn't have yellow tags and they weren't scrounging in the campgrounds. They were foraging along the forest floor, scratching their way north, unused to human beings.

I didn't find my mother. Around midnight, I lay down near the Wine Boulder in central Camp 4. My eyes opened to the sky above me, to the stars I knew. I started picking out the shapes of the familiar constellations, my father's stories in my head. The Hunter. The Husband. The Wife and the Bear.

I thought of my father in a hospital bed in Merced, no name for the doctors and nurses. I imagined the medical tent at Wawona, but knew a hospital must be different. I thought of the smell of humans, of sweat and feces. Of blood. The tube I had seen them put into his arm.

No cloud night and no moon. I watched the stars until my eyes closed.

I say, "What's in the trunk?"

My father eyes me like a marmot eating a climber's shoe for salt. "Nothing," he says.

"Nothing?"

He says again, "Nothing. Never mind that."

I'd never seen inside the rear hatch of the car. "Why?" I say. "What's in the trunk?"

"Listen to me, Tenaya. It's not important," he says. "Don't worry about it, okay?"

In the morning, I found my mother. She was on the Little Columbia Boulder. She had a cut on her knee that was open two inches. It looked like a river oyster, dark on the outside and mushy in the middle.

"Mom?"

She didn't answer me. She was sitting on top, eight feet up, rocking, her legs pulled in, her knee bleeding a seep. She had a wet paper bag in her hand, and she was humming again, but this time her humming was loud. It was the closest she'd come to talking in fourteen years, this sound of almost singing.

She put the bag to her face and took a long breath. Her eyes flickered, then slitted, reminding me of a raccoon's eyes when the animal has forgotten that it is nocturnal.

"Mom?" I said.

She hummed. She sucked on the bag.

I stood below her. Her right eye zagged, then her eyes crossed.

I climbed up the rail. When I touched her shoulder, she didn't flinch or pull back. She didn't lean in. I tried to take the bag from her, but she was holding it in her fist. The bag was wet, and when I grabbed it, it tore all the way around, the bottom half sticking to my palm. My mother held the top now, open to nothing.

She didn't notice. She took a deep breath in and out, her fist still clutching the torn rim.

I pulled the glued bottom of the bag off my palm, felt the gumming as my mother continued to breathe through her fist, nothing but the Valley.

Carlos was waiting by my parents' car when I went back for it. I'd taken my mother to her camp, and returned for the car. Carlos said, "Hi, Tenaya."

I stared at the slither down his face, the curve at the middle. I listened for the snake's rattle.

He said, "Drive with me?" He pointed to his Park Service patrol car.

"No."

"Don't worry," he said. "We'll be invisible in there. People hide from cops. They really do."

"But why would I ride with you?"

"Because," he said, "this is important. I have to show you something. It's not good, but you'll understand."

Carlos wasn't arresting me.

He said, "You should know about this. Really, you should." He leaned across and opened the passenger-side door. I got in. Carlos handed me a Park Service shirt and hat. "Put these on."

We drove the Valley Loop Road. With the traffic, the loop took half an hour, but we didn't talk. I watched all the familiar locations pass. Then we drove up through the tunnel, past Inspiration.

Carlos stopped the car on the side of the road at Wawona. He said, "Twin Burgers. Thompson. The new deal. There's no Delaware North anymore. Do you know what I'm talking about?"

"No," I said.

He took off the hat he was wearing. Smoothed the curve in the bill. He said, "You and I are looking for the same things here. There's a development plan in play and it's all connected. Every single one of the companies and deals, they're all connected. And the Park Service is going to make big money off this."

"Money for what though?"

"Money to keep this park number one. Money to fund more of everything. Other parks. More money coming back in again."

I said, "But for what? I don't understand."

Carlos said, "The more money they put into the park, the more money they'll make. The more money they make, the more money they can spend. So this will be the richest park. It'll have the best of everything. And corporate sponsorships will ensure protection forever. Plus, Yosemite will fund more than Yosemite."

I said, "So the park is being sold?"

"Basically. Highest bidder situation. You probably don't follow sports, but we're talking sports-like, big-time corporate sponsorship. Location and naming paramount. Branding. Merchandise sales. You get it?"

"So what does that mean specifically?"

"It means that this park is going away," he said. "Or at least the park we know. This is all going to change more than you already see. Everything's going to change. And I'm supposed to be a ranger, protecting what we have."

I said, "Shouldn't you arrest me then?"

"Well, that's where it gets interesting. Are your fires the real enemy?" Carlos reached into the middle console and pulled out a can of Copenhagen. He popped the lid and pinched a dip, packing it in with his fingertips.

The fake mint smell filled the cab. I said, "So you don't care if I burn Miwok longhouses?"

Carlos spit into an old coffee cup. He said, "I don't care if you burn everything anyone builds here. You understand?"

I looked out at the road where we'd parked. Carlos had stopped before the yellow caution lines, the burned houses down in front of us.

He said, "Do you know what those two were doing?"

"Which two?"

"Lucy and her father?" he said. "Do you understand everything that was going on?"

"No," I said.

"I didn't think you did, but I did. I found them out. I discovered their deal, and it was like the old stories, like Vowchester. Do you know that one?"

"Yes," I said. "The betrayal."

"Right." Carlos pointed down the road. "Burning the forms, the fake longhouses up here. That's a good start. And that's why I brought you here."

I didn't say anything.

"But Lucy's father . . . both of them actually. Their deal with Thompson and Motel 4? The Park Service? That was them. They started that deal. Well, he started it, and she jumped in. And now no one can unstart what they started. Can't be undone. The Park Service is moving, and it's much more than saying that the Miwoks had 'original rights,' or anything like that. It's much more than that. They're designing a new Disneyland."

"But you're the same tribe," I said. "Same ancestors. You'd win."

Carlos readjusted his dip. He said, "You know better than that. This place owns us. Not the other way around." He lifted the cup and spit again. "I'm going to stop the deal. Fuck everything up."

I looked at where two ponderosa pines grew close together off the side of the road, how the smaller pine twisted around the larger trunk trying to find sunlight.

"You can be bitter," Carlos said, "and I was for a long time. But in the end, we have to make choices. It doesn't matter how we feel. We have to do what's right for the Valley." He put the car into gear and spun a U-turn. Then he drove back down the Chinquapin road.

When we got to my parents' car, Carlos pulled over onto the shoulder. I took the Park Service hat and shirt off. Set them on the dash. Then I opened the door and got out. I walked around the front of the car, across the road.

Carlos rolled down his window. "Hey," he said. "You have to know this."

"Yeah?"

He said, "I started the fire."

"What fire?"

He said, "The one at North Wawona."

"You what?" I said. I was holding the car's door handle.

Carlos popped his car into gear and rolled onto the road. He said, "I loved them, but I had to stop it."

PART III
Delilah

CHAPTER 11

We are living off the entrance road, pulling fish from the river twice a day like the Depression families who lived in the Valley year-round in 1932. The little money we make from selling grass mats and arrowheads is spent on butter, hot dogs, potatoes, and cheese. I am in the store, and your mother is alone in the car when a man taps on the glass. Your mother rolls down the window.

This man says, "You and your husband will have a child."

"What?" your mother says. She is forty years old. "I can't have children."

The man closes his eyes. He says, "Yes, you will. And he will be set apart for the Valley. Pure. His hair uncut. His name will mean, To Dream."

The man hands an envelope to your mother, then he walks away.

When I return from the store, your mother says, "I can't eat the hot dogs." She points to the envelope. "It's a map."

"A map to where?"

She says, "To Lower Merced Lake."

There is no time and there is all time. Water dries like light disappearing in the trees.

I was four years old when my sister was born. I saw her come out, blood and mucous, blue turning to pink with one scream. That is my first memory. Her hair like black goose down, wet as from water, but not water. I touched her as she turned her face back and forth against my mother's chest like she was trying to rub her nose off.

My mother whispered, "Shh, shh, shh, shh," and tapped her fingers on the little back.

My sister toddled early, and walked at eight months.

"That was you too," my father said. "We could not keep you down." But I knew that I'd walked at a year, exactly. My mother had told me that once when I was little, one of the last things she ever said to me, and I did not forget it.

She said, "You crawled everywhere, and your shoulders were so strong. Then two steps right on your birthday. Then ten the same day. You walked on that day exactly, your birthday, like it was a rule."

I used to watch my sister wander around camp, busy with her jobs, scraping sticks into a pile, organizing the screwdrivers on the backseat of the car, tipping over water cups.

She was with me for two years, everywhere I went. Slept in the same tent, the same sleeping bag. Bathed in the same creek. She toddled the flat trails with me, her face turned up, lips set, hands out to her sides, her goose wings.

And I remember nothing of myself before her. My father said that I was not nervous until that evening.

* * *

Kenny returned from Truckee. He walked into the Ahwahnee cave boulders. "It was beautiful," he said.

I watched him pull his gear out of his backpack. Lay his sleeping bag out to dry. Pile six books on top of each other. He'd found a headlamp somewhere and he placed that on top of the stack of books. "Got rained on hard," he said. "Epic rain. Biblical."

I said, "Were you here during the flood?"

"No," he said. "I didn't see that."

"It was like the Valley trying to reclaim its ground. My father said that the Valley would reclaim itself someday."

"I imagine," Kenny said. "And I've seen that road sign thirteen feet up. So I know that flood was huge." Kenny had his hands on his hips and he was staring off. He said, "I'd like to see that."

I took his down coat and hung it over a branch. It smelled like a bear, the wet fur stink of the soiled down. I took a shirt from his pile and wrung it out for him. Kenny did the same with another. We hung them on tree branches outside the cave.

Kenny said, "Want to go find food?"

I hadn't eaten much in the last week. I said, "Okay."

We walked the hotel road, past the Church Bowl, into the mosquito hatch, the black clouds that hang there, May until August.

Kenny was dirtier than ever, covered in old sweat, and the mosquitoes landed all over him. He slapped a few and said, "I hitchhiked some. I didn't just walk."

I looked at him. It was hard to imagine a driver picking him up. Kenny looked worse than homeless. Wild dreadlocks and bloodspots where the mosquitoes had found bare skin. His bloodshot eyes.

I slapped a mosquito on my left arm. I said, "A couple nights ago, I heard that you were a major college wrestling recruit, that in high school you won five national titles."

Kenny said, "How'd you hear that?"

"Greazy told me. Said he'd wrestled you at the campfire once and you threw him all over the place."

"Greazy said what?"

"Yeah, and he told me about you being ranked number one in the nation for three straight years."

"Oh," Kenny said.

"He told me he thought that he could take you 'cause you're short."

Kenny said, "I did wrestle pretty small. One twenty-six at the end." His left ear was cauliflowered, spiraled to a close. I hadn't noticed it before. He slapped a mosquito behind that ear.

I said, "Greazy told me that you wrestled in college too."

"For a while," he said.

"Then you just stopped?"

"Yep," he said, and he waved his hands around, trying to keep the mosquitoes from landing. "College wrestling wasn't fun."

"But I heard you were the best."

Kenny nodded. "In high school, I was. I wasn't the best in college." He picked dead mosquitoes off his palm with a black fingernail. Then scraped a body off his elbow.

I said, "So why'd you quit?"

"The coaches," he said. "They weren't good people."

"No?"

Kenny blew dead mosquitoes off his fingertips. "No, and I didn't want to be around that negativity anymore."

I waited for him to explain more, but he didn't. We walked and waved our arms, trying to keep the bugs from landing on us. At the end of the hotel road, we turned toward the falls, and within fifty feet, the mosquitoes were gone.

I said, "I hate that patch there. The swarm."

"Yeah, it's weird how they sit right there and stay. The second you walk past it, they're gone."

Both of us picked bug remains off our necks and arms.

Kenny said, "Did you ever have a girlfriend, Tenaya?"

"Yes."

"Was it serious?"

I said, "I had a wife."

Kenny stopped and looked at me. "Wait, what? A wife? How old are you?"

"Twenty."

"Twenty? Did you get married at fifteen?"

"No," I said, and kept walking, "I got married at twenty."

I realized that I hadn't thought about Lucy that day. I'd woken up, washed my face in the stream, boiled oatmeal, stolen coffee from the Ahwahnee, read part of a book, and never thought of Lucy.

Kenny said, "What happened?"

I didn't know how to explain. The story was too complicated. I said, "She died."

"What?" Kenny said. "She died?"

"Yes," I said. "She died last fall, right after we got married."

Kenny was staring at me. He had a dead mosquito under his left eye. "Wow," he said. "I'm sorry, man. I'm really sorry."

We kept walking west on the Loop Road. Kenny said, "Tell me the story, Tenaya. Tell me about her."

The sun was up now and it was hot. I looked back at the Church Bowl cliffs behind us, their struts of vertical black and gray, water lines in the granite. I began telling the story. From the beginning. From when I first went up into the Tuolumne country at fifteen, to returning to Tuolumne to work the summer before. I didn't tell about the superintendent, or Carlos, not everything, but I told most of it. I told all about Lucy until the burn.

Kenny listened as we walked the north side road toward the Village, 140, then the Lodge.

Later, after we ate, Kenny said, "Something I want you to see: my favorite bear."

"Your favorite bear?" I said. "What's that?"

"A bear," Kenny said. "My favorite."

"So he's a real bear? Where is he?"

"Not far off 140. He's always scrambling down from this ledge to pull stuff out of tourist cars. It's pretty funny to watch, actually. You want to come?"

"No," I said. "I might go back to the caves for a while."

Kenny said, "I understand that. Wanting to be alone. I'm sorry, man."

"Yeah, but I'll try to find you later."

"Later sounds good."

I walked back toward Church Bowl and noticed the cirrus clouds disappearing without weather, the scrub jays dipping to steal food messes at the Village. At the Ahwahnee, ground squirrels ran the road lot like they were being chased by dogs. I was watching the movement, walking back up the drive, and a young woman ran toward me in shorts and a bright pink sports bra. She was almost as tall as me, thin and strong, and she ran hard. Passed me. I turned to watch her until she disappeared at the turn.

Carlos was leaning against his patrol car at one of the first Ahwahnee parking spaces. He said, "I was hoping to see you here."

"Fuck you," I said.

Carlos said, "I know how you feel. But there's nothing to be done about that now."

"Nothing?" I said.

"Not really," he said. "You could hurt me again. We could go on like that."

A ground squirrel loped out onto the asphalt, took something from underneath the car, turned and ran. I walked past Carlos, toward the middle of the lot.

"Hey," he said, "have you thought about what's going on? Have you thought about everything I told you? The new contracts?"

"No," I said.

"Everything's linked, Tenaya. It matters. This could change the Valley forever."

I stopped and turned around. My father was in a Merced hospital room, no name or information on his chart. No insurance.

Carlos said, "They're coming into this Valley. And they'll do whatever they want unless we stop them." Carlos licked his finger and rubbed something off his front windshield. Then he used his thumbnail to scratch at a dead bug in the corner. He said, "Think about it. And think about what we're going to do." He reached in his pocket and pulled out a card. "This is my number."

I took the card.

Carlos opened his driver's door and got in. He backed out of the parking space and drove away. I saw him arc the vehicle across the yellow lines to make room for the runner girl who was running a sprint back toward me.

She smiled as she passed. I turned and watched her slow to a walk, her hands on her hips. Then she disappeared into the entryway of the hotel.

Kenny said, "I might be gone a while."

"Where are you going?"

"I don't know. Going to take a big walk. Bigger than before."

I said, "But to where?"

Kenny said, "I don't know. Maybe to the coast. Through Tuolumne. Maybe to the summit of Mount Whitney."

"You might walk to the summit of Mount Whitney?"

"Yeah, can you imagine that? How pretty it'd be?" Kenny closed his eyes and tilted his head back and forth like he was smelling something cooking. He said, "Twenty miles a day on the John Muir Trail. It wouldn't take that long. Back in three weeks, and really fun."

"Are you going to do that?"

"Yeah," he said. "I think so. Want to come with me?"

The next morning, I was alone in the Ahwahnee Boulders, climbing traverses and variations. I'd been climbing for an hour when the runner girl walked up. She was wearing black spandex leggings now and a bright red tank top. She looked as athletic as the day before.

She said, "I've been watching you climb the last few minutes. Sitting on that boulder over there." She pointed to the flat rock by the bear boxes. "My name's McKenzie."

I jumped off the low side of the boulder. "I'm Tenaya."

We shook hands. We were under the oaks, and McKenzie squinted against a line of light that came through the branches. She said, "Do you give climbing lessons?"

"No," I said.

She twisted her lips to the right, making a crinkled W. "But would you make an exception?" she said. "I want to learn to climb."

I thought about her running the day before, the way her body moved when she sprinted.

She said, "I'd pay you, of course. Say, $200 a day?"

I said, "I don't really need $200."

She shook her head. "Two hundred dollars is nothing for private lessons. You could make a lot more if you wanted to."

I looked at my hands. Picked at the callous of an old flapper on my index finger.

She said, "Or we could just have fun. We could just climb together as if we were friends."

She didn't smile. She moved her lips around and made little noises by sucking in her breath.

"Okay," I said. "But it's going to be hot this afternoon. Let's start in the morning, tomorrow, early, when the rock is more sticky."

"How early?" she said.

"Six-thirty."

"Okay," she said. "Six-thirty sounds good. Meet you right here." She pointed to the ground.

I pointed too. I said, "What's your shoe size? I can borrow a pair for you."

"Don't worry about that," she said. "I bought a new pair before I came to Yosemite. I figured I'd pay somebody to teach me once I got here."

I borrowed a rope, two harnesses, belay devices, and trad gear from the dirtbag group bins at the caves, and set them next to my sleeping bag before I went to sleep. When I walked down to meet McKenzie the next morning, she was there waiting for me.

She said, "I thought you might not show up."

"Am I late?" I said.

"No, but I still thought you might not show up."

We hiked down to the Swan Slabs where I knew I could set up an easy top-rope for her.

I picked up a harness. "We'll start here, with the gear."

She stepped close.

I explained harnesses, rope strength, and belay friction. She distracted me with her coconut sun lotion. When I put on her harness, she sucked in her stomach and I felt the hardness of her abdominals as I doubled back the belt loop.

Her face was serious. She said, "What creates a factor two fall?"

"That's a good question," I said. I had to think for a moment to come up with multiple scenarios. Then she asked about leads and gear placement. As I explained, she listened and looked right at me. I never had to repeat myself.

I scrambled up a 5.1 gulley to set a top-rope on the nearby 5.7. When the anchor was set, I rappelled down. "Ready to climb?" I said.

"Yes," she said.

"Okay then," I said, "keep straight arms and look at your feet, roll your feet onto holds, keeping your hips in, weight directly over the balls of your feet."

McKenzie mimicked everything I did, pretending to climb as she acted out my directions. Then I tied her in with a figure eight, locked the biner on my belay device, and pretzeled the tail. She stepped onto the slab and began to climb, and she climbed well, with careful footwork and complete trust in the system.

When she was thirty feet up, I said, "Have you ever climbed before?"

"No," she said as she moved toward the anchors.

"Are you sure?" I said.

"Yes, I'm sure. Maybe you're just a good teacher."

I said, "I've barely taught you anything yet."

After she finished the climb, I lowered her back down. I said, "To be honest, there's nothing very difficult on this slab. This place is for beginners. Do you want to hike over to the Books?"

She said, "I don't know what that is, but okay."

I loosened her harness and slipped it down over her hips. She stepped out of the loops. I coalesced all of our gear and stuffed it into my pack.

In the afternoon, we climbed Munginella and Selaginella, and McKenzie was as comfortable 400 feet off the ground as she was at 10 feet. I'd never seen someone so fearless.

We were standing on a ledge at the end of a pitch. McKenzie had just climbed up to me. I said, "Doesn't this scare you?"

"Not really," she said. "I like this sort of stuff."

"You climb like you run, straight and fast," I said. "Is everything this easy for you?"

"No," she said, "and when I struggle, I really struggle. And I hate it."

"Do you ever really struggle though? That's hard to imagine."

"I do," she said. "Sometimes. But mostly I get what I want." She wiped her nose on her shoulder and smiled. She looked up at the next pitch. "Should we keep climbing?"

The next belay anchor was a hanging belay, our feet together on a protruding block, gravity pressing our bodies together.

I re-racked gear, and to get the cams off her harness, I had to reach behind her back. I could hear her breathing next to my ear, smell her coconut skin and her sweat, feel her breasts pressing against my shoulder as I reached around.

She said, "This is really fun."

"Yeah," I said, "I like it."

I adjusted my short-rope in front of me and my forearm brushed her stomach, knocking her off balance. She grabbed a fistful of my shirt and pulled herself in. I thought of Lucy, and Lucy's finger.

I said, "Sorry about that."

"It's okay," she said. "It's a small ledge."

I readied McKenzie's belay device, our foreheads together. I said, "Ready?"

"Ready."

I began leading the next pitch. McKenzie paid out rope as I moved, plugging gear, protecting the climb.

After, when we were hiking down the descent trail, I said, "What do you do for your job?"

"Public relations."

"Oh," I said.

She said. "Do you know what that is?"

"Not really. I've only read about it in the newspaper."

"You're cute," she said, and bumped into me like a coyote shouldering a pup. She'd insisted on carrying the rope, and she had her thumbs hooked in the backpack straps.

Her nose was sunburned pink on the end. She had a black smear of rope-grime across her forehead. She said, "PR is easy and complicated. I talk to people for a living. When they like what I have to say, it's an easy job. When they don't like what I have to say, it's a difficult job."

"That makes sense."

"Right," she said. "But that also makes it sound like any other job, a good job. But my job's not a good job."

"Why not?"

"Because . . . " she adjusted the backpack straps, "because it's . . . I don't know. It's a long story."

I said, "You don't have to explain."

"I know I don't," she said. "But I sort of want to. Or I would want to if it wasn't such a really long, complicated story. That's all. It'd take a while to explain."

We got to a wide space in the trail, and we stopped. I pulled out my Nalgene bottle. "Want some water?"

"Thank you," McKenzie said, and drank. She still had that grime mark across her forehead, and I liked that. She said, "Can I buy you a real drink? I'm staying at the Ahwahnee, and they have a lobby bar."

"Umm . . . " I said.

"Oh come on," she said. "You don't have to play hard to get. Or is it because I'm so dirty?" She held up her hands. They were dark gray from rope-grime.

"No," I said. "I like that. Dirty's good."

"Right, and would you like an even dirtier girl?" McKenzie clicked her tongue.

But before I could say anything, she said, "You could use a beer. Let's go."

I put my water bottle back in my pack and we hiked down to the Falls path.

The Ahwahnee was as ridiculous on the inside as it was on the outside. It looked like a billionaire's log cabin. My father had prohibited me from going inside when I was younger, saying the hotel was haunted by throat-cut Yosemiti.

In the lobby, McKenzie said, "I've got to talk to the bartender for a second, then I'll wash up and meet you back here. Bathrooms are down there." She pointed.

"Okay," I said, "I'll go wash my hands."

I walked down the stone-floored hallway to the restrooms. They were air-conditioned. Clean. The counters were waxed granite.

I peed, then washed my hands, turning the sink black with my hand grit. I ladled water back on the sink's sides to wash off some of the gray-black smears.

When I came out, McKenzie wasn't waiting in the hall, so I walked the other way, looking around. This section of the hotel had been rebuilt after the Arches rockslide a couple years back. I'd read about the construction of the new Great Room. The room was a recreation space, the only part of the hotel not built in the 1930s. The new Great Room included a stone-arched roof held up by two side-by-side ponderosa pine pillars, each twenty-four inches in diameter, standing four feet apart. The Great Room circled around these pillars like a meadow.

I walked down the stone steps and into the main portion of the room. All around me were tables, people on laptops and phones, clicking and talking. Two little girls played checkers. A boy drew in a coloring book. And above all of us, a black-and-white photography exhibit chronicled "The First Inhabitants: The Miwoks."

I walked underneath these pictures all the way around the room, reading captions of basket weaving and flint knapping, two chiefs' names and a woman grinding acorns. All the pictures were of Yosemiti, not Miwoks.

Standing under a picture of Captain John, a Yosemiti warrior, I read, "The Miwoks hunted game in the Valley for centuries." But Captain John wasn't carrying hunting gear. I stood under that picture for a long time and tried not to think about my father in the hospital, my father telling me stories, my father warning me.

"Here's part of that story for you," he says. "They buried the treasure in the lake."

I say, "The lake?"

"Yes," he says. "In a basket thatch. They lowered it down with ropes."

"You mean the river?" I say.

"No." He looks at me. "Why?"

"Because you said it was in the river when I was younger."

"No," he says. "I didn't say the river. You have to listen better than that."

"I did listen. You said the treasure was in the river. You said that they buried it in the bank on the side of the river."

"No, no," he says, "the treasure was always in the lake."

I went back to the Ahwahnee bar.

Cheeseburgers, French fries, and four pints of reddish beer were already on the table. Two pints next to each plate.

McKenzie pointed to the cheeseburger she'd ordered for me. "I hope that's okay. You were taking so long that I went ahead. And they cook things right away here."

"Yeah, sorry," I said. "I was looking around."

She said, "I thought you might've snuck out. Stood me up."

"No, no. Thank you for the food."

The smudge was gone from her forehead. She took a bite of her cheeseburger and looked at me. "Are you okay?"

"Yeah, I'm fine," I said. I took a sip of the nearest pint. Strong and cold and bitter.

McKenzie chewed with her mouth slightly open. Wiped her lips with her napkin.

I took a bigger drink and picked up my cheeseburger. I was hungry and the cheeseburger was fresh and hot, with crisp lettuce and tomatoes underneath the bun. The cheese dripped out onto my finger and I slurped it off.

I hadn't had good food or a cold beer in a long, long time.

"I hope you like it," McKenzie said, and took a big bite of her burger.

I took a bite and said, "This is so good."

We ate, both hands on our burgers, not talking. The food was greasy and the beer was cold, and I forgot about the Great Room and the native photographs on the wall. With each gulp of beer, my father drifted.

I said, "Thank you again. This is too good." I took a few French fries and dipped them in ketchup.

"You're welcome," McKenzie said. "It's the least I could do. Thanks for the climbing lesson today."

She pushed the last bite of her hamburger into her mouth. It barely fit and she chewed slowly. She smiled and her cheeks bulged.

I started my second pint of beer. The beer was rushing my brain.

McKenzie said, "Are you going to leave those fries?" She reached for them.

"Go for it," I said. "I like people who enjoy eating."

She took a few of my fries, and I dumped ketchup on the remaining pile. Mustard after.

McKenzie said, "Climbing was just so fun."

"Good," I said. "I'm glad you liked it."

We were finishing our food. Drinking our second beers in gulps now. McKenzie flicked two fingers and a waiter brought us each another beer.

I said, "Maybe I should get going."

"Really? Why?"

"I don't know," I said. "Maybe let you get back to your own stuff."

She said, "This is 'my stuff' right now. This is it." She pointed at the table.

I took another drink, finished my second beer.

She said, "Where are you staying right now?"

I said, "I'm camping near here."

I was a little buzzed. Drinking strong beer fast. I'd started my third.

She said, "Why don't you come up to my room and hang out." Her foot touched my ankle underneath the table. She said, "If you don't have anything else to do right now."

I picked up my last few French fries and ate them. "Okay," I said, "we could do that."

I was sitting on the end of the bed in her room. McKenzie pulled new bottles of beer out of the mini-fridge by the television. She handed me one and I took a sip.

She said, "I need to use the bathroom for a moment. Be right out." She closed the door and I heard the sink running.

I looked around her room. She had one suitcase and a small bag. Everything put away. The bed made. The room smelled like store cleaner and soap bins.

When she came out of the bathroom, her hair was down, wavy and thick brown, just below her shoulders, the ends at the top of her tank top. She sat next to me, her elbow touching mine. She said, "I've never taken a climbing lesson before."

"Yeah?" I said. "Well, you couldn't tell."

"Thanks," she said.

I said, "It's true. I've never seen a beginner climb better."

She tapped the top of her beer against mine. "Cheers, then."

"Cheers." I swigged my beer and wagged my index finger back and forth. "And I've never been in a room at the Ahwahnee."

"Really?" she said. "Cheers to firsts then."

"Yep." I was feeling good and buzzed now. On my fourth beer. We both drank.

She said, "So that means you've never ended up on an Ahwahnee bed with a woman before?"

I looked at her.

She smiled.

I said, "Not even close."

She leaned over and kissed my neck, her lips staying on the skin for a moment as if she was drinking there too.

I turned and kissed her. She tasted like toothpaste and beer.

We kissed for a minute on the end of the bed, still holding our drinks. Then she took my beer out of my hand and set both of our bottles down on the table. She stood and leaned over me. I was sitting, and we kissed harder now, McKenzie pressing down into me. I put my hands on her hips, feeling the skin just above her waistband with my thumbs. Her hipbones. I ran my hands along the tops of her legs, felt her long, thin muscles flexing against my hands.

She said, "You smell like pine needles and dirt." She laughed. "I like that."

I pulled her into me. We kissed harder. Her tongue. Her breath faster.

She pushed me down onto the bed. Kneeling above me.

I was hard underneath her, on the bed, and she pressed down. Pressed and moved.

I ran my hands up her tank top. She stopped kissing me and peeled off that shirt, showing a crisscrossed white bra.

I put my hands there, on her high breasts. And we were kissing again.

When I awoke, she was turned away from me. Late evening, light coming through the window. I looked at the straight line of her spine and the curve of her hip. The covers had slipped down to the bottom of her back. It was warm in the room and she didn't move in her sleep. I wanted to be inside her again, but I didn't want to wake her.

My head felt like tree pollen. Floating. I knew I should leave. I considered waking her and saying goodbye but I didn't know what she would say. What I would say.

I slid out of bed and put on my clothes. Tried not to make any noise.

She'd left $200 on the nightstand, and a paper note that said my name. I stared at the money. Then I looked at her sleeping. I didn't take the money.

I wrote on the bottom of her note: Thanks for lunch.

The door clicked as I closed it, so I jogged to the stairs and down the bottom hallway. I walked through the boulders behind the hotel, toward the caves. I saw no one near the trail. No one at the caves either, camp quiet. I'd stashed the borrowed climbing gear in the bear box at the parking lot and I went back to get it. I returned the gear to the group bins, then went to my cave.

I lay down on my sleeping bag and tried to read. But I stayed on the same page, staring off as it got dark.

CHAPTER 12

The seventh year. Plenty and famine. Seven a holy number. The cycle.

The rule of the seventh year: the acorns will not fall heavy and berries fruit a short season. Animals wander in search of food. Bears eat thin meat in the fall, not fattening before hibernation.

The people ration stores. Count the days to a new season. Mark the door pole.

At the end of the seventh year, there is a year of plenty. You must look for this. Berries on the ground in piles like ready jam, fermenting before they can be eaten. Acorns scattered at light green, the squirrels heavy-bellied. The fish in the river come fat in spring as if mayflies hatched through the winter.

Your people store in preparation for long snows, years when the white drifts crest the banks of the Merced in April, when creeks run off to drown.

Wovoka knows all of this. He whispers truths in his dreams, men bending their ears to his lips. And Nevada, 1889. Wovoka speaks in the mountains on New Year's Day, during a full eclipse of the sun. He says, "When the sun died, I went up to heaven and saw God."

I held my thumb up for an hour as I walked down the Merced toward El Portal. I was near the 120 Junction when an old car pulled over in front of me. The driver leaned across and popped the passenger-side door open. He said, "Get in, man. Get in." He had a blunt between his front teeth.

"Thanks," I said. I sat down and closed the door. The car filled with smoke.

"Where are we going?" he said.

"Merced. But any ride in that direction's great."

"Cool, cool. I'll see what I can do. This old baby's been dying all afternoon though." He patted the dash, then he puffed on his blunt. He said, "Something wrong with her alternator."

We didn't make it to the park boundary. We made it a mile, maybe. The dash lights turned on and the man jerked the car onto the gravel shoulder. He said, "Got to get her off the road quick 'cause that power steering holds her straight like a motherfucker."

We got out of the car and the man popped the hood. "Maybe we can get another jump," he said. "What did you need to do in Merced?"

I said, "See somebody in the hospital there."

"Oh, damn. That's not good. Sorry about this car, man. She really is a piece of shit." He puffed on his blunt and waved his arms at a passing car. It didn't slow down.

We waved at cars for half an hour until someone stopped to give us a jump. Then we drove another mile before the car died again. This time, it got dark without anyone pulling over to jump the vehicle. The man said, "Want some of this splif?" He'd started a new one, his second.

"No thanks," I said. I sat next to him on the embankment while he smoked.

"Yeah, sorry about my car, man. She really doesn't care about what a man needs, you know?"

"Right," I said. I stood up and stretched. "I think I'm going to walk."

"A hundred miles to Merced?" The man laughed.

"No," I said. "I'll walk back to the Valley."

The man held in a deep breath, then exhaled smoke. "That makes more sense," he said. "Hell of a lot more sense."

I was reading about the debate in the *Chronicle*. Protesters in the city, on Market Street in San Francisco, as a symbolic gesture. I wondered that there weren't any protesters demonstrating here in the Valley.

The insects scrabbled, and the cars shuffled like pinacate beetles through the lot, edging forward into parking spaces. Putting their back hatches up. Easing their scents.

I was standing at the T of the North Loop and Ahwahnee Drive, watching hundreds of cars pass by. The infestation growing toward July 4th.

I hadn't seen McKenzie for a week when I ran into her at the ranger booth in Camp 4. Late morning.

She hugged me. Said, "Hi, Tenaya."

I felt her body against me. Remembered the swell of her breasts, her nipples in my mouth. The smell of coconut lotion on her shoulder blades.

She said, "How are you?"

"Good," I said. I wanted to taste her. Put my hand on her throat. I crossed my arms.

She said, "Thanks for leaving a note. And you forgot to keep your money."

"We agreed to climb for fun," I said, "remember? But I'm sorry I had to leave so quickly."

"No, really, it's fine." She touched my forearm. "Although I was pretty sure I'd have to buy another climbing lesson just to see you again."

"Yeah, well, you wouldn't need to."

She said, "I'm kidding. You didn't even take the money the first time." She laughed.

I said, "What are you doing in Camp 4?"

She pointed to the booth behind me. "I was just leaving a note for you on the message board." She read it aloud to me. "A girl named

201

McKenzie seeks a climbing instructor. He must be roughly six-feet-two inches tall with wide shoulders, dirty hands, long black hair, a scar next to his eye, smelling like pine needles, and preferably named Tenaya. If interested, call this number." She handed the note to me.

I said, "You want another climbing lesson?"

"Absolutely," she said.

"Okay. But we'll just climb again for fun. No lesson this time either."

"Unless you need the money," she said, and pointed at my T-shirt. It was dirty and had one sleeve torn off.

"No," I said, "I think I'm good."

We bouldered in Swan Slabs for three hours. I showed her my favorite moderate problems on the Bridwell Boulder and the short cracks, and she climbed well. I didn't teach her many techniques because I could tell she liked to figure things out for herself.

In the late afternoon, she said, "Want to get some food?"

I shook my head.

She said, "Let me just buy us a little food. Please. It's a lot cheaper than a $200 climbing lesson."

"No," I said. "I'm fine. You don't have to buy food."

She was tying the laces of her climbing shoes together. "Look," she said. "I'm going to buy extra food, and I'd like you to hang out with me while that extra food is just lying around." She squinted and wrinkled her nose. Waited.

"Okay," I said, and we walked back to the parking lot.

McKenzie said, "I know climbers don't eat at the Ahwahnee Hotel. So where do they get their food?"

I didn't want to explain scrounging at Curry, how dirtbags ate unfinished food at the Lodge, or out of dumpsters, so I said, "All different places. All around. Housekeeping?"

"Housekeeping?" she said.

"There's a cheap store there."

We drove in her rental car over to Housekeeping, across from the LeConte Memorial. Inside the store, I showed her the 99-cent microwave burritos. Free hot sauce.

"I know I'm not paying for the climbing lesson," she said, "but I can at least pay for this fancy meal, right?"

"Yeah. That's fine," I said. I didn't have any money with me anyway, and I was hungry. I'd been planning on making an excuse not to eat, but I gave that up.

McKenzie bought four microwave burritos and a six-pack of Miller Genuine Draft cans. She said, "Look, it's *Genuine.*"

"Whoa," I said, and held up my hands.

We microwaved our burritos using coffee filters as plates, and took our lunch down to the Housekeeping beach. Tourists were gathered at the turn in the river there, taking pictures of a black bear. The bear was sitting on her backside in the sun, looking confused.

McKenzie set the food down and said, "I should get a picture of that bear. He's huge."

I took a bite of burrito and burned my tongue. I said, "She."

"She?"

"The bear," I said. "She's a female."

"Oh," McKenzie said. "How do you know?"

"Narrow head," I said, "and bigger ears."

"Oh. Well, she's pretty close to us."

"Yeah," I said. "If she came after someone, a social bear like that? What if she wanted our burritos? Have you ever seen a bear rip a car door off its hinges?"

"No," she said.

"Well, it's incredible. They're three times as strong for their weight as humans, so that bear right there is like a 900-pound person who's not obese. Just muscle strong."

My burrito had cooled, and I took a bite without burning my mouth. McKenzie cracked two cans of beer and handed one to me. The bear walked off and the crowd dissipated.

We ate our burritos and drank our beers. We were at that turn of the river by Housekeeping, where the old floods stacked downed trees on the north side. The water cut on that far side, and the bottom fish congregated under the fallen logs.

McKenzie said, "Do you like it here?"

"Yeah," I pointed at a swirl in the current. "See the bottom fish?"

McKenzie sighted down my arm. "Oh. I didn't see the fish at all."

I said, "I used to catch them right here in the fall."

"Wait," she said. "How long have you been here in the Valley?"

I took a swig of beer. I said, "A long time."

"And always camping?" she said.

"Yep. Always camping."

We watched that black-green pool for the flashes of the foot-long bottom fish, for the quick break from the school, then the drift to white and the return.

We drank our second and third beers, then went back to McKenzie's room at the hotel.

We were in bed afterward. I was thinking about the protestors I'd read about in the *Chronicle*. I said, "Do you know about Multi-Corp?"

McKenzie lay on her side next to me in bed and she pulled the covers up to her throat.

I said, "The big corporation. They want to develop here in the Valley. Tie everything together."

"Oh," she said. She rolled onto her back and straightened the sheet. "Which company is that again?"

"The parent company to Thompson Food. Have you ever heard of it? I don't know how much people talk about it away from the Valley."

McKenzie said, "Yeah, yeah. Thompson Food. The new concessionaire. I've heard of that."

I said, "They're here in the Valley."

She was lying on her back, staring at the ceiling. "You read about a deal?"

"Yes. I'm just trying to remember what I read."

She said, "I've heard that negotiations are going on."

"Negotiations and protests," I said.

"The protests in San Francisco?"

"Yes. And I think they're pretty big now. Three thousand students and young people sleeping on Market Street. People bringing them food to support them. And that crowd is growing."

"Hmm," she said. "Sounds intense . . . and complicated."

I said, "How so?"

"Well, these deals bring a lot of money into the Valley, fund a lot of conservation in a national park," she said.

"But they destroy so they can conserve. It doesn't make sense."

She said, "Maybe they destroy 1 percent to save ninety-nine. Then it would make sense."

"No," I said, "it's worse than that. You have to spend more time in this Valley. See the traffic jams. Watch animals get put down. See people throw candy wrappers in the river."

She said, "So you agree with the protesters?"

I said, "I'm pretty sure they're right."

"Really?" she said.

"Yes," I said. "Are you serious?"

She said, "But if Junior's won the contract instead, it'd be worse."

"Junior's?" I said. "What are you talking about?"

"If Junior's and its motel chain won that contract, to put motels here in the Valley, it'd be much worse. There'd be branding everywhere. Junior's signs. Renaming: The Junior's LeConte Memorial Museum. Junior's El Capitan. Junior's Half Dome . . . "

"Wait," I said, "I've never heard of Junior's."

"That's the competition."

"Multi-Corp's competition?"

"Yes."

"But what if nobody got the contract? What if everyone was told no?"

"Everyone?" She laughed. "That's never going to happen. Progress will progress. Development will happen in this Valley. That's inevitable."

CHAPTER 13

Wovoka waits in the Sierra Nevadas. People arrive from the east, representatives seeking the prophet. He was raised Jack Wilson, Bible-reading on a western Nevada ranch, but he is Wovoka now, the Paiute Messiah, and people will wait for weeks to hear him speak. He preaches the Ghost Dance, peace, and continental disappearance.

A Sioux messenger rocks back and forth on his feet. He looks away, his attention captured by a coyote on a rise. Two coyotes. Then the way the wind sounds coming through the branches of a nearby juniper. The raven on a branch, cleaning its talons. The messenger does not hear all of Wovoka's words. He hears only the Ghost Dance and the ghost shirts, and so he believes in invincibility, invincibility that is as good as truth.

The Sioux messenger returns to South Dakota. Then his bands ride to violence, a frozen creek in December, bodies like twisted sticks.

This is your end if you do not listen to every word.

Greazy saw me in Camp 4 at the Pratt Boulder. He said, "Bro, you should lay low for a while. I had two troopers and an FBI dude visit me at the Bees. They asked a lot of questions about you."

"What did they ask?"

He said, "Where you were. What you liked to do. Who you hung out with. Lots of shit like that."

"Did they say anything else?"

Greazy rolled a cigarette, twisted each end. "Yeah," he said, "I think they asked about the fires. Not sure what they meant though, and I said that. Plus I told them that you'd left the Valley."

"You did?"

"Hell, yeah," he said. "I got your back." He pulled out a plastic Bic lighter. Flicked and lit his cigarette. Inhaled and exhaled. "Fuck the feds," he said. "I told them you'd been gone a while, might never come back."

"Did they believe you?"

"Not at first," he said. "But then I said you'd left to chase a girl, and that this sort of shit can take a while. Those dudes seemed to get that. At least they wrote it down and didn't ask me any questions after that."

"Thanks, Greazy."

"No problem, man. But stay low, okay?"

The rear Ahwahnee caves were less caves and more hollows in the jumble of the granite. The drop-off of the Arches. I moved to the most remote natural lean-to, where I'd never heard of anyone staying. There was no mattress moldering, no pine-needle bed arranged, no stove parts crushed into the dirt. I didn't find any bottle caps or cigarette butts. There was a black drip on the west wall, a fungus growing at the seam of the rock.

Greazy gave me a mattress that was wintered. Folded over my head, it smelled like gin gone wrong. I hiked it up.

Early the next morning, I pulled a hat on low over my eyes and I snuck into the hotel bathroom to fill water. Scrubbed nickel faucets, hot water, free soap. Upstairs, six coffee urns silver as mercury. Cream in a mini-pitcher. I took a big gulp of cream straight out of the pitcher, before I poured myself a free coffee.

I walked past the Great Room on my way out, my ancestors hung as tapestries while 3 million visitors drove through the Valley. Men and women held bags of ice and Popsicles in store lines, ramen noodles and microbrews. People set up in campers, kids watching Disney movies on laptops in their tents.

I still had the nightmares but I didn't wake up. I slept through. In the morning, I snagged coffee again from the hotel urns, got the rhythm of my day. I walked outside and scrambled up on a little boulder at Ahwahnee West, on the backside, careful not to spill my coffee. Faced away from the parking lot, the Arches above me.

"What are you up to?"

I turned around. McKenzie was at the base of the rock.

I said, "Drinking coffee."

She held a cup too. "Mind if I join you?"

"Sure," I said.

She scrambled up the slab and sat down next to me.

We both sipped and looked out at the rocks and the forest, the green trees and the red-brown of the loam.

"So you're still around here?" She raised her eyebrows.

"Yep," I said. "Living close." I looked uphill toward my lean-to cave.

She touched her paper cup to mine like she was toasting me. "And I'm still here as well," she said.

We sipped at our coffees.

McKenzie stuck her lips out and made different shapes with them, a duck bill, a fish mouth. I watched her in my peripheral vision.

She said, "Were you mad at me?"

"No," I said, "not really."

"So a little bit?"

I shook my head. Swallowed a gulp. "Not at you. Maybe at the people bringing in Twin Burgers and Motel 4."

"Oh," she said.

"But I don't really know what I believe," I said. "Some days I think that there's all this bad stuff, all these forces working to wreck this place, Yosemite and the Valley, and then other days I just think there are people. Only people. And all of these people do people things. That's all."

"Huh," she said. "That makes sense. And how do you feel about it right now?"

"I don't know. Maybe that there are people that sometimes do bad things? Or often do bad things? And other people who do bad things less often? I mean, I don't know. I don't know what I'm doing half the time," I said. "I don't know where I want to go or what I want to do. Do you?"

McKenzie looked into her coffee cup. She said, "I don't even know where to start. If you make mistakes, they're probably no worse than anyone else's."

"No," I said. "I've made horrible mistakes."

"Well, I doubt that," she said. "Do you do worse things than all of these people coming through this Valley? Do you really? Do you do worse things than me?"

"Yes," I said. "I'd guess so."

"No. You don't. You don't really know all of the mistakes that other people have made. The things we still do."

"But you don't know mine."

"It doesn't matter," she said. "We make mistakes, but we move on. We try again next time. I don't spend a lot of time with regret. Where will that get me?"

I said, "But what if a mistake can't be fixed? What if it's final?"

McKenzie didn't answer right away. She sipped her coffee and thought about it. "Well," she said, "maybe some mistakes can't be fixed. But there's nothing you can do about that afterward, right?"

I said, "There are things that can't be undone."

"Maybe," she said. "Maybe and maybe not."

I said, "You know, I was born here."

She was finishing her coffee and she swallowed quickly. "You were born in the national park?"

"In the Valley," I said. "In a car."

"What? Really?"

"Yes."

Our feet were dangling off the edge of the boulder. The boulders around us looked like the boulders near my parents' camp.

I said, "I don't know if all of his stories were true."

McKenzie said, "Whose stories?"

"My father's," I said. "I don't know if they were true, but I think about them all the time."

McKenzie bit a fingernail, clamped it between her teeth, and tore it off. I saw that all of her fingernails were jagged. She said, "What makes you question his stories?"

"A couple things. First, they're long stories and old stories," I said, "so they sound like myths."

"Myths," she said. She still had her fingers to her mouth, trying to find another nail to bite. She clicked her teeth together and spit out a corner. "Maybe myths are as real as anything else."

"But one of his most important stories changed," I said, "changed from a river to a lake, became something that wasn't as far in the past, that had to do with my father's own life. His time. But I don't know."

I found the tools as I was flattening the cave floor to make a space for my mattress. The line of black mold had grown along the cave wall, and I could smell it in my sleep, so I decided to move to the opposite wall. I turned the mattress so my head was farthest from the black.

The dirt was wet and thick underneath, claylike, and I scraped at it with a two-foot-long stick. That's when I found the cache. Hollowed out and a foot deep, like a box inserted into the clay, the cache was half-full of stone implements: a pestle and mortar, three hand-sized blades, nineteen red obsidian arrowheads.

The obsidian was not from this Valley. I'd never found any red obsidian, and I wondered at the thin, maroon-colored glass flaked in half-circles on both front edges. All the arrowheads were similar in size.

My father told me that the Yosemiti had hidden up here in the rocks and caves along the wall when the 36th Wisconsin entered the Valley. They'd waited until the food stores ran out. Then the band had marched down to meet the soldiers. Arrows and spears against rifles. The soldiers had tied the mothers' hands together. Little children crying. The Valley full of the smell of burning acorns.

We hadn't set up another time to meet, but McKenzie was in the Ahwahnees the next day after finishing a run. She walked a cool down through the boulder weave, and found me as I was climbing a traverse. I dropped off when I saw her.

She pointed above us to the wall, 1,500 feet tall. "Has that ever been climbed?"

"Yes," I said. I pointed to the line on the right side of the Arches. "Royal Robbins climbed up through there in 1956. Thousands of others have since."

"And you've always climbed too?"

"Me?" I said. "Yes."

"Is it part of living here?" she said. "Part of living in the Valley?"

"I guess that's probably true."

She tucked my hair behind my ear. "I like you, Tenaya. Will you take me climbing again?"

"Climbing?" I said.

"Just climbing." She held up her hands. "I'm so innocent."

"Right," I said.

"Come on . . . "

"Okay," I said. "Meet here tomorrow at 6:30."

She gave me a hug and walked back toward the hotel. I smelled the coconut of her sunscreen all day.

I'd reburied the tools and dragged my mattress over the top of the cache. I didn't want anyone else to find them. In the afternoon, I lifted my mattress and dug the ground open again to make sure everything was still there.

I was holding one of the obsidian pieces when I heard someone say, "Hey."

I set it down and spun around. It was Kenny.

He said, "A little jumpy, huh?"

I said, "I didn't know it was you."

Kenny stepped over and hugged me. "I just got back," he said.

"From Whitney?"

"Yep."

Kenny looked thin and dirty. I said, "Did you take enough food?"

"Oh yeah. The day before I left, I went through three campgrounds: the Curry tent cabins, Lower Pines, and Upper Pines. And every abandoned bear box item went into my 70-liter pack. Then I stuffed backup socks, a hat, and my sleeping bag on top, and good to go. I ate the whole time."

"Nice," I said. "I'm glad."

"And the snow," he said, "that was intense. Got an ice ax from a PCT free box and I needed it for probably fifty miles."

"But you made it to the summit?"

"Oh yeah," he said. "You can do anything if you want to. You know that."

Kenny was still wearing that orange down jacket, even though it was hot in the Valley. The jacket was filthy now, one huge red stain smeared down the front on the right side.

He saw me looking at it. He said, "My coat might need a dip in the river. That's sweet and sour sauce from packets. Found thirty of them in Curry. I'd suck on them as I walked. Instant energy."

We talked for a while. He told me about weathering a windstorm in a debris shelter, about crossing a corniced ridge, about sun so bright that he pulled his hat over his eyes and walked blind up a snowfield. I showed him the cache of stone tools I'd found.

Kenny examined the mortar and pestle. "These are amazing," he said.

"Yeah, I think so."

"But why are they here?" He held up one of the thinnest obsidian arrowheads.

I said, "Maybe someone buried them when the army came in 150 years ago."

We looked at each tool carefully. I kept coming back to this one symmetrical arrowhead. I held it up. It was so thin at the blades that the sun almost glowed through it.

Kenny said, "It's so beautiful."

I handed it to him and he examined it. He said, "Are you going up on the wall with me?"

"The wall?" I said.

"Yeah," he said. "Go up on El Cap and just chill for a long, long time?"

We hit up the Curry pizza deck, scoring half-glasses of beer and soda, half-eaten pieces of pizza. Kenny found a whole slice of sausage and mushroom, and I found a slice of pepperoni with only one bite out of the crust. We toasted his return.

The place was so crowded in the evening that people didn't seem to notice us trolling through the tables. Kenny piled scraps in his coat pocket. I collected food in my left hand, piled up until the food got to the point of tipping.

Kenny said, "Let's play Chicken Wing Friday. First person to find one wins."

I said, "We'll never find one, you know."

"I know," Kenny said. "First person to find a wing—at any time tonight—gets free coffee deliveries to the cave for a week. Other person has to hit the urns, add cream, sugar, whatever he wants. Bring it to his sleeping bag."

"Okay," I said.

We played for an hour. I drank a dozen half-finished beers, and Kenny did the same. We ate at least a medium pizza's worth of food. But we didn't find any chicken wings.

Kenny said, "To be continued," and snagged a quarter-beer from an abandoned table. He swigged it down. "Maybe I'll go to the Curry showers and shower in my clothes. Got to clean this coat somehow."

I wasn't tired. Beer-buzzed and awake.

The night expanded with clouds and I hiked down the Valley past the hotel, the Village, the Falls Trail, Swan Slabs.

No moon or stars, and the white granite patterns of the Camp 4 boulders were elephantine, unpronounced as snowdrifts. I could feel the strength in my legs, but I was moving slowly. Awake. I didn't know what I was looking for. Past Arizona Avenue.

I stumbled around a low oak, then across the Falls Trail. I hit the signpost there, in the dark, knocking it loose. The post was rotten at the bottom and I felt it teeter as I hit it. I turned and walked up the other trail past King Cobra. Wound through the blocks toward the Energy Boulder. The night closed with clouds over the moon.

I caught the smell of wet dog again, another bear. I smelled him even though I couldn't see him, and I stopped. The bear was close, too close, his smell everywhere around me. I rubbed my eyes but couldn't see anything. I stood and waited. Listened to a sound like gravel turning underneath truck tires. Wetter. Of mud and gravel, wet suck and grinding, the breaking of small sticks.

I didn't move. I closed my eyes and opened them to find the differences in the shades of gray. I couldn't see the bear, but I could see my mother. She was hunched in the front seat of my parents' car, cutting rectangles of paper with shears. Letters in her lap, scissors in her left hand. Chewing on her hair. She had a twisted lock running across her cheek, dividing her face, wedged in the corner of her mouth. Chewing again. Cutting letters. She sucked her hair and worked her scissors *swick-swick* through the papers held in her right hand. I watched her cut, turn the letter, cut again. Left-handed and the scissors backward, flipped upside down.

I waited because I knew bears, and I knew this bear.

My fingertips tingled and a numbness went up my arm. I blinked again to see him. He was ten feet from me, in front of my eyes, appearing like the black growth of a 600-pound mushroom.

A young male, a grizzly, and grizzlies did not exist in Yosemite, not anymore. This bear could not be here, but he was here, next to the Lower Falls Trail, out of Camp 4, in the Valley, and the grizzly was sitting on his backside, eating and chewing.

Both my arms were numb to my shoulders now and I crouched, dropping down onto my heels, letting my arms fall useless to my sides, fingertips dragging the ground, no feeling in my hands.

I didn't know what this bear was eating, but then he shifted and I saw the outline, the fir, the silver and light-brown of the coyote, the grizzly tearing at it with his claws. Holding up a paw and looking at that paw as if he were learning shapes.

And he ate.

I saw the bear and the coyote, and then the glow, odd on the side fur of the coyote. I blinked and that fur was painted orange, spray-painted, and I knew this coyote then too.

I could hear my mother and her scissors again. Behind me now. I turned around but saw nothing.

I sat on the dirt, in the middle of the trail, ten feet from the grizzly, and my arms were numb all the way to my neck, behind my ears, like worms crawling on the back of my scalp. I could hear my father explaining the bear's life. "The betrayer becomes the greatest bear, spends his next life in this form," he says. And so this bear is

Vowchester, Chief Bautista, who helped Savage capture Tenaya in the Valley. Allowed the murder of Tenaya's son. And now, the first grizzly in the Valley since 1925.

I'd promised to meet McKenzie, to climb the Grack on the south side. I never slept late and this morning was no different.

The nightmares woke me early. Day just begun.

We were going to meet at 6:30 in the morning to get a head start, to avoid waiting in line behind other climbing groups at the first pitch.

I'd slept two hours. My eyes itched like springtime and I felt like throwing up. I pounded a quart of water. Brushed my teeth with my fingers and a dab of Greazy's toothpaste.

McKenzie had breakfast burritos and coffee waiting for me at the parking lot at 6:30. She pointed to the food. "Because you won't let me pay you for a climbing lesson."

I swigged water. "Thank you."

"No big deal," she said. "It's just a friend buying a friend some breakfast."

"Sounds good," I said.

We ate our burritos. Sausage and potatoes, beans and cheese, and the sounds of the grizzly were still with me. I could hear the crunch of wet bones.

We hiked over to the Grack and were the first people on. But the climb was too easy. McKenzie floated the climb.

My hands were not numb now but strong again, and the cool insides of the rock smoothed me, took the bear and the coyote away. Took away my mother and her scissors.

McKenzie smelled the same as ever, better than good, as we huddled at the hanging belays, her hair and skin and sweat and sun lotion. Nothing I didn't like.

We were climbing in the daylight and then we were not climbing. She was coconut sun lotion underneath me, and the dark hair smelling of clean and her breathing like the sweep of trees back and forth in summer. The wind rushed upriver in catching gusts and the tops of the trees swayed green and smooth and rhythmic, back and forth, up and back, and then the wind stopped and everything waited in the bright sunlight glaring white, in that moment, that single wait, thinking about the wind that came before, and I wondered if a tree ever makes any choice at all.

I woke up to McKenzie making a noise. I didn't know what it was.

I rolled over.

She was looking right at me.

I said, "Are you okay?"

She didn't say anything.

I said, "What is it?"

"I didn't tell you everything the other day when we had that long talk."

"What's everything?" I said. "What do you mean?"

She said, "I work for Thompson."

"I don't understand," I said. "What do you mean?"

"Thompson," she said. "I'm here in Yosemite doing PR work for Thompson, Multi-Corp, the parent company. That's why I'm here in the Valley. That's what I meant when I said I work in PR."

"Oh," I said.

"I know," she said, "it's bad. I didn't tell you before, when we talked, because I didn't know what you'd think about it. Or I knew, and I didn't want it to be like that."

"Yeah," I said. "You should've told me."

She said, "But I really like you. And I didn't want you to know what I do."

I said, "Do you think it's wrong then? Your job? Is that why you don't talk about it?"

"I don't know," she said. She lay back on her pillow. "I don't know anything. I feel like you do sometimes, like sometimes you know. Do you?"

"Do I what?"

"Do you think my job is wrong?" she said.

I nodded. "Probably," I said. "Probably, yes."

She said, "I've thought about that, about it being wrong. But I don't know what's right and wrong here. Not anymore. Or not really ever. I mean, my mom used to tell me not to smoke when I was little. She said it all the time. Told me that smoking could kill me, that it cost a lot of money, that it was a stupid habit. Then, one night I came out of my bedroom—I was maybe nine or ten—and my mom was smoking a cigarette right there in the kitchen. We had a little slide-up window and she was leaning forward and blowing the smoke out the window, and I stood there and watched her for a minute before I said anything."

"And what did she say when you caught her?"

"She said it was the first time she'd ever tried smoking, that she didn't think she'd ever do it again. And I believed her until the next time I caught her a few weeks later."

I said, "They're really putting a motel here?"

"Yes," she said. "They're really putting a Motel 4 in the Valley. It's going to happen. I should have told you."

"Yeah," I said, "you should have told me."

Kenny asked me to go up on the portaledge with him again. "We'll be flying above it all, man. Hang out for days and days."

I said, "I don't think so."

"But I really want you to come," he said. "Remember what I told you about last time?"

"Yeah," I said. "You said you suffered. Called it 'long-term suffering.' Then you said that lightning came in one day and scared you to death."

"Right," he said. "Exactly. We need that long-term suffering in our lives. That struggle. That abject fear. We need the carabiners humming with electricity against the anchor bolts, bright blue and shaking. Remember that I had to crouch in a fetal position for more than four hours?"

"Yeah," I said, "you told me."

Kenny said, "You don't understand, man. It was great."

"I don't know, Kenny."

He said, "I like to think about the orbit of the sun. You know? How it's moving too, a lot faster than we can imagine. It's not just us moving out here. Everything's expanding. Have you ever thought about the universe?"

August snow at 4,000 feet on the Valley floor. The only time ever.

My father wakes me up. "Tenaya, come out here."

It's early morning. Not yet light.

He says, "Come on. Get out of the tent."

I see his bright teeth in the dark. I pull my blanket around my shoulders. Get to my feet. Step out.

White dropping all around me. Huge, wet flakes piling, the ground already covered.

My father says. "It's an inversion. Cold air stuck down in the Valley."

"An inversion?"

My father laughs. He holds out his hands and opens his mouth to the sky. He says, "Tourists are going to drive out of here so fast today. This is the Valley's way of saying 'Leave. Just get out.' Sometimes the Valley gets its way."

Kenny was staying in my cave until he went up on the wall. He had a sleeping bag that matched his down coat in both puffiness and grime. He'd found the bag on the El Cap slabs, near the area of poop drops, where climbers threw their loaded Ziplocs from the Nose route. Kenny didn't own a sleeping pad. He was lying in the dirt next to my mattress in the wet. I knew he didn't even need the bag around him. Kenny was like a crow.

At Curry Village, two days earlier, he'd said, "Hold on a minute," and hopped down off the rock. He lay down on the dirt, on his side, scraped a pile of pine needles and leaves over himself, and went to sleep. When he woke up five hours later, I was sitting next to him reading the book he'd brought out for the day.

He sat up and blinked. He said, "It's horrible what they're doing to this place, huh?"

"What?" I was finishing reading a poem.

"Don't say 'what' to me." Kenny scratched at the corner of his eyes where the sleepy was stuck. He said, "I know you know what I'm talking about. You're the guardian of this thing, right?"

I said, "How am I the guardian?"

"You are," Kenny said, "and you know it." He laughed at me.

I said, "You want to walk down to Housekeeping and swim?"

"Okay," he said. "I could afford to be cleaner than this."

We were walking along the bike path near the Curry bridge a few minutes later when Kenny saw the paper bag. It was sitting on a log under an oak, by the path. He stepped over and looked inside. "Oranges," he said. "It's a whole bag full of oranges."

"That's weird."

He pulled out an orange, smelled it and rotated it in his hands. "Yeah, these are good," he said. He pulled out another orange and inspected that one too. "This is a bag full of perfect oranges."

I reached down and took one. Smelled its thick peel.

Kenny said, "Do you think these belong to someone?"

"Not anymore," I said. I looked around. "Plus, the bears won't leave them for long." I pointed up into the trees behind the last cabin. "I know of at least three full-grown bears who live up there, and 'Yellow Tag 12' is notorious."

Kenny giggled. He spun an orange in his hands. "Not even one bruise here. I mean, a whole bag. Can you believe it?" He bit into the peel and started tearing it off.

He ate that first orange so fast that some of the peel was still sticking to the sections. Mouth full, Kenny mumbled, "These oranges are all ours. Yours and mine. Sometimes I don't even know what to say." Juice ran down through his scraggly beard.

I started eating my orange too. Then we were both laughing.

As Kenny peeled his second orange, he said, "Some people are just luckier than everyone else."

CHAPTER 14

During the flood, the bears come out of hibernation, woken like ghosts. They drop down off the scree slopes underneath El Cap to see the river for themselves, to know if the flood is real. They will tell their grandchildren that they saw the water up close, that the current was as powerful as people said.

You know this.

The bears come down and paw at the brown water, water weaving between trees like lines in a birch mat.

There are no fish to catch, no suckers in the shallow pools, no rainbow trout, no caddis fly hatches, no stoneflies.

There are no berries.

The bears search through tents and cars. Check the locks on the boxes. Snatch grocery bags and unguarded Coleman coolers.

Plastic and aluminum are scrunched in their scats, duct tape and pieces of Ziploc bags.

How do I explain the beginning of this? Of the end? My arms tingled. Fingernails covered in wax. Maybe Kenny was the wildlife that tourists were not supposed to feed.

Kenny said, "Mishmash." He put a slice of chicken on top of his waffle, forked them both, and took a bite. He said, "Always different."

I was eating a breakfast of hamburger halves.

Kenny said, "The dumpsters in the rest of this country are crazy." He had that Camp 4 squirrel look in his eye like when he'd just found an unopened can of beer behind a boulder. "They've got good food in them, full sometimes, not even dented cans. Pizza and bread. I've gone behind Safeways and found enough food to eat for a month. No joke. But here—" he waved a French fry in the air—"here we have to worry about the bears. So there are no open dumpsters. No big scores. Then, places like this cafeteria become our dumpsters. The Curry deck. And box-diving."

I said, "No trouble with those though."

Kenny pointed his fork at me. "Are you going up on the wall with me next week or what?"

"I don't think so," I said. "But I'll see."

"You'll see? Why? You're not doing anything down here. There's no reason for you to stay the next few weeks."

I hadn't told Kenny about McKenzie. I hadn't talked about her at all, how I couldn't stay away from her. How I didn't want to. She was still working in the Valley, and I was meeting her in an hour.

Kenny said, "Name one thing that's keeping you here on the ground."

I took a big bite of hamburger bun.

After dinner and drinks.

Many drinks.

McKenzie didn't know that I was still awake. I was watching her through the bathroom door. She stood naked in front of the mirror, examining herself.

I lay there, wanting to watch her without being noticed.

Over dinner she'd told me about her childhood, her parents' divorce, her father taking her car camping once a year in Sequoia. How her father would be drunk the whole time.

She told me the story of her shoplifting postcards from the general store, thirty glossy images, and handing those out to her friends back in Long Beach, telling them that her father was the photographer, that he was a traveling photographer, and that was why he was never in town. None of her friends had ever met her father, so they believed her story. Or at least they pretended to.

She told me about sneaking away from the tent one summer night and meeting up with some college boys, about going into one of their tents with them, feeling a blond-haired college boy through his pants. She told me about the sound of his zipper. She was fourteen.

I watched McKenzie in the mirror. I closed my eyes and opened them again. I was trying to put all of the pieces together.

McKenzie found a hair on her face and plucked it with tweezers. She stood back and examined herself. Touched the light brown mole on her hip, tapped it with her index finger as she shifted her weight from left to right. The muscles in her butt and hips flexed one way, then the other. She looked thin in her underwear. Even taller. She'd told me that she'd been a middle-distance runner in college.

I'd said, "I don't know what that is, but it must make a person strong."

McKenzie ran her thumb underneath her left eye, wiping something away, but I couldn't see it.

I was watching her, and I wanted her to never put on clothes again. She said aloud, "Pale and blobby," to the mirror. But she was neither pale nor blobby. I pictured her at fourteen. Shorter? Skinnier? With a college boy running his hands all over her body. I blinked.

McKenzie didn't look drunk. Five strong drinks after dinner in the bar though, and I knew she was drunk. Seven and Diet Sevens, and she didn't weigh much.

My alcohol was fluttering.

McKenzie leaned toward the mirror and pushed her breasts together to make cleavage. She frowned. Then she grabbed a loose T-shirt, slipped it on, and stepped toward the bed. I could see her nipples through the cotton as she turned.

I closed my eyes.

She got in under the covers, scooted back against me, the backs of her legs touching the fronts of my thighs. Her back against my chest, and only that thin T-shirt between us.

I pulled her hips closer to me and reached up under her shirt with one hand.

She said, "Are you still awake?"

I didn't say anything. I slid my other hand down and pulled her underwear out of the way.

I went out into the meadow and the yellow jackets were there. At a lightning-split pine, the downed trunk across a runoff, natural bridge over the sand cleft. Two crows, disease-twisted, one foot of each to the sky as if they were pointing sunlight, sundial lines with claw points.

The yellow jackets went in and out of the beak of the second crow like drippings of metal. They tumbled from the opening until their wings caught and they lifted.

I leaned down and saw the pulsing of the crow's insect-pregnant belly. The arthropods pushing out like vomit building.

I let a yellow jacket land on my forearm and watched as it turned to an upside-down V, ready to bite and sting. Then I crushed it with a slap, starting a pheromone war, the other yellow jackets coming up in an armored cloud, chasing me for a few hundred feet. I ran as they stung my shoulder and neck, biting at the smell I'd caused.

I went to visit my mother, but she wasn't in camp.

I walked up the creek until I heard her, the humming, and the song slow as the Merced run in August. I waited at the white pine near the big pool in the creek. I didn't want to scare her.

Her head listed and she stumbled. Still humming the song but rickety on her legs, her knees turned out. She played pat-a-cake on the surface of the water to right herself, slapping like a little girl, then she waded over to the bank and dried her hands on the grass. She blew her nose into her hand and wiped that hand on the mud. Washed it with water.

Then she picked up the metal tube of glue and squeezed a pea-sized drop on two fingers. She put half of the glue under her right nostril and the other half under her left. Then she waded out into the water again, turned her palms up to the sky.

I put my feet in the water and waited for her to turn around.

I said, "Do you want to go visit him?"

But she didn't hear me.

I went back to her camp and started the fire. Heated a small amount of water in the pot on the grate and dropped in a handful of oatmeal and brown sugar.

Six years old at the river, and the water cold, prickly as ponderosa cones. The snow is in the water, but I know we can swim it. Both of us swim well.

We're in an eddy, and my father isn't far behind us. My mother said she was coming soon. I wade out to the current line, deep as my waist, stare at the submerged boulders out in front of me.

I'm not holding her hand like I used to because she can swim now. I've seen her swim the eddies. But when I turn around and look, she isn't there.

I see her hair on the surface, down at the far end of the eddy, and then her hair sucking under. I try to swim to her, but the eddy is in a reversal and the river pushes me upriver. I put my head down and swim out into the current, but when I come up I'm past the spot where she went under.

Then the water, dark in the shade like blackberry pulp, a thin coating of mud on the eddy stones. I swim back to the bank and stand up. I lose my balance and slide off a rock. Land on my elbow. I stand up and scramble the shallows back to the bottom of the eddy. Look in every direction. Hear the water. Where the water is lapping the stones it sounds like an animal drinking.

I search the eddy again. Yell her name. My father comes. My father falls in the water, gets up, turns around, swims out and back.

He scrambles up on shore and runs down the bank. At an undercut by a riffle, I hear his choke. He pulls an arm. Smaller than mine.

Her foot is turned underneath where her ankle is broken, her foot jagging right like she's trying to run away, to go somewhere the rest of her doesn't want to follow.

CHAPTER 15

Wovoka has not given a time. He only knows that they are still coming. He points to a tree with his right hand and a boulder with his left. He says, "They come riding horses of sickness. They swell past us to the ocean where they rot like dead fish on the shore. Then they return to this place where we Ghost Dance."

But there is no Ghost Dance, and no one is listening. No one has listened for two decades. The Sioux rot on the pine ridge, while the Paiutes stay at Pyramid Lake. Commodity food.

Then it is 1932, and Wovoka walks with God.

In a tent on the Hetch Hetchy shoreline, I am born, and I will come here to bring you to this Valley. That is the end and also the beginning.

Summer. The early night heat pushed into the cave like the warm tongue of an unbrushed animal. Kenny and I lay on top of our sleeping bags.

He said, "I'm going up in two days. There's supposed to be a lot of wind, you know?"

"Wind?" I said.

"Yeah," he said. I could hear his dry lips crack into a smile even though I couldn't see them in the dark.

I said, "I don't know if that's a good idea, man."

"Think about it. On a portaledge, just getting hammered. Feeling the power and the glory."

I looked at the black line of the cave mouth where it severed the night's stars like a cut of aluminum. "No," I said, "I still don't think so."

Kenny rustled around on the top of his bag. He said, "I wish you'd change your mind and go with me, 'cause I'm going up no matter what."

I spent the day in Stoneman Meadow. Sat and watched the grass breathe. Locusts popped on the stalks, and I caught one in my hand and wondered about honey. I ate the bug and it wasn't bad, the rear legs crunching after the thorax. I caught another and ate that too.

There was no air near the floor of the Valley, the meadow grass yellow and papered. Ninety-five degrees and the wind that breathed was like the exhale of a burning log. I counted RVs that passed on the loop. Stopped at seventy-seven.

My mother would leave too, one way or another. I pictured her with a sticky bag in her hand, heard the rasp of locust legs, and wondered at the sound of my mother's voice.

I knocked on McKenzie's door late that evening. She opened it. Her smile was crooked in the space and I knew she'd been drinking again.

"It's wrong," she said. She opened the door all the way.

Her white blouse was untucked from her skirt and unbuttoned most of the way down. I could see her lacy bra. She stepped back and waved me in. Closed the door behind me.

She said, "Why are we doing this? It's fucking wrong. And me? I don't even know what I want. Or why I'm still here."

"Neither do I," I said.

"But that's not good enough," she said. "You're here. You know?"

I said, "I don't know what that means."

"This," she said, "this place. Right? This place. And you're actually here. All of you. And you'll stay here where you were born."

"Well, I don't know now. You know what I did today?"

"No," she said.

"I sat out in a meadow. I ate locusts."

"Locusts?" she said. She stepped over to the table and swigged from an open fifth of Maker's Mark.

I still stood in the doorway. "Yes," I said, "locusts. I ate them like in the old stories, when the people ate honeydew and locusts, the honeydew rolled from the trees and the locust swarms caught as they traveled."

"See," she said, "I don't know those old stories. I don't know any stories. Nothing." She took a long drink. Then she handed me the bottle.

I took a big drink and handed it back. The whiskey was warm and went down like a handful of sparks.

"And this?" she said. She wagged her finger back and worth. Took another drink.

I said, "Thompson?"

"No, no," she said, "you and me. We can't do this."

I leaned back against the wall.

She handed me the whiskey again, and I took two big gulps, one after the other. My eyes watered. I watched her walk toward the TV, her fingers playing with the buttons of her blouse. Then she stood still.

The alcohol thickened like moss in my empty stomach. I took another big swig and set the bottle down on the nightstand.

McKenzie said, "Do you know what you want?"

"Here?" I said.

"Everywhere," she said. "In general."

"No, I don't know anything about that. Do you?"

"Nope," she said. "I don't either. Do you ever just feel . . . " She was still standing by the television. " . . . I don't know." She turned and walked over to me. Kissed me hard. Then she said, "I try not to, but I want to."

I kissed her back.

She was swaying. She said, "Am I beautiful?"

"Yes. Of course, you're so beautiful."

"And you want me?" She unzipped my pants.

"Yes," I said, "I do."

She pushed me back against the wall. Started kissing me again, her thumbs hooked in the waistline of my pants.

I turned her around and pushed her up against the wall, her face against the plaster. I smelled her hair and kissed the back of her neck.

I stripped her shirt, peeling it to her wrists. Undid her bra. Pressed her nakedness to the white. I kissed the back of her neck again, listened to her breathing and the sounds of her nails scritching against the wall.

In the morning, McKenzie brought a large glass of orange juice back to the room. I watched as she did a workout. Push-ups, jumping jacks, sit-ups, then a drink of orange juice. She repeated the sets.

Afterward, she took a shower.

She was drying her hair with a towel around her waist. Nothing on top. She brushed her teeth. Applied mascara and lipstick. Her nipples were hard as she leaned toward the mirror, and I watched.

She stood back and put her hands on her hips.

I came up behind her and put my arms around her. Felt the goosebumps. Then her breasts.

She said, "We have to make a plan. We can't just do this forever."

I said, "Okay." I had my hands on her breasts.

"No," she said. "I mean it. We have to decide what we're doing."

My father came from Hetch Hetchy when he was a teenager. He had his own time alone in the woods, then hitchhiked down the 120, came into the Valley and never left again, reclaiming his home from the Wisconsin 36th.

I could see the face he made as he gutted browns at our eddy. "This is dinner, Tenaya. Dinner and breakfast, huh?"

I waited all morning while McKenzie was at a meeting. She was taking notes that she promised to share with me. That was our first plan.

I talked to myself. I said, "Should I?" and waited. I expected my father to answer me somehow. But he was a hundred miles away.

I watched a ground squirrel drag a Kraft macaroni and cheese box around the side of a boulder. The box was unopened and heavy, and the squirrel worked the corner.

McKenzie and I met for lunch.

She was outside the deli, waiting. She said, "I ordered us grilled sandwiches so we could take them somewhere else. We should talk in private."

"Right," I said.

We took our food out on the back path. The summer dust puffed underneath our feet. McKenzie said, "How old are you, Tenaya?"

It's funny that she'd never asked me that before.

I said, "I'm twenty."

"Shit," she said, and sucked in her breath. "Really?"

"Yeah," I said.

"Oh my god. I thought you were at least five years older than that."

I said, "How old are you?"

She took a bite of her sandwich. "Twenty-nine. I'll be thirty in a month."

I said, "I'll be twenty-one soon."

"Right," she said, and took another bite. "I guess that doesn't matter. Or at least that's not the most important thing right now. But this thing with the meeting . . ."

"Yes."

She said, "Two weeks from now."

I said, "I know. I've been thinking about it." I looked at her. There was no one else around. We were in the trees. I said, "I've been thinking that we have to end it somehow. Get them out of the Valley forever."

"But how?"

I said, "The meeting and the hotel. They're both symbols. So we have to do something big."

She said, "I'm not sure what you're talking about."

"I'm not sure either," I said, "but we have to stop it."

Kenny and I hiked along the base of El Cap to the start of Tangerine Trip. I carried his second haul bag full of water. Ten gallons in reused milk jugs. Eighty pounds of water on my back.

He had all of the climbing and camping gear plus food on his back. We were both sweating hard.

Kenny said, "I really appreciate your help. You've got to go up with me, huh?"

"No, Kenny. I really can't."

Kenny dropped his pack at the base of the route. He shook out his arms.

I dropped my haul pack and leaned it against the wall.

Kenny picked up a pebble and threw it out in front of us. "The water would make it ten days with both of us. Maybe longer . . . "

"Yeah, I know."

He said, "And there's that convention in town."

I raised my eyebrows.

"Yeah," he said, "developers gunning for the big contracts. You don't want to be in the Valley with those people. Motel 4 and Thompson. Have you been paying attention to that?"

I started chewing my thumbnail.

Kenny said, "And there's this new superintendent of the park."

"Yeah," I said. I picked up a rock and threw it downhill. It bounced off a boulder below us.

"I mean . . . " Kenny snapped his fingers like he'd just remembered something. But he didn't finish his thought. He started pulling out gear, laying it on top of his rope tarp. He piled his gear in a big jumble, and I began sorting through the pile to give my hands something to do. I racked cams, hexes, and chocks in order. Then beaks, hooks, and angles. I said, "You sure you have everything you need?"

Kenny kept snapping his fingers. He was thinking about something. He kept squeezing his eyes closed.

I pulled a sling. Opened and closed the trigger of a cam.

Kenny looked at me. "What?"

"What?" I said. "No, what were you thinking? I can tell you were thinking about something."

He fingered the gear I'd put in order. He said, "I'm not really sure."

I straightened the cams on the sling, turned their carabiners so the draws lay flat. Untwisted each one.

Kenny looked out toward the Cathedrals.

I looked across the Valley too then, to the three Cathedral spires to the south. To the west, I saw the round hump of Turtleback Dome.

Kenny picked up a small flake of rock between his index finger and thumb. He said, "So what's the deal, Tenaya?"

I cocked my head sideways to see between two fallen pieces of talus downhill, trying to sight the river. But the boulders blocked my view.

Kenny waited.

I said, "I don't know if I can explain it all."

"But you can try." Kenny was still holding that little flake of rock. He flicked it with his opposite index finger and it made a tick sound. Spun in his hand. He said, "Start at the beginning. I know it's not just burning the forms of one longhouse. There's a lot more to that story."

"The beginning?" I said. My sister. My mother on the boulder and the sticky bags in her hands. My father in a hospital room in Merced.

"Wherever you want," Kenny said. "I'll listen to any of your stories. Pearl for pearl. Give me something."

I put my hands down on the granite sand next to me, fine-grained, white with flecks of yellow. I said, "Do you ever feel like everything's coming together for a purpose, like there's some reason you're supposed to do something, or be somewhere?"

Kenny smiled. "Everything is for a purpose."

"Well, if that's true, and sometimes it seems like it's true, then why can't I figure everything out? Sometimes I think about . . . I don't know, putting everything together, everything, and I can't make it work out in my head."

Kenny said, "That's the best place to be, don't you think?"

"Confused?"

"Yes, confused," he said. "Humbled. That's the best place to be. Every time I get like that, I think it's good."

"Maybe," I said, "but I've felt like that for a long time, maybe my whole life. So the question is, is it the best place to stay? Should I always be confused?"

Kenny began reracking his gear in his own order, different from mine, the blue cams in a row of five and the yellow cams next. Then the oranges.

He said, "I was in a cave once on the east side of the Baja peninsula, in there for two weeks just looking out at the ocean. I'd go fish off the cliff in the morning, then come back. And there wasn't anything around me. Or anyone. Just me. And I thought, I could go back to the rear wall of that cave, burn my clothes, and lie down. Die right there. And no one would ever find me, not for hundreds of years. They might carbon-date me or something, thinking I was peter brown hoffmeister

a caveman from the prehistoric, but then they'd be all confused when the numbers came back and I was only dead a little while."

Kenny set the red cams next to the oranges. Blacks next. I was watching his hands. I said, "But what about now?"

"Right," he said, "this is where we are. Right now. Here. We're not anywhere else, and I had to learn that."

I still had my hands on the sand, palms in the heat. I was moving my fingers apart like miniature snow angels. Hand-size sand stars.

Kenny dropped the green cams next to the black, everything adding up to him. He reached across me to the water pack. Grabbed a gallon.

I smelled the sharp reek of his armpits.

He said, "Come up with me. We'll have time to talk up there." His teeth were covered in plaque, dark yellow at each joint. Brownish.

I piled all the light-blue cams while he gulped water. I said, "I'm not coming up, Kenny. This is a bad idea. There's weather coming in, heavy weather. Plus, I have to be in the Valley. That's one thing I think I know."

"So I'm going to suffer up there alone?" Kenny said, and smiled.

It was getting dark. I took the gallon jug and had a drink, a smaller drink than I wanted, to conserve Kenny's water supply. Then I handed it back to him.

He held out half of a peanut butter Clif bar that he'd found earlier. I ate it slowly, then took another small drink.

I stepped off a few paces to pee and Kenny went the other way. We met back at the packs and pulled out our sleeping bags. Put them down on the sand.

Kenny said, "Do you need anything else for dinner?"

I was hungry but I knew how little Kenny had for his twenty days up on the wall.

"No," I said. "I'm good."

"Yeah," Kenny said. "Me too."

I stayed awake. The stars filled like a glittering sandbar above us, suspended, the grains reflecting the lost heat of the day, mirroring the sand around our bags.

Sometimes I tried to count the stars in a small section of sky, a box between any four constellations. But not on a night like this. In the high dark, the stars procreated like white flies, their new young filling spaces, exponential sparkling.

I told stories to Kenny.

I was arrested two nights later.

"Can I give you a haircut?" McKenzie's eyes glittered from the whiskey.

My nervous system surged. I took a sip from her plastic cup. We'd been drinking all evening.

"Please?" she said.

It was one of the things I'd never done. My mother's voice about the man at the car. A boy set apart for the Valley. Uncut.

I said, "Okay." Sipped from that cup.

She said, "You'll look so good with short hair."

I put a towel over my shoulders like a blanket. My fingers tingled as the scissors touched my scalp. I felt the weakness. My arms numb up to my elbows.

I rolled over in bed and saw the outline of McKenzie's shoulder. I couldn't go back to sleep.

I sat on the edge of the bed looking at my hands in the faint light of the moon through the window shades. I opened and closed my fingers. After a while, I slid back underneath the covers. Then I fell asleep again.

McKenzie must have snuck out to go for a run or to get orange juice for one of her quick morning workouts. I was alone when the door rattled. McKenzie lurched through the door.

"Tenaya," she said, "the FBI's coming. Quick! Quick!"

I sat up. "What?"

But they were already at the door. Pounding.

McKenzie said, "Just a minute." She put one finger to her lips and pointed to the bathroom with the other.

I ducked in. Locked the door behind me. But there was no way out. No window in there.

They came in the room, and one of them said, "Where is he? Is he under the bed? Is he in the bathroom?"

They knocked on the door. Said, "Open this up, now."

I unlocked it. I couldn't think of anything else to do.

There were two men in suits and one park ranger behind them. One of the men in a suit said, "Do you have a weapon, sir?"

I was in a pair of boxers. I held up my hands. "No," I said.

I didn't try to run or fight, and the numbness was above my wrists when they zip-tied my hands behind my back. I couldn't feel the plastic.

An agent put a badge in my face. "You have the right to remain silent."

I sat in my cell. Waiting. Gray walls, a toilet, a sink, a bed, and a small window. There was no one in the cell with me. No one in the cell next to mine.

I asked the clerk as he came down the hall.

"Arson," he said. "That's a federal."

"A federal?" I said.

"Yep. A federal charge." He turned and continued walking down the hall.

I was alone in the cell all day. I lay back on the bed and looked behind me at the wall. At that angle, I could see, scratched in faint lettering, the names of people who had spent a night there before me. The etchings covered the wall, more than a hundred, and I wondered how many of those names represented the living. I saw the names of five dead climbers I knew, climbers who had died in the park in the past ten years. One who had died in the Karakoram. One in the Himalayas. These stories got back to us in Camp 4, told over the fire while we drank boxed wine or King Cobra Malt Liquor.

I looked for something to scratch my name, but I couldn't find anything. I didn't have a pen, a spoon, a rock.

I did push-ups on the floor. Then three-quarter lever pull-ups on the bars, my forearms in line with the steel. Sit-ups on the floor, my bare back collecting the grit. My fingertips still numb, but less so. Then I slept.

Day two. The FBI agents came in again.

The taller one sat next to me on a wooden chair. The shorter one walked around the cell. I'd seen this on a TV show at the Curry Village buffet once when it was snowing outside and I felt like being underneath a roof. I wondered which agent would hit me with a phone book, but there were no phone books in the room.

"How long have you been living in the Valley?" the shorter one said.

"A long time."

"About how long, would you say?"

I said, "A long time," again.

"In the Valley?" he said. He clicked his pen.

I looked over my shoulder. The tall one still didn't have a phone book. He was leaning against the wall now.

The shorter one repeated the question. He said, "In the Valley?"

"Yes," I said.

"And you know that it is illegal to live in the Valley long-term?"

I said, "Huh?"

He clicked his pen twice. He said, "And you know that it is illegal to live in the Valley long-term?"

I said, "I don't know."

"You don't know?" he said. Then he laughed. "I think you know." He clicked his pen again. Then he talked about camping laws in the National Park System. The seven-day, fourteen-day, and thirty-day rules. Permits. Tent tags. He said, "So how many days have you been camping?"

I said, "I don't know."

"You don't know, or you won't say?"

"I don't know," I said.

The taller one was writing on a yellow pad behind me. His pen scratched quickly on the paper. He never sat down. He leaned against the wall or paced back and forth while he wrote notes.

The shorter agent said, "Do you know about the Miwok longhouses?"

"The what?" I said.

"The Miwok longhouses."

I said, "What are those?"

"A new housing and tourism program. Do you know anything about them?"

I said, "I don't know. Tell me more about them."

"No," he said, "I'm asking if *you* know anything about them."

I said, "I've heard that there's a new housing and tourism program."

"You have?" he said.

"Yes," I said. "You just told me."

"Oh," he said, and his lips came up on his teeth like he wanted to bite me. His teeth were very clean and white. He said, "So it's going to be like that, huh?" He clicked his pen. "So did you know anything before I told you?"

I said, "Before when?"

He didn't click his pen. He tapped the table in front of me. "I'm sorry. Maybe you don't understand what I'm saying to you. Would you like an interpreter, sir?"

He sat back in his chair. His tie looked too tight, as if his neck was constricted. I turned to look at the tall one who stood next to me now, writing. He raised his eyebrows. His tie fit him better. He looked more comfortable.

I said, "Why would I need an interpreter?"

"Well," the shorter agent said, "let's try it from this angle. Where's your social security card? Where's your driver's license? What's your full name? What country were you born in?" He paused. He leaned forward again. "I said, what country were you born in?"

"The United States?"

"Really," he said. "Do you have a birth certificate? And can you show it to me?"

The taller one was writing faster now on the page just behind my head.

The shorter agent said, "I said, can you show me your birth certificate?"

I still didn't say anything.

He stood up. Walked to the wall and touched it where the names were scratched in. He said, "You have no rights here. You're not a citizen here. We might keep you. We might deport you." He shrugged. "We might let you go. We might let you walk out of here. But it's up to us. Do you understand?"

There were no books in the cell but I got the newspaper each day with breakfast. The clerk handed me the *San Francisco Chronicle* and said, "Sorry there's no TV, man."

I said, "It's okay." I was looking at the free oatmeal and bacon and juice and coffee and newspaper.

I read an article about a well-known actress who had left her husband to sleep with a man who was twenty years younger than her. I read an article about a bond measure that would allow four businessmen to build casinos on private properties near San Francisco. I read an article about the link between the Tamil Tigers and

242

the Chechen rebels, how they both trained and employed suicide bombers, sometimes children and women.

That night, I was sitting on my bed in the cell when the feeling crept through my fingernails to the backs of my knuckles. It felt like caterpillars wriggling on the chrysalis. I tried to do another workout to make it disappear.

Squats and lunges. Shoulder stands. Curls with the metal bed frame.

The numbness lessened and I lay down. Went to sleep a little while after.

Day three. I scratched my name with my fingernail, chipping the first layer of paint. I used a different fingernail for the second.

McKenzie came to see me.

She said, "I didn't tell them."

"No?"

"I didn't tell them anything," she said. "I'm not sure how they knew."

"Knew what?" I said.

She leaned in close to the bars. She said, "About the longhouses."

"What about the longhouses?"

She said, "They told me you burned them."

"They did?"

"Yes," she said. "They told me that the night they arrested you."

"Oh," I said. I didn't say anything more because I didn't know if they were recording what we were saying. In the TV show that I'd seen at Curry Village, they'd recorded every conversation.

McKenzie said, "There's going to be more building than I thought."

"How?" I said. "What do you mean?"

She said, "They're going to put two Twin Burgers and two Motel 4s in the Valley. One of each at each end. Four total."

"How's that possible?"

McKenzie drew the Valley on her hand with her finger. "Motel here at Bridalveil, and Twin Burgers here, north side. Twin Burgers here on the south side, and Motel 4 here, just past Curry. The sponsorship money is in the tens of millions, but Thompson isn't worried at all. Everything will be double-priced. Their advisers are saying that they'll recoup in fewer than five years."

"And this new superintendent?"

McKenzie said, "He loves it. Says we can go from three million visitors a year to five million. New growth model for all of the parks."

I looked at the paint chipped under my nails. Gray, almost purple. I said, "Now you think it's wrong?"

"Well, that's too much. Clearly," she said. "So I'm driving to Los Angeles today to try and talk to my boss. I'll see if we can slow everything down. But it doesn't look good."

"Slow it down, huh?"

"Yeah," she said. "I don't think it can be stopped. But we can slow it down."

I said. "That's not good enough, but I guess that's where we'll start."

McKenzie leaned in close again. She said, "One more thing, and this is important: they haven't charged you."

"What?" I said.

"They haven't charged you with anything."

I said, "I don't know what that means."

"With a crime," she said. "If they don't charge you, you don't have rights. No due process. No phone call or lawyer. They might keep you or let you go. They can make you disappear."

Day six. I was reading a newspaper story about the homeless population growing in San Francisco. A sheriff's deputy came to get me. The agents put me in a new room, a room with a table and two wooden chairs on either side. This looked more like the TV show I'd seen.

The shorter agent said, "What would it look like if we were to let you go?"

"What would it look like?" I said.

"I mean," he said, "have you ever left this Valley?"

"Left this Valley how?"

"Stop that," he said. "Stop repeating my questions. You understand me perfectly well. Have you ever left this park? This national park? Yosemite?"

"No," I said, "I haven't."

He pulled his pen out of his pocket and clicked it. "No?" he said. He pointed his pen at me and looked me in the eyes. We both looked at each other. Then he said, "You're telling the truth. I can see that. I know these things."

The taller one scratched on the paper again. He still didn't talk.

The shorter one said, "But would you leave the Valley now?"

I looked back and forth between the two of them.

The shorter one said again, "I'll repeat the question. Would you leave the Valley now?"

I wanted to say yes, but I said, "No, I wouldn't leave."

"That's what I thought," he said. He clicked his pen and put it in his pocket.

We're at the campfire eating marshmallows. My father says, "You are a warrior."

My fingers are sticky with burnt marshmallow. I lick them. I look at my mother. She doesn't say anything.

My father says, "That's why I came back, why I reclaimed this Valley." He fumbles in the marshmallow bag. Pulls out two more.

My mother's family played tourists in the pines in 1929, blending in, waiting through the Depression, living out of their car. Her father fished three times a day for food, trout for breakfast, lunch, and dinner. She told me the stories when I was little, and I didn't forget.

My father puts another marshmallow on my stick. He says, "You're a warrior, and you'll protect this place. Right?"

I say, "Yes," my hands sticky, the roasting stick hanging out over the coals.

Day eleven. I read about the storm in the paper. Snow on the cliffs, almost to the Valley floor, the Camp 4 climbing ranger worried about teams up on El Cap. He ordered helicopter rescues for everyone who'd filled out a permit.

I knew Kenny hadn't filled out a permit. I counted back, figured out how many days he'd been up there: thirteen. Maybe he'd decided to retreat early. Hopefully he'd run out of water.

I called down the hall. I said, "Hey. Is somebody there?"

No answer.

I said again, "Is somebody there?"

The unit buzzed, and the clerk came through the door. He said, "Yes?"

I said, "I need to log a missing climber report."

"A what?"

"I need to log a missing climber report. My friend is up on El Cap."

The clerk had his hand on the door. It was halfway closed. He said, "On El Cap? You mean the big cliff, El Cap?"

"Yes," I said. "Up there in the storm, and it's raging. He probably needs a helicopter rescue."

The clerk nodded. "Okay," he said, "I'll let people know. What's his name?"

"Kenny Cox. Cox with a C," I said.

"Got it," he said, and started to close the door.

"Quickly," I said.

He put his head back around the door. "What?"

"Quickly," I said. "He didn't file a permit, so nobody knows he's up there. He's on Tangerine Trip, and he probably needs a rescue immediately."

He said, "A tangerine tripped?"

I tried not to be impatient with him. "No, no. On Tangerine Trip. The famous climb. The rock climb. Write it down. Kenny Cox is on Tangerine Trip. He needs a helicopter rescue. He's probably halfway up at a hanging belay somewhere. He needs help immediately."

The clerk wrote it all down.

Later, I looked at the cafeteria tray underneath my food in my cell, and wondered if the trays circulated the Valley, if all of the trays went somewhere central to be washed. Maybe Kenny and I had eaten on this tray before, maybe in the Lodge dining hall. I thought of Kenny's dirty hands on a leftover waffle. His stained down coat. Orange with the one big, red mark.

I couldn't get the numbness to leave my fingertips that day no matter how many push-ups I did.

On day twelve, I made my workouts harder. One-handed push-ups. One-legged squats. I waited for the guard to come.

"Did you file the report?" I said.

"About the climber? Yeah, I did," he said. "I filed it yesterday, right after you told me. They sent it down to Camp 4, to Search and Rescue."

"Good," I said. "Thank you. Did you hear anything?"

"About him? No," he said. "Not yet. But they wrote it all down. I know they took it seriously."

"Okay, good," I said.

"No problem," he said, and walked back down the hall.

I lay on the floor with my shirt off. Arms outstretched. The numbness almost gone from my fingers. I could feel my hair beginning to grow again.

McKenzie came on day thirteen.

She looked small in her clothes, like she wasn't eating well. "I was wrong," she said.

"What do you mean?" I looked at her through the bars.

She said, "I'm so sorry."

"What do you mean?"

She touched my hand. "Have they said what they have you on?"

"Arson. Also, they questioned whether or not I'm a U.S. citizen."

"Can they prove that you're not a citizen?" she said.

I said, "Do they have to prove that I'm not, or do I have to prove that I am?" I shook my head. I kept thinking that they were listening to us, that they had the cell set up for recording. "But maybe I am one," I said. "I was born here, and this is the United States, right?"

She said, "Here in the Valley? You were born right here?"

"Yes," I said, "in a car."

She was holding my hand. "Have you told them that?"

"No."

She said, "Why not?"

"Because of my parents," I said. I looked around for cameras but didn't see any. I didn't know where they could hide microphones.

McKenzie was tapping her fingers on the bars. She said, "I'm going back to L.A. again. This will be my second time in three days."

I said, "How did that work before?"

"Not well. My boss was gone on a business trip. I called him. We talked, but this needs to be something we meet about. I can be more persuasive in person," she said. "He's coming back to L.A. tonight, so I'll drive there today. Give it one more shot."

The clerk opened the hall door and walked up. He said, "They want to talk to Tenaya again, so ma'am, you're going to have to leave now."

I said, "Good luck, McKenzie."

"I'm sorry," she said. "I really am."

The guard said, "Ma'am, it's really time to go."

"Okay," she said, and stood up. "Goodbye, Tenaya."

"Goodbye."

She started down the hall, then turned around. She said, "I'll come see you as soon as I get back, okay?"

"Okay," I said.

She left through the door and a deputy came back for me. The deputy unlocked my cell and let me out.

The agents were waiting for me in the other room. They were both standing. The shorter one pointed to the chair by the table, the one I always sat in. I sat down. The taller one still had that pad of paper. I didn't know why they kept doing this, always the same thing.

The shorter one said, "This doesn't mean much."

I waited because that wasn't a question.

He said, "But we'll have to wait. Be patient."

I said, "Be patient for what?"

"Right," he said. "We'll have you back in here soon."

I said, "In this room?"

"In here," he said. "And then you'll let us know what else is going on." He was clicking his pen again. I wanted to rip it out of his hand. My fingers were less numb each day now. Three good meals, lots of sleep, time to get strong.

"Yes," the agent said, "you'll let us know the whole scope. Who else is involved . . ." He waved his pen around.

I started to reach toward the pen but made my hand go back down to the tabletop. I spread my fingers on the Formica.

"For example," he said, "that McKenzie Johnston?"

"No," I said. "She's not involved."

"We'll see about that," he said. "And this Kenny Cox?"

The man behind me scratched for ten seconds then stopped.

The shorter one looked at me. He said, "Maybe someone else too? We'll figure it all out though. Gather more evidence. Then bring you back in. Do you understand what I'm saying?"

I looked back and forth between the two of them. I said, "So I'm getting out?"

They looked like campers who left out food to bait a bear. But I knew how that always worked out. I'd seen a bear break a man's face with one tap of his paw, no effort at all, just a pat, and the orbital bone dented in an inch, the man's face crushed.

The agent said, "So we're going to let you go for a little while, but we'll have you back in a week. You'll be required to check in every two days. Can you do that? Because if you don't, you'll be impeding a federal investigation. Do you understand what that means?" he said. He smiled.

"Yes," I said.

"All right then." He clicked his pen one final time. He said, "I guess that's it. So if you'll wait here, we'll go notify the clerk."

They left the room and I sat for fifteen minutes alone in the room. I rubbed my hands over the top of my head where my hair was growing. In the last couple of days, it seemed to have grown a quarter of an inch.

I didn't know which direction to walk as I came out of the building. I knew I was lucky to be out, and I wasn't sure if I should go back to the caves at the Ahwahnee. I knew someone might be following me, or waiting there.

McKenzie was gone. If I'd been released an hour earlier, she would've still been at the jail.

My mother is there with us, outside of camp, the day after it happened. I'm six. My mother is standing with her eyes closed while we dig the hole.

The blanket, wrapped, lay off to the right, next to a tree, as if it holds belongings for a picnic, food and clothing. It looks so small, a family blanket rolled three times and folded at each end, less than three feet long.

We take turns digging, my father and I, although my turns are shorter. The ground is rocky, and I can't move much earth. Even the small Army Surplus shovel is too heavy for me. When the hole is deep enough to stand in, my father does all the digging and I sit on the ground next to him as he deepens the hole.

My father walks over and picks up the bundle, holding it to his chest.

I say, "Can I put her in?"

My father looks at me, his eyes gray, more gray than brown.

We both look to my mother but she isn't looking at us.

My father says, "Okay."

I hold out my hands, flat, palms up, elbows pressed to my sides, as if my father is about to load my arms with firewood. He rolls the bundle over my hands, into the right angle of my elbows against my chest. I pull my hands in tight, hold the bundle close, and my father slips his hands out from underneath the blanket.

Even though I know it is not true, the blanket feels as heavy as I am, as if I am burying myself.

At dusk, I jogged back to the Ahwahnee caves, the sun dropping like a fire-sharpened stick. It was almost dark when I walked into camp, found my cave at the meeting of the two boulders, my sleeping bag moist from the ceiling drip. I lay down on top of my bag.

After a while, I got up. Drank some water and peed. I thought about when I first saw what was inside the trunk of the car.

My father and mother were down the hill, walking toward the river. That morning, I'd seen where my father had stashed the keys, and I waited all afternoon for this opportunity.

I read my book until I was sure that they were gone. Then I lifted the rock, pulled the keys out, and walked over to the car. Seventeen years old, and I had never seen the inside of the car's trunk.

I slid the key in the slot. Turned it and the trunk popped, came open, and rotated on the hinges. Inside were stacks and stacks of money, rubber bands around each stack. I picked up one stack and counted it. Five hundred dollars in twenties. And all the stacks looked the same, more than one hundred of them rubber-banded.

I remembered the story of Lower Merced Lake. The divers. San Francisco trips to sell bricks from the Lodestar fuselage. This was no river treasure.

In the morning, Greazy told me about Kenny, but I already knew. I'd seen his face against the wall in my sleep, seen it blue and hard, and I didn't want to hear about the helicopter and the YOSAR crews rappelling. I didn't want to hear about the portaledge ripped in half, Kenny's hands stuck to the chains, white-blue and hard.

I was sitting against the back wall of my cave, on the old mattress, my sleeping bag wrapped around my shoulders.

Greazy said, "I'm real fucking sorry, man."

"Yeah," I said, "me too."

Greazy said, "He was a good guy, a great guy. I'm real, real sorry. You know that, right?"

I felt the back of my head against the granite of the boulder. The cool. The slick of the rock. "Yeah, I know," I said.

Greazy kicked one of my water bottles left to right with his foot. Rolled it over. He said, "Kenny was . . . " but he didn't know how to finish the sentence.

I said, "Yeah," again. I couldn't think of anything else to say.

"I know," Greazy said. He rolled the water bottle back with his toe. "Hey, man, I was thinking . . . I mean, some of us saw you come in last night all upset looking. Before all of this. You know?"

I had been trying to read all morning, but I hadn't gotten anywhere in the book. It was folded closed next to me, and I realized that I'd made up my mind. I knew what I had to do.

"You know," Greazy said, "no offense or anything, right? Just hoping you're okay, you know?"

"Right," I said.

"Okay then. If you need anything," Greazy waved. Then he left.

I called Carlos from the pay phone in the Ahwahnee because I wanted them to trace the call there later.

I went to the Curry deck and collected newspapers. Read all I could, memorized the names of everyone and everything. I ate pizza leftovers while I read, ate without tasting, food as a reflex, a habit. The CEOs, presidents, and the superintendent were meeting at the Ahwahnee, in the Great Room. The next meeting would bring them all together to form a "plan of conduct," a future for the Valley. They were meeting in ten days.

I had never done much of anything that I'd planned. I looked at my hands for a mark of the superintendent's blood.

The wet mattress. Mist. The drip at the north corner of the cave making a sound like two marbles kissing. The night-quiet of the middle hours, nocturnal animals in bed now, and diurnal animals still asleep. I heard him scream.

I rolled over onto the wet patch of the mattress and soaked my shirt at the shoulder. Sat up. Heard him again. Then the muffled scraping sounds, leather against granite. A rasping. I stood up and left the cave.

He was up in the talus fifty yards away. I found him wedged between two boulders shaped like obtuse triangles. The hole in his head was half the size of my fist. He stopped thrashing. Rolled and looked at me.

I said his name. My own name.

He looked like a darted bear. Didn't blink. His eyes were open and watery, twitching at the corners.

I knew this story, his death at the pass in the high country. Trying to cut through the mountains after the invasion, the ambush came from above, and the rock broke a hole through his skull.

I put my hand on his chest and felt his breathing, the suck of his lungs. I leaned down next to the hole, hearing his soul's whistling as it came through the skull.

A middle-aged man brought in the truck full of fertilizer two days later. The truck was an old silver Nissan with a tinted-windowed canopy. The bales were wrapped in the back, wound in dark plastic, only visible if I leaned in and looked with my hands cupped around my eyes.

The man said, "This stuff has sat for a week now. But you've got to let it sit for a few days more. After that, it's volatile. Timing is everything, right?" He looked like a university botanist on a Valley hike. He had leather patches on the elbows of his tweed sports coat, long, gray hair, an enormous mustache.

I paid him with the money Carlos had given me in an envelope marked "Food." The man didn't count the money, but slid it in the pocket of his coat.

We got in the truck and he went over the remote. He said, "Don't mess around with this. Only flip this lock when you're ready to go. The caps are all in place. They're set. So you make a mistake here, and you go with it. Do you understand?"

"Yes," I said.

"All right then. You take care now," he said. "Big boom."

He got out of the truck and closed the door behind him. Then he walked up the road and put his thumb out to hitchhike.

I started the truck and drove it across the road into the overflow parking lot. I nearly stalled the vehicle twice in a hundred yards, my driving skills not good enough to captain any other car than my father's.

I went to see my mother. There was no wet bag coated in solvent, no glue underneath her nostrils, but it didn't matter. She stumbled around camp, tripping over the bench log each time she passed as if that log hadn't been there for twenty years.

"Are you okay?" I said.

She smiled at me with her eyes closed. She teetered, fell again, and I caught her.

I said, "I think you need some food, some water, then sleep."

I fried fish for her. Cooked thin slices of potatoes that I found on the backseat of the car. They were growing roots but they still smelled good. I fed her one bite at a time.

Then I put her to bed in her tent. She insisted on sleeping in my father's sleeping bag. I lay down right outside the tent, guarding the door, guarding her escape.

In the morning, I made her drink more water. Then I boiled coffee. Sprinkled cold water on top to settle the grounds. Gave her a mug full with a teaspoon of sugar.

I drank a cup too. We sat on the bench log.

My mother's eyes opened all the way. I said, "We should go visit the hospital today. He would want that."

My mother shook her head, no.

"You don't think so?"

My mother looked at me and didn't blink. She didn't say anything.

The rains started the next day, on the Fourth of July, the most populated camping and visitation weekend of the year. People crawled through the Valley like wet locusts, hands and heads bent over cell phones to protect them against the sky.

The rain came down, clouds piled low, black and roiling, one storm stacking the next from the southwest, none passing the buttresses of North Dome. The air thickened in the Valley, pressed against the points of the pines, everything wet.

In the afternoon, the rains turned harder still. Drops the size of hail, but nothing frozen, the sky pounding stone-size warm water, and I laughed as I saw it splatting against the Park Service's tin roofs, the storm making the sound of a snowplow throwing gravel against a windshield.

People hid in tents, the Lodge, bathrooms, kiosks, the Village Store, at Curry, the LeConte Memorial, Housekeeping, and at the Buffet. Visitors waited all day for the storm to end.

When the evening came, people ran for their cars and hid, the sandy mud three inches high on their shoes and socks. They scraped the mud onto their floorboards, took off their shoes, and curled their feet up underneath them. Some slept in their cars that night with the rain pelting rhythms on their rooftops. Tents were no longer waterproof. The cement doorways of the bathrooms deflected rain inside, stall floors flecked with the spray.

And it rained.

It was only the second day of the rain when people started to leave. I went to check on the fertilizer truck and saw people packing their tents in Camp 4, across the road. At the ranger's box, the ten-day forecast from the National Weather Service predicted ten days straight of rain, a summertime record for the Valley. I saw climbers shaking their heads. Two-thousand-mile destination road trips ending here in the rain. No chance to climb for more than a week.

I focused on the truck. The meeting. What I would do. I went over my plan. Drive the truck up and leave it in one of the front parking spaces. Walk away. Get to the Village. Walk behind the store complex to the midsize boulder. Flip the lock on the remote and press the button, then slide behind the boulder as the blast wave moved out.

The smell of cologne and cigar smoke. My fist inside the mountain lion. The green bottle in my hand. My hand on a remote.

On the third day of rain, the Merced River rose suddenly like an opened dam. Tenaya Creek fed from the east, joining the melt from Vernal and Nevada. The Arches' streams became three runners, then five, then seven. The explosions of water off Bridalveil Falls could be seen from Northside Drive. And the Merced rose above its banks like a man stepping over a fence.

I saw the Merced at North Pines, where the river floods first, at the long bank, the water circling around campsites before dropping into the flats. The rangers sandbagged at the first sign of overflow, yelling to each other and throwing bags in the rain. But the river snuck behind the wall and moved on. Then it took the south side, at the Lower Pines, slashing a line to the watershed across, spreading to create a backwater up and down behind the camp.

Campers packed wet everything. Stuffed the backs of their cars with soaked gear.

The river took the first of the meadows next, below Housekeeping and up, rising across the southeast beach, collapsing muddy banks on the northwest. This was the highest I had ever seen the river, bigger than the two huge snowmelts, April floods, but this was not April, and the rains would not stop.

I went to get my mother, but she wasn't in camp. I looked in all her usual places near the creek, the clearing, down on the trail by the road. I yelled for her in the rain but the wet ate the sound.

I walked back up the hill and got into the car. Reached under the seat for the keys. Turned the ignition and heard the engine catch. I blasted the air to clear the condensation, then I drove downhill, the car sliding at each turn, sliding sideways on the rained-out ground. The third turn proved too tight. The car skidded sideways, caught for a moment, then skidded some more. I pulled the wheel, but the car followed the slope, sliding downhill sideways until it crushed against a tree, the left side rear door denting in against the tree trunk.

I couldn't get out on my side. The door wouldn't open. So I crawled across, opened the passenger-side door, and slid out. Then

I walked back down to the Loop Road. The north side. Put my thumb out in the rain.

A car pulled over in front of me. The driver rolled down his window. He said, "Where are you headed?"

"Merced. The hospital there."

He said, "Are you hurt?"

"No," I said. "I need to visit someone."

"Well . . . shoot. We're not really going that way. We're headed up out of the other park exit, not going through El Portal at all, and nowhere near Merced."

I said, "That's okay. I can flag down another car."

"Sounds good," he said. "Good luck."

I waved and he pulled back onto the road in front of me, driving west. I put my thumb out once again.

Car after car passed, trying to leave the Valley before the flooding covered the road. But it was too late. I saw the return cars first, then I walked up on the traffic jam an hour later. The river had crested, spreading a lake at the west end of the loop before the 120 split. One car at a time was trying to turn around and head back east. I didn't see the car that had pulled over for me. It was somewhere up in that traffic line, sitting in the rising water, now partway buried.

I was standing at the Book Cliffs, looking up the Valley, the waves of the Merced light, but the river coming north now, licking and extending, four times its normal width.

The fifth day of rain.

Water wedging and the rockfall starting. Rockfall off the Nose of El Capitan first, to the west, the collapse sounding like dynamite in spring to clear slides on the Tioga Road. I hiked down into Camp 4 and heard dirtbags discussing the rockfall in the bathroom.

One said, "I think that's off the Great Roof, huh?"

"Yeah," the other said. "Just sucks. That route is gone, bro."

The first climber shook his head while brushing his teeth at the sink. There weren't many climbers left in the campground now. Camp 4 held ten people at the most.

The same day saw a piece of Sentinel come down. Black rockfall at the lichen smear, a buttress on the west side of the north face heaving into the trees below, and the rangers warned all hikers and climbers back from the cliffs. They wrote on the signboard, "Don't scout climbs." "Don't even look up from below." "Wear helmets." "Stay near the river." The climbing ranger circulated through the sites, yelling and smiling. But his smile looked like he was sipping turned milk.

And the river crept toward us on the Lodge footpath, moving like a rattlesnake over the asphalt.

Day six. The Arches heaved, trembling like an earthquaked building. I'd cleared my gear from the cave, and was standing near the hotel dumpsters with the arrowhead collection in my hands and my soaked sleeping bag around my neck. Then the first slide came down, and the roaring followed.

Three men were getting into a red Cadillac in the parking lot. It was morning, a malignant gray under the rain, and the three men looked like hikers, wearing new, Day-Glo, waterproof gear.

The rockfall rushed the trees, turned pines like broken saplings, huge boulders hurtling fifty feet off the ground. A boulder hit the Cadillac from above, landed on the roof, a boulder weighing four or five tons, exploding three of the Cadillac's doors all the way off, and the men were crushed inside. Only one of them screamed. The other two never made any noise at all.

That was the small rockfall.

The hotel was evacuated. As people walked out along the entrance road, a ranger yelled, "The Village is okay, but stay away from the river! Don't go to Curry! Do not go to Curry!"

The hotel had been evacuated only an hour when the second and third rockfalls came down off the Arches, washing through the abandoned structure.

I heard it, an avalanche of loose rock against the set stone of the walls, the grating and collisions reverberating through the Valley even in the rain. Nothing could stop that sound as the two rockfalls, ten minutes apart, took the boulders, the caves, the parking lot, and the hotel itself. The great Ahwahnee that had stood for nine decades in the Valley was gone.

There was no job for me then, the hotel gone. I couldn't destroy what the rockfall had already taken, and the meeting wouldn't happen. I'd left the fertilizer truck to sit in the rain in the Camp 4 overflow parking lot. The river was licking at its wheels now, rising little by little up its black tires.

I recovered the remote and dropped it in the dumpster.

People massed at the Village store, crowded like elk against winter, yelling into their cell phones.

I saw her against the wall, hunched over her phone, reading.

I said, "McKenzie."

"Oh my god," she said. "I've spent six days trying to find you. I've been everywhere. Seriously. I thought you might have left."

I pointed to the sky. "Crazy, huh?"

"Yes," she said. "Have you seen it like this before?"

"No," I said. "Never."

"But weren't there floods before?"

"Not like this one. Not even the big flood. Nothing like this. I don't even know what I'd call this."

"Evil?" she said. "Deadly?"

"Deadly maybe."

McKenzie said, "And angry."

We watched the sky drop its wet. Listened to the pounding on the corrugated metal roof above us. The people near us kept walking out to the edge of the awning, checking to see if it could still be raining as hard.

McKenzie said, "They're going to re-evaluate, my boss and the others. They're going to wait a while on everything. This storm's supposed to stay, to wreck a lot of things. Everyone is freaking out."

"Yeah," I said. "This flood might do some lasting damage to structures."

"Are you kidding?" she said. "Do you know what it's done already?"

"Yes. The rockfall at the Ahwahnee was incredible. I saw it."

McKenzie looked at her watch. "I've got to go call them. Give a report. Will you still be here in a while?"

"No," I said. "I don't think so."

She was holding her phone. She put it to her lips. "Where will you be?"

"I don't know. I have to find my mother."

"Your mother? Is she here? And is she out in this?"

"Somewhere," I said.

"Okay, wow," McKenzie said. "I didn't even know that she lived here. Where do you think she is?"

"I'm not sure. But she's somewhere in the Valley. I have a few ideas. Might not be that hard to find her."

McKenzie flipped her phone open. Checked for messages. Then she closed it. She said, "I guess you better go find her."

"I will," I said. "I'm going."

McKenzie kissed me quickly. She said, "What is it that the Spanish climbers say in Camp 4?"

"*A la muerte?*"

"Yeah, that's it. *A la muerte*, Tenaya."

It wasn't a long search. My mother was back on the Little Columbia Boulder again, where I'd found her before. She had no glue bag this time. She huddled underneath my father's green rain poncho, sitting on top of the boulder, looking out at the abandoned west end of camp, oriented toward the Search and Rescue tents.

I helped her slide down the ramp-side of the boulder, made her jump to me at the short end.

"We've got to get up and out of here, okay?" I said. "I've packed food and blankets for us, so we can hike right out of camp."

We hiked in the white sludge, the high granite mud. The Falls Trail ran rivulets down past our feet, no summer acorn dust as my mother kept slipping.

I said, "Do you remember when we used the grind holes to make acorn flour? How you taught me?"

My mother stopped. I put my arms around her and hugged her. She hugged me back, then turned and kept walking. I looked over my shoulder but I couldn't see anything yet. We were still in the oak forest, low on the switchbacks.

After a while, my mother stopped again. Looked back over the Valley and Camp 4. We were halfway up to the rim, at the midway switchback, the one little iron rail for the overlook. I gave her water, then drank some myself.

Underneath us, we saw the lakes of brown water, the green trees spiking, and the white gray of the big boulders still above the waterline. The flood lapped the edges of Camp 4 now.

My mother looked shriveled next to me in her poncho, the outline of her small shoulders, and the rain pressing everything tight.

I said, "I don't think this is rain anymore."

My mother held out her hands, palms up, and caught the splats.

I said, "I've seen it rain here thousands of times, and you have too. But this isn't rain. This is something else." I could feel the lakes in the Valley rising up to meet the water falling from the sky. Water to water.

My mother licked at the rain running down her face. She held her palms still and turned her face upward, into the heavy drops. She closed her eyes.

I did the same. Tilted my face and let the rain welt my eyelids. It was not softening. We stood like that, together with our eyes closed, standing above the Valley lakes.

After a while, I said, "Should we keep hiking?"

My mother dropped her palms and started walking uphill again. I followed her. She was not fast or slow, but steady, walking at the same pace regardless of the pitch, no matter how steep. When she lifted a foot, I set mine down in its place. I watched her feet dent the trail, and I stepped in those dents.

I'd loaded my pack at the bear boxes, more food abandoned in the camp than I could ever eat. If the boxes didn't flood, we'd have food stores forever when we went back down.

We didn't need to bring extra water. Water was everywhere around us. I knew of three natural cisterns that would be full and overflowing above us.

My mother and I sloshed through the traverse at the girdle of trees above midway, then up the steep switchbacks again. The incline was difficult in the slick. The Upper Falls crushed next to us, in the void between the cliffs, the sound of the falls concussing. I had never heard it like this before, not even at a quick snowmelt in April. The sound of a new Valley being born.

Then we were on top of the rim, hiking along the iron-wired edge and looking out, wondering at the water everywhere, pools in each hole at our feet, rivulets running down stone, splatting at every flat.

The storm kept on, and the clouds massed. Electric and grating, they stacked above us. In the south. Then to the west, like dark cars filling a lot, people wedging into spaces between. Filtered light growing dim.

Sideways lightning started behind Glacier Point, on the high plateau behind the Valley, behind the Cathedrals, crackling like magnesium-dipped yarn. White illumination of the dark. The three spires light and dark above the water.

My mother pointed.

"This is nothing like anything," I said.

My mother kept pointing.

The lightning strikes were short at first, high ground to sky, the cumulonimbus inching north, ready to drop the rim. Sideways lightning like fingers wiggling.

My mother took my hand.

"Are we staying here when this is over?" I said.

She didn't look at me. She watched the lightning, the Valley's three elements: iron, water, and electricity.

In between the lighting, everything turned to dark gray, the night coming. I felt the nerves at the ends of my right hand like a color. Sparks of yellow. I felt my mother's small hand in my left. She was cold and she began to shiver like an animal coming out of a creek. I put my arms around her. Walked her toward my favorite cave at the slab summit.

There, we looked out on the running lake below us. And it rained still. In the west, the metallic glint of cars floating among low tree branches. The water turned to black at the end of the day, and the river lake spread laterally across the Valley, the reclamation of the meadows, the roads, the buildings.

Rockfall broke off the Shield, shearing like a cornice, but louder than a snow cornice breaking. The waves of sloughed granite washed into the Curry tent-cabins just before dark. White buried beneath thick gray, the dust cloud beaten down by the rain. Darker gray now and the trees sticking like clipped wire ends.

I scanned down the Valley. Tried to see the silver of the fertilizer truck in the overflow lot, but it would be floating on the current now, floating down toward the mouth of the Valley where the soldiers of the 36th Regiment Wisconsin first entered near El Portal.

I knew the white jumble of scree boulders on the south side loop there, at the mouth of the Valley where the Merced cuts a W at the west end. In the morning, the boulders would mix with the new wrecks of brightly colored tourist cars.

We stood above the Valley with the screaming of the water and the stones falling, the storm, the lightning, the throating of thunder.

And the Valley rose. Water and water and water.

My mother huddled against me.

In the beginning I was. And I was with the Valley, and I was the Valley. We were with the Valley in the beginning.

ACKNOWLEDGMENTS

To Jennie Hoffmeister. How can I say what I mean here? You read bad drafts, vet ideas, challenge me, support me, stay up late reading, and make me feel capable of anything. You are my Maxwell Perkins.

To my friend Kenny Cox. The way I see it, you and I were even after the third round. But that's not what I wish for you. No more wrestling. Instead, I hope you're given raw congress with the natural world. Life in the canyon. Hiking the desert. Swimming in the river. Your hair dirty always.

To Dr. Lafayette Bunnell, post mortem as well, for your book *Discovery of the Yosemite: And the Indian War of 1851, Which Led to That Event*. Your vivid, anti-36th account started me on this strange deer trail. Did the soldiers of your regiment know you didn't agree?

Thank you also to the Northern Paiutes, greater Paiute People. If the National Park Service continues to make things up, we'll continue to talk. This book and others will spread the truth.

To Miriam Gershow who read the short story that led to this book three and a half years ago. Thank you for saying, "There's too much good stuff happening in these twenty-five pages."

Next, to Adriann Ranta, an excellent agent because of your honesty. When you say it's bad, it's bad. When you say it's good, it's good. And that is the most an emerging writer could ever ask for. Thank you for hating so much of the third draft.

To Ben LeRoy. The King. You got it. You understood this big thing that I was attempting. And *Graphic the Valley* wouldn't have happened without you.

To John Galligan for perfect editing and revision advice. Thank you for finding my egregious plot hole and for explaining structure. You made me better.

Ashley Myers, all-things-girl at Tyrus. Thank you for helping me clarify those little details, and for finding my one, overused simile.

To Haley, Hillary, Cooper, Maddie, and Ellis. Thank you for the love and support, for the wild fun of this big, messy family.

To my mother, Pamela Hoffmeister. You made me want to be a novelist when I was young. For all of the books, art, and imagery.

Again, to my father Charlie Hoffmeister for your early morning work ethic. It is your model that I always follow. Plus watching baseball together doesn't hurt.

To Betsie, Aimee, Carrie, and Sarah for so much love. You four are incredible. I am truly blessed.

To my brothers-in-law, Nate, Caleb, Jay, and Dan. You guys just get it.

To Courtney Stubbert for the interwebs and the absinthe. The cover. My kitchen or your kitchen, it doesn't matter.

To Mike Wilt for blood. To Pris Wilt for love.

To Sonja Jameson for always reading and encouraging.

To everyone I've climbed with in Yosemite over the years, but especially to Garrick Hart, Lee Baker, Jennie Hoffmeister, and My-Only-Friend-in-the-Entire-World Jeff Hess. Any time. Let's go. And apologies on Pywiack Dome. I know there's no route with that line, but I needed it. Same with the Yosemite jail.

To my friends and fellow writers who inspire me, Michael McGriff, Dorianne Laux, Tina Boscha, Lidia Yuknavitch, Alexa Lachman, Katie Meehan, and Jose Chaves. A writer needs writers. And y'all are good.

To Ingrid Bodtker for calm. We shouldn't be this busy, but somehow we are. Working with you makes it all better.

Finally, to my girls, Rain and Ruth. I love coming home every day.

ABOUT THE AUTHOR

Peter Brown Hoffmeister is the author of the memoir *The End of Boys*, the nonfiction manifesto *Let Them Be Eaten By Bears— A Fearless Guide to Taking Our Kids Into the Great Outdoors*, and the story album *The Great American Afterlife* (produced with Mankind). He has climbed and bouldered and camped for more than a decade in Yosemite Valley, Yosemite National Park. Hoffmeister's fiction collection *Loss* earned an Oregon Literary Arts Fellowship and his first book was chosen as a Goodreads Memoir finalist. Hoffmeister blogs for the *Huffington Post* and runs the Integrated Outdoor Program at South Eugene High School. He lives with his wife Jennie, and daughters Rain and Ruth, in Eugene, Oregon.